Tree of *Pearls*, Queen of Egypt

Middle East Literature in Translation

Michael Beard and Adnan Haydar, *Series Editors*

 Syracuse University Press and the King Fahd Center for Middle East and Islamic Studies, University of Arkansas, are pleased to announce TREE OF PEARLS, QUEEN OF EGYPT as the 2011 winner of the King Fahd Center for Middle East and Islamic Studies Translation of Arabic Literature Award.

Previous winners of the *King Fahd Center* prize

Blood Test: A Novel
    Abbas Beydoun; Max Weiss, trans.
The Pistachio Seller
    Reem Bassiouney; Osman Nusairi, trans.
The World Through the Eyes of Angels
    Mahmoud Saeed; Samuel Salter, Zahra Jishi, and Rafah Abuinnab, trans.

Tree
of
Pearls,
Queen
of
Egypt

Jurji Zaydan

Translated from the Arabic by Samah Selim
With an Afterword by Roger Allen

Syracuse University Press

Library of Congress Cataloging-in-Publication Data

Zaydan, Jirji, 1861–1914.

  [Shajarat al-Durr. English]

  Tree of pearls, queen of Egypt / Jurji Zaydan ; translated from the Arabic by Samah Selim ; with an afterword by Roger Allen.

    p. cm. — (Middle East literature in translation)

  ISBN 978-0-8156-0999-5 (pbk. : alk. paper) 1. Shajarat al-Durr, Sultana of Egypt, d. 1257—Fiction.   2. Zaydan, Jirji, 1861–1914—Translations into English. I. Selim, Samah.   II. Title.

  PJ7876.A9S3813 2012

  892.7'35—dc23   2012034829

Jurji Zaydan (1861–1914) was one of the most important Arab writers of the late nineteenth and early twentieth centuries. Born in Beirut in 1861, he emigrated to Cairo in 1882 and died there in 1914, on the eve of World War I and the collapse of the Ottoman Empire. In Cairo, Zaydan founded *Al-Hilal* (The Crescent), the longest-lived cultural and literary journal of the Arab world (1892–), which he edited and to which he frequently contributed. He authored two canonical multi-volume histories of Arabic literature and Islamic civilization, and twenty-three historical novels that span twelve centuries of Islamic history. Many of these novels were translated into a variety of Asian and Middle Eastern languages throughout the twentieth century and they continue to enjoy the same popularity today throughout the Arab world as they did one hundred years ago.

Samah Selim is a scholar and prize-winning translator of modern Arabic literature. Her translations include Yahya Taher Abdullah's *The Collar and the Bracelet* (2008) and Miral Al-Tahawi's *Brooklyn Heights* (2011). She currently teaches at Rutgers University.

Contents

Translator's Note

JURJI ZAYDAN IS OFTEN COMPARED to the great eighteenth-century novelist Sir Walter Scott. Like Scott, Zaydan wrote novels at a time when the novel itself was still a new genre in Arabic. Like Scott, he introduced the historical novel to Arab audiences, conceptualized as a political and didactic project but also as a medium of entertainment for a newly emerging middle class. Both authors were, moreover, highly popular in their day, and yet ultimately the comparison is a somewhat misleading one. In the English-speaking world, Scott has survived as an academic curiosity on university syllabi and the bookshelves of dedicated aficionados. Today he makes for difficult reading outside of these narrow, specialist circles and the dense, ornamental, and extraordinarily rich diglossic language of his fiction—consciously rooted in the rhythm and texture of medieval romance—no longer speaks to the broad audience for which it was originally intended; it has become quaint and irredeemably dated.

Unlike Scott, Jurji Zaydan's historical fiction remains as popular today as it was a century ago, both in the sense that it is still widely read across the Arabic-speaking world, and in that it remains firmly rooted in a popular space and sensibility. Zaydan's novels never made it into the literary canon. They are not read at school or university, and had elicited no real scholarly interest until quite recently. Nevertheless, very few educated Arabs today have never heard of Zaydan's novels, and most will have devoured at least a couple as young adults. The novels have been regularly reprinted in Egypt over the past century, and numerous editions continue to appear in markets from Rabat to Damascus. Translations into a plethora of regional languages have been made across the decades: Persian, Urdu, Azeri, Turkish, and Uighur, to name a few.

Part of this continuing popularity has to do with the continuing accessibility of Zaydan's language. Zaydan was part of a literary project that consciously broke with tradition and that undertook the radical renovation of both classical Arabic and its late medieval hybrid vernacular forms. Zaydan's precise, streamlined, and lexically undemanding prose, along with his clever rationalization of the temporal schemas of popular romance and epic, deliberately targeted a new readership situated "in between" elite circles and the quasi-literate audiences of oral, vernacular narrative forms. His language and style were the basis of later literary realisms and are still readily accessible to readers today.

Another important reason for this remarkable longevity has to do with pleasure: the kind of old-fashioned readerly pleasure born of the satisfying union of knowledge and entertainment. Taken together, the twenty-two novels make up a cycle: the story of worldly Islam from the conquests to the fall of the Ottoman Empire. Each of the novels represents a distinct adventure in this cycle—adventures that unfold in richly exotic locations scattered across a nonetheless familiar geography whose most famous monuments continue to exist today: from the martial tents of Bedouin Arabia to the palaces of imperial Baghdad, from the hallucinogenic secret grottoes of the Assassins in the mountains of Syria to the court of the Ayyubid Sultans in Cairo. Throughout all the novels, romance, intrigue, and above all politics make up the well-proven recipe that draws the reader into a distant world that continues to live in and through the present. In Arabic, Jurji Zaydan's novels are what we would today call "page-turners," with lively dialogue, fast-paced action, and short, cliffhanger chapters, but they are also mini-history lessons that directly reflect on the troubled contemporary moment of the Arab world.

It is this sense of pleasure that I have tried to reproduce in the present translation for the English-language reader, and the choice of language register was a central part of this process. As mentioned above, Zaydan's spare and efficient prose compellingly draws the reader into a world that is both distant and present, exotic and yet familiar; a medieval world, moreover, of princely courts and valorous warriors, that is already available to the modern English literary imagination in various articulations, from Scott's crusader fictions onwards. The present translation deliberately draws upon the "archaic" rhythms and diction of Scott's prose in order to activate this familiar/distant imaginative space for the English-language reader, while at the same time weaving into it the simple and decidedly modern texture of Zaydan's Arabic phrase. My hope is not only that this strategy will teach and entertain in English as it does in the original Arabic, but that it might offer the English-language reader a vibrant and layered sense of the histories and fictions that we share across time and place. My thanks go to Michael Beard for his unflagging support for this project from day one, and to Tamer El-Leithy for his generous and invaluable help with the intricate titles and protocols of Ayybuid court culture.

Tree of *Pearls*, Queen of Egypt

The Ayyubid Dynasty

A HISTORICAL SUMMARY

WE HAVE ELSEWHERE recounted the story of Saladin and how Egypt came into his possession. It was Saladin who constructed the Citadel of Cairo, took it as his royal seat, and therein founded his dynasty. His sons and brothers, their children, and their grandchildren shared between them dominion over the lands of Egypt and Syria until Al-Salih, son of Kamil, the Good King, ascended the throne in Egypt in the year 1239. This king acquired over a thousand Turkish Mamluks and built for them a fortress on the *Rawda*, or Garden, Island. There he made them dwell amongst his own slaves, his family, and his court; and this fortress he chose as his sovereign seat in place of the Citadel.

During his reign, the Crusaders under the command of Louis IX, King of France, invaded Egypt. Al-Salih had fallen gravely ill, but the instant he received news of the offensive, he commanded his troops to make ready for war. The Crusaders nonetheless managed to seize Damietta, thanks to the treachery of some of its inhabitants and the flight of a number of its princes. Al-Salih died soon thereafter and was succeeded by his son, Ghiyath al-Din Turan Shah, who became known as the Exalted King, Al-Mu'azzam. Real power, however, rested in the hands of Tree of Pearls, a concubine of the late King, and it was she who managed the affairs of the state after his death, carefully concealing news of this event from the populace until his son, Ghiyath al-Din, was brought to Cairo from Damascus and invested in the year 1249.

Meanwhile, the Egyptians made war on the Crusaders and, being victorious, drove them back upon their heels after many a bloody battle. Louis IX was captured, along with a large number of his knights and soldiers. Deadly dissension then spread between the officers of the Exalted King Ghiyath al-Din and his father's Mamluks, who rose up in rebellion against the son. Fearing for his life, Ghiyath al-Din fled Cairo but was captured and died a horrible death near Farskur. The victorious Mamluks conferred amongst themselves and agreed to invest Tree of Pearls with the royal title, and thus it was that she became the first Queen in the history of Islam. A bitter struggle for power ensued between this Queen and a number of Mamluk princes, along with the remaining members of the Ayyubid dynasty and other ambitious parties. The struggle finally ended in the victory of the Turkish Mamluks, who thereupon founded a new dynasty. During the reign of this victorious dynasty, the Tatars under the leadership of Hulagu invaded Baghdad and killed the Caliph al-Musta'sim, and the Caliphate was transferred to Egypt, the details of said history being the proper subject of this novel, God willing.

The Garden Isle

ON A MOONLIT NIGHT long ago, two women of exceeding grace and beauty, though far apart in age, sat gazing at the silver waters of the Nile from their fragrant bower on the famed Garden Island of Al-Salih, Egypt's Good King.

"The moon shines so brightly tonight, Shwaykar," mused the elder pensively.

"Indeed my Lady, and yet it is nothing compared to the radiance of your presence and the sparkle of your conversation," the young girl sweetly replied.

"You flatter me, Shwaykar, and speak not the truth. Which of us derives the most pleasure from the other's company? Can it be you, when I have nothing to speak of but the worries and anxieties of politics? Or is it I, God having endowed you with everything a singing-girl requires of beauty, intelligence, richness of voice and graceful conversation? While you are in the full flower of youth, I am on the threshold of middle-age and time with its burdens has laid me low."

The handmaiden blushed at this gracious compliment. "Do not speak so, my Lady. Indeed, you abash me with your praise. Who am I, that I should be counted a creature worthy of notice next to Tree of Pearls, consort of Al-Salih—may God have mercy on his soul—and mother of his child? God has favored you with a genius that has no equal amongst mankind. There is none amongst women who would dare aspire to even a small part of your blessings, may God exalt your rank and—"

Tree of Pearls interrupted her slave by affectionately placing her hand over the girl's mouth and bestowing a gentle smile upon her. There was anxiety, and foreboding too, in that smile, and the Lady's eyes glowed darkly with the great burden of her thoughts. She sighed heavily. "Do you then envy me for what you imagine to be a distinction conferred by fate? Indeed, this is the very source of my troubles." She bent her head while saying this, a frown suddenly creasing her brow and making Shwaykar's heart tremble.

Tree of Pearls reclined on an ebony couch richly upholstered in patterned brocade. The terrace on which mistress and slave now sat, and which belonged to one of the many palaces that Al-Salih had built on his Garden Island, overlooked a vast expanse of the Nile. This islet was the most beautiful of the verdant patches of green that sat like jewels in the great river between Old Cairo and Al-Jazira. Many a king of old had made it his pleasure-garden. It was Al-Salih who moved his royal seat there from the Citadel, where his predecessors had resided and from whence they had ruled. On this island he built a magnificent fortress that became known as the Fortress of the Measure, in reference to the ancient Nilometer nearby. It was also known as the Garden Fort or the Salihiyya Fort. Numerous palaces, mosques, and naval workshops had formerly existed on the site, and it was home to the famous pavilion that the Fatimid Sultan, Al-'Amir bi Ahkamillah, had built for his concubine. The Good King demolished all these structures and raised the Fortress in their place, expending a vast fortune in the process. The palaces and mosques that he caused to be raised rested upon great columns and arches fashioned from the venerable granite and marble taken from the ancient ruins surrounding the city. He planted orchards with flowering trees of all kinds, and he erected sixty towers for his armories and for grain and sundry foodstuffs against the possibility of a Frankish siege, for the Franks were intent on invading Egypt in those days. So lavish was he in constructing this fortress that each one of its stones was said to be worth a whole dinar. The King himself had supervised its construction, and when it was completed he moved his womenfolk and his slaves there, as well as his Mamluk horsemen, their number reaching one thousand hardy warriors. Finally, outside the walls he built a vast zoological garden in which he gathered all sorts of savage beasts—lions, for instance, and tigers.

Tree of Pearls was Al-Salih's favorite concubine, and when she gave birth to a son, the King drew her even further into his confidence. Being a woman of surpassing astuteness and intelligence, she acquired great influence over the King and so, when he was killed in Mansura in 1249, she carefully concealed his death from the populace and ruled in his stead, signing decrees and military commissions in his name, for the war against the Crusaders still raged. Her secret she confided to none but the leading princes and commanders of the army. 'Izz al-Din Aybak the Turk was her most particular confidant, for there was love between them.

Upon discovering the death of their King, the great princes commanded that his son, Ghiyath al-Din, be conveyed to Cairo from the Fort of Kifa, and they appointed him King and pressed on in their battle against the Crusaders.

Tree of Pearls's heart was heavy with secrets, and on this moonlit evening in particular, her apprehensions crowded in upon her. In spite of her confidence in Shwaykar, she could not bring herself to reveal her thoughts to the girl, though she derived great pleasure and comfort from her company. Shwaykar was exceedingly comely and possessed of a rich, melodious voice, and was moreover a masterful lute-player. When Tree of Pearls felt the sharp stab of anxiety assail her as she did now, she would summon the girl to her side, the better to be soothed by her presence and charmed by her voice.

Tree of Pearls was dressed in a simple garment and wrapped in a silk shawl. She sat gazing abstractedly at the Nile, while all around, nature lay perfectly still. The breeze had died down but for a few puffs that now and again stirred up her long dark hair, which she had gathered into an insouciant mass that tumbled luxuriously around her shoulders. She was not a woman like other woman. She had both the courage and the ambition of the greatest of men. If once she resolved on a course of action, she paid not the slightest heed to any obstacles placed in her path. She knew well how to conquer, by any and all means necessary.

Her handmaiden Shwaykar was, like her mistress, of Turkish origin, but still in the flower of youth. Tree of Pearls loved her dearly. She was the eager repository of her mistress's little secrets, for the great lady trusted her in spite of the native cunning that made her loath to reveal her thoughts to a living soul. It was for this cunning that the Mamluk princes feared and respected Tree of Pearls. She had conquered their hearts with her grace and she now commanded their awe and admiration with her indomitable will.

Shwaykar strummed her lute and sang her mistress's favorite songs while Tree of Pearls sat wrapped in her thoughts, gazing at the Nile which the moon's rays, glancing across its surface, had given the appearance of molten silver. Indeed, if not for the shivering ripples that broke across its waters from time to time, one would have imagined the river to be formed of a single pure sheet of the precious metal, like a massive mirror sparkling in the night (for in those days, mirrors were crafted from silver, and not from glass as is the custom today).

She turned her eyes to the opposite bank of the river at Giza, where the rows of tall palm trees reaching up to the heavens assumed the appearance of phantom maidens bearing parasols as they gracefully peered over the water's edge and gazed in wonder at the flowing current of the great river. The shadows of the palms were reflected in the water. There, they trembled and undulated, as though the water-maidens had now gone in to bathe, their lithe bodies shivering from cold or from vestal modesty. The Pyramids of Giza loomed large behind the palm groves like mighty mountains victorious over the accidents of fate.

Noting her mistress's drawn, fretful expression and the heavy sighs that from time to time escaped her, Shwaykar finally cast her oud aside. She knelt before her mistress and kissed her icy hands. "What is it that disquiets you, my Lady?" she entreated. "Do you no longer trust in me, though I have ever been the repository of your secrets and have no concern in this world other than your well-being?"

Tree of Pearls smiled wanly and reached out to stroke the girl's hair and face, much as an enamored youth will tenderly caress his beloved. She was reluctant to confide her fears to the dear, innocent child. She wrongly supposed Shwaykar to be entirely ignorant of the momentous matters that troubled her, this being one of the favorite illusions cherished by the possessors of secrets. So does the lover take pleasure in concealing his passion, though it may well be the talk of the neighbors from morning till night. Nothing remains safe from people's watchful eyes, though they be constrained to hold their tongues. Household servants, especially, are all-seeing and knowing, the sole occupation of these folk being to discover, dissect, and discuss the secrets of their masters and to embellish and embroider the truth of a matter.

Shwaykar was aware of the cause of her mistress's cares. She feigned ignorance, however, and begged Tree of Pearls to unburden her mind.

"I conceal nothing from you, as you know, but the subject that fills my thoughts cannot be of any great importance to you."

"I beg not your confidence because the matter may be of importance to me personally. I only wish to relieve the burden that weighs upon you and to soothe your heart by drawing out your complaint."

At this, Tree of Pearls laughed tenderly. "It would seem, child, that you have long dealt with secrets and the pleasures of disclosure."

"I have no secrets either to hide or disclose, my Lady," she shyly replied, "and any such store would most certainly be beneath your notice. But I know this to be true of other people—am I then mistaken?"

"Indeed no. You speak the truth. But leave this subject for the time being and give us the rapture of your sweet song."

Shwaykar did not consider this refusal final, for she had read otherwise in her mistress's eyes, and eyes are ever truer than tongues. "I am at your service, my Lady."

Tree of Pearls truly desired that her handmaiden should further provoke her to speech, and so she fretfully replied, "What then do you imagine to be the cause of my unease?"

"How might I know such a thing?" Shwaykar was quick to reply. "I know nothing of your affairs, other than that which can only inspire delight and pride. Even in matters of the heart, I know that you have attained a rank to which no other woman may lay claim. All our noble princes court your pleasure and count your notice of them a great boon. A single glance of favor from you is enough to win the heart of any of them, though you may dispense with them all, due to your pride of place in the heart of the greatest of princes, my Lord 'Izz al-Din Aybak, who ever longs for a sign of your special esteem."

The blood rushed to Tree of Pearls's cheeks at the sound of this name. "That is not a matter that merits the concern of one such as I, Shwaykar, but rather it is a subject in which a young maiden like you may take pleasure."

Like many at court, Shwaykar was certain of the ties of love that bound her mistress to 'Izz al-Din Aybak, Commander in Chief of the Mamluk princes. She changed the subject, however, and said, "Forgive my presumption and pardon my error, my Lady. Perhaps you are preoccupied with affairs of state since the death of his Highness the Good King, may God rest his soul."

"You have guessed correctly, Shwaykar. The Franks continue to threaten us in Mansura and Farskur, and I fear the tides of war may turn against us."

"But the news that reaches us is good, is it not? Did not a great bird come to us from afar with omens of success? Did not a messenger thereafter alight with news of our soldiers' victory over the French, and recount how they had dispatched thirty thousand of their men, captured their king, Louis, and imprisoned him in the mighty fortress of Ibn Luqman? Did not yet another messenger come, bearing the cloak of the King of the Franks himself, a red velvet cloak trimmed with pale grey fur, and his golden crown, at which the city of Cairo bedecked itself in joyous ornament the likes of which has never been seen? Do you then put no faith in these tidings, my Lady?"

"I have no doubt but that they are true."

"Then, what is it that disturbs you so?"

Tree of Pearls sighed and shook her head anxiously, "You have constrained me to speak, Shwaykar, and I shall share a small part of my troubles with you. I fear not the Franks, for our armies are valiant and unyielding, not least those Turks for whom our Sovereign the Good King built this fortress. Their courage has been well proven in these wars. No, it is dissension in the ranks of the army that I fear, a deadly discord brought forth by the foolish actions of Giyath al-Din, the Exalted King."

"Does my Lady permit me to speak, though I may know nothing of politics or of statecraft? I fear that you have made a grave mistake in bringing this Sultan from the fortress of Kifa and giving him the reins of power, while there are amongst our own princes many much worthier than he."

"And yet the people would have a scion of the ruling house of Ayyub as their king. If it were not for this, or if only Giyath al-Din were a prudent ruler, all would be well. But he is a mere youth: ignorant, thoughtless, and a drunkard, no less. If once he is intoxicated, he acts in a manner unbefitting even a child. I have heard that he sets rows of lit candles in front of him at night, and taking up his sword, cuts them down one after the other, crying all the while 'this is how I shall deal with the Bahri Mamluks!'—meaning, of course, our own Turkish Mamluks. Since he arrived amongst us—and that was a mere two months ago—he openly favors his Kurdish troops over our Turks, declaring this aloud in his assemblies for all to hear, though our victories against the Franks have been won thanks to the valor of our brave Turkish champions, 'Izz al-Din Aybak, Rukn al-Din Baybars, Sayf al-Din Qutuz, and their peers. I fear that this controversy will only deepen, allowing our enemies to take advantage of this strife and attack us once again." Tree of Pearls fell silent and bowed her head in thought. Then she took a deep breath and whispered, "But I have devised a plan that, if successful, shall save us from destruction!" She rose abruptly and, turning her back, fell silent once again.

Shwaykar understood by this gesture that her mistress wished to terminate the conversation, and so she took up her oud and began to strum it softly. Suddenly, she perceived in the distance the sound of movement on the waters. Her eyes scanned the moonlit river and she made out a large, shadowy shape sailing towards them from the north. "Look here, my Lady," she cried. "A vessel approaches! Surely its advent at this late hour bespeaks some serious matter."

Tree of Pearls turned towards the approaching vessel. She recognized it immediately. "It is 'Izz al-Din's craft!" she exclaimed. "I wonder what news he brings." She hurried towards the harbor, pulling her shawl tight about her, while Shwaykar trailed behind eagerly.

The vast garden surrounding the Fortress contained a small harbor at which vessels had formerly docked back in the days when the garden itself had been a shipyard. A short path ran between this harbor and the castle walls. Excitement and curiosity had sent Tree of Pearls hurrying down to the river's edge to meet the vessel that was just now docking, but suddenly remembering herself she stopped short, turned about, and soberly proceeded to the Great Hall in which Al-Salih himself had been accustomed to receive delegations, princes, and ministers in the days of his glory.

Rukn al-Din Baybars

THE GREAT HALL, to whose elegance and ornament the Good King had devoted his greatest energy, was one of the most gorgeous in the palace. It was a vast chamber raised on marble columns, its ceiling decorated with frescos and engravings in the *Qurnus* style and its walls of colored marble covered in exquisite gold-leaf calligraphy. The entire effect was designed to arrest the eye and delight the soul. Tree of Pearls had not entered the Hall since Al-Salih's death over two months past, but she now had her own reasons for taking her place there to await 'Izz al-Din's messenger. She therefore commanded the palace eunuchs to make it ready. Noting her mistress's agitation, Shwaykar suddenly stopped at the doors and said, "I beg your leave to withdraw, my Lady."

"Whither to, my dear?" Tree of Pearls replied in surprise.

"To wherever you command me to go, for I fear that my presence may lie heavy on you."

Tree of Pearls signaled to her to follow. "Come, Shwaykar, I will keep no secrets from you." She arranged herself upon a magnificent couch of solid gold that stood on a large dais occupying the center of the room. It was from this very spot that Al-Salih had presided over his subjects. She motioned to Shwaykar to take the gilt chair next to her. The Great Hall was lit by candles that illuminated its gorgeous engravings. As Tree of Pearls reclined on the royal couch, Shwaykar gazed at her mistress and suddenly let out a peal of musical laughter that provoked Tree of Pearls to inquire archly as to the cause of it.

"My Lady, I rejoice to see you seated upon this couch, and I take it as a good omen. Indeed, it suits you well."

Tree of Pearls's heart trembled at this propitious augury, for the truth was that she desired dominion with all her soul, being well worthy of it. She said nothing, however, and summoning the palace Steward, she ordered him to make haste to the harbor and fetch any message that the newly arrived vessel might bear. Her immobile and stern features did not in the least betray the fires of anxiety burning within her. Shwaykar attempted to engage her in conversation about the priceless ornaments that graced the Hall and the extravagant sums that Al-Salih had expended on its construction, and Tree of Pearls in turn feigned interest in the subject, recounting to Shwaykar various anecdotes about the King's great care and exactitude in erecting the building. While they were thus engaged, Tree of Pearls heard the distant trumpet blast that heralded the vessel's arrival. Her heart pounded anew and Shwaykar noticed the sudden tremor of uneasiness that passed over her mistress's face. Shortly thereafter, a page entered and solemnly announced Prince Rukn al-Din Baybars. "Let him enter," Tree of Pearls commandingly replied.

A tall young man swept into the hall. He removed the woolen cloak in which he was wrapped from head to foot, to reveal a handsome form and a radiant face whose mien combined the poise of manly maturity and the freshness of youth. He was just twenty-three years old at the time of which we speak, and he was helmeted and dressed in a full coat of mail, as though still in the battlefield from whence he had come. As soon as he entered, he greeted Tree of Pearls with unusual ceremony. She immediately guessed at the reasons behind the peculiarity of his address, but she pretended not to notice, and merely said, "What news, Rukn al-Din?"

In response to this question, Rukn al-Din looked about him as though fearful of being overheard. Taking note of this gesture, she immediately dismissed the servants, keeping only Shwaykar close by. She then signaled to Rukn al-Din to approach. "What news, young Prince?" she repeated. "Speak, and have no fear of my dear Shwaykar. Indeed, her presence at this interview is fortunate, for she has long been an admirer of your courage and gallantry. Speak! What news?"

Shwaykar wondered at this odd pleasantry on her mistress's part, but she remained silent and gravely waited to hear the Prince's message. He, on the other hand, turned to gaze curiously upon her. He had heard tell of her wonderful voice, which was famous throughout the palace. He now discovered her to be exceedingly comely, with great limpid eyes in which intelligence and charm were perfectly united. He promptly turned back to Tree of Pearls. "I bear news of great importance which I know not whether it shall please my Lady to hear."

Tree of Pearls started at this, and her eyes bored into him. "Speak then! Tell me your news, and fear not my reaction, for I have ceased to expect any good of this world!"

"It is this: Giyath al-Din Turan Shah, the Exalted King, son of our Lord the Good King, met his end this very morning. My Lord Prince 'Izz al-Din Aybak sent me to you with this news ahead of the time when he shall arrive here in person on the morrow. He trusted no one but myself to deliver the message, and he charged me to place this sealed note into your hands." And with that, he took a small folded paper out of his pocket and, bowing deeply, offered it to her.

Tree of Pearls's heart leapt at this news, but she remained coldly impassive, her face a lovely mask chiseled in stone. She unfolded the note and began to read.

I hasten to inform you of these good tidings. The spoilt child has departed this world. Prince Rukn al-Din Baybars al-Bunduqari, the bearer of this letter, will describe to you the details of his death, in which the hand of this selfsame Prince bears the greatest glory and for which he deserves your notice. I have further news, of which I will inform you in person upon my arrival in Cairo tomorrow, God willing.

She slowly raised her pale face. "Are you absolutely sure that the Exalted King has been slain?"

"Yes my Lady."

"Was he taken by stealth?"

"He was openly and publicly dispatched."

"And who is responsible for this?"

"It was we who slew him. He was a tyrant, a fickle and reckless child. He insulted and provoked us incessantly, we the Bahri Mamluks, his father's own. He disdained us, though we are the Bearers of the Sword and Defenders of the State: we who repelled the Franks from these lands. In his rashness, he imagined that he might continue thus unopposed, and that we were nothing but vile insects to be crushed underfoot. We patiently bore his tyranny, nonetheless, until we heard of the displeasure of our Lady Tree of Pearls, mother of the Good King's son. So we waited and plotted against him until the moment was propitious. This very morning he was holding court amongst his entourage, princes, Kurds, and partisans, his chief officers arrayed before him carrying golden scepters, his whole manner proclaiming his insolence, as though he were like to say, 'I am your Sultan, whether it please you or not!'

"We waited until he had dismissed his party. The table was laid for his meal and he took his place at it as usual. Then a group of us approached him with our swords drawn and struck off the fingers of his right hand. Terrified, he rose and fled into the Wooden Tower, sealing the door behind him. When we fired on the tower, he fled yet again and threw himself into the sea, swimming for dear life. The archers assailed him from all directions, and he cried out, 'Take your kingdom and give me leave to return to the fort of Kifa!' but none came to his aid. Thus was he slain, by fire, water, and sword! We dragged his corpse from the sea and left it to rot on the shore. May he never know a true grave!"

An Amorous Interlude

THOUGH TREE OF PEARLS remained perfectly still during this account of the death of Giyath al-Din, her eyes betrayed the deepest interest. "Turan Shah is then truly dead!" she whispered when Rukn al-Din had finished speaking. "God have mercy on his soul. He erred in his judgment. He was unworthy of the kingship that we bestowed upon him, and the king who is incapable of ruling must needs be overthrown!" She cast a glance at Rukn al-Din, adding, "And have you any other news, Prince?"

"Verily I do, but my Lord Prince 'Izz al-Din Aybak will himself inform you of it tomorrow morning, my Lady."

"Perhaps, then, it is of the utmost importance, this news he brings?"

Smiling, Rukn al-Din replied, "It is so."

Tree of Pearls guessed his meaning, but she changed the subject and said, "You have mentioned nothing of the brave officers who dispatched the Exalted King. Are you perchance one of them?"

"I am, my Lady, though I am but the lowest in rank, and was merely commanded to action by my Lord 'Izz al-Din," he replied.

Tree of Pearls was well pleased with this modesty. "Do you then shy away from this act, as though you considered it a crime? Indeed, it is a great deed, with which you should be well satisfied. You have saved our lands from ruin, for this King was unworthy of his title. Fear not! 'Izz al-Din has informed me of your bravery and I myself have long marked your courage and daring. I doubt not that a great future lies before you, and if my speculation be well placed, I hereby pledge to bestow upon you my most precious possession." Having made this speech, she glanced at Shwaykar and laughed. Shwaykar guessed her meaning and was overcome by shyness, for she had never yet given her heart to a soul. Her whole world revolved around the pleasure of her mistress. She blushed and bowed her head, and suddenly regretted her uncovered face. She was not, however, in the habit of veiling in the presence of princes.

As for Rukn al-Din Baybars, he was well pleased with Tree of Pearls's compliments. Though greatly taken with Shwaykar's beauty, he would never have imagined that she might one day be his, and he was uncertain how to respond to Tree of Pearls's veiled conditions for this unexpected prize. Finally, he replied, "I thank my Lady for the kind words she has deigned to bestow on her slave and servitor, and I hope one day to prove worthy of her confidence. I am at all times hostage to her least command and my very life is her ransom." Tree of Pearls rejoiced at this declaration, for she was desirous of winning Rukn al-Din to her cause and anxious to employ his cool and unswerving courage for her own ends. Shwaykar, too, was moved by the Prince's words. She felt a new and exquisite sensation, the likes of which she had never before experienced. Her eyes reflected her inner agitation and her heart skipped in the most curious manner, but she kept her head bowed and said nothing.

Tree of Pearls was well satisfied with the success of her plot, for it was she herself who had incited the Mamluks to slay Turan Shah. Had it not been for her direct command, they would never have dared such an undertaking. Her paramour, Prince 'Izz al-Din Aybak, had been her accomplice in this. It was he who had instigated them to rebellion, and Rukn al-Din Babyars had been in the forefront of the revolt. Many a time, Tree of Pearls had heard 'Izz al-Din recount his courage and his fealty to their cause. By promising Shwaykar to him she hoped to redouble the young Prince's loyalty to her person and her ambitions. "When, then, can we expect Prince 'Izz al-Din's arrival?" she resumed.

"I believe he will arrive tomorrow morning with the princes and officers of the army. The news he brings shall effect a great change in the affairs of our state, but Prince 'Izz al-Din has reserved the bearing of these good tidings as his own prerogative, he being our lord and master."

Tree of Pearls smiled as she rose from her couch. "I congratulate you on the great prize you have won, Rukn al-Din," she said as she looked at Shwaykar, "and I pray that you will indeed fulfill my hopes of you."

Rukn al-Din understood that she dismissed him with these words. He turned to depart, first casting a farewell glance at Shwaykar, who dared not look up to meet it, but the two hearts had met and taken stock of each other—a simple exchange when natures be mutually inclined. Bowing deeply, he now took his leave and immediately returned to the tower in the Citadel that he occupied with a number of his fellow Mamluk officers.

'Izz al-Din Aybak

AFTER RUKN AL-DIN'S DEPARTURE, Tree of Pearls rose and gathered the long train of her robes behind her. Shwaykar rose in turn to await her mistress's command. Tree of Pearls was not entirely easy in her mind as to whether she had done well by her handmaiden in pledging her to Rukn al-Din. She wished to ascertain Shwaykar's opinion on the matter and sound the inclinations of her heart, and so she approached the subject directly. "I hope you are pleased with your suitor, Shwaykar?"

Blushing deeply, Shwaykar raised her eyes to meet those of her mistress and saw that her expression was full of teasing affection. She struggled to overcome her shyness, and with some effort finally brought herself to offer a hesitant smile in reply. "It seems that my Lady has grown weary of my company."

"What nonsense, child! I only wish to secure your future, and a woman with your beauty, education, and accomplishments must needs make a fit match. I am certain that this brave young man is a gem amongst his peers and has, moreover, a brilliant career before him. If I am wrong in this, and he is not the man that I imagine him to be, I will never give you to him in marriage. Fear not, Shwaykar, for I am as jealous of your interests as though they were those of my own daughter. I am confident that you know this to be the truth. And now I shall retire, for I am quite fatigued by the day's events."

"And yet you are surely satisfied with this conclusion, my Lady? The man who was the cause of all our troubles has met his end, and government shall now resume its proper course. Who shall now take up the reins of power, I wonder? I trust we shall no longer be forced to submit to the House of Ayyub. It seems that the days of this dynasty are well past."

"Perhaps you are right, Shwaykar," she smiled. "'Izz al-Din Aybak shall certainly enlighten us on the subject when he arrives tomorrow." She then bade her goodnight, and Shwaykar kissed her mistress's hand while Tree of Pearls placed an affectionate kiss in return on her handmaiden's brow.

As soon as Shwaykar had quit her, she hurried through a secret door in the Great Hall that led directly to her chambers. The hour had struck midnight and the servants had long since lit her splendid apartments, which were hung with heavy tapestries of silk brocade richly woven with verses of poetry, ornamental designs, and wonderful martial and pastoral scenes of most brilliant and varied color. She threw herself onto her bed and surrendered to her turbulent thoughts. "Turan Shah is slain—may God resurrect him not!—and this by the hand of my own 'Izz al-Din." She sighed deeply as she pronounced his name. "He is my love, but he is secretive and cunning, and I yet doubt his loyalty. So it is with men, ever untrustworthy! And what does it matter?" she shrugged, "let him act as he pleases! Has he not served me well in this affair? All that now remains is for the kingdom to be delivered once again into my hands. 'Izz al-Din has promised me this! I wonder, then, if he will honor his pledge. I shall be the first Queen in the history of our Empire, and I shall reward him well if he serves me faithfully."

She spent a good part of the night thus reveling in her plots and fancies. When finally she slept, she dreamt that she had been made Queen and gripped the royal scepter firmly in her hands. Tree of Pearls desired dominion, no matter the cost. This appetite for power had possessed her upon the birth of Al-Salih's son, Khalil, for she had dared to hope that he would one day be the means through which her ambitions might be fulfilled. Would he not be the future Sultan and she his Regent? But the boy had died in his infancy, and Tree of Pearls's budding hopes with him.

The next morning, a eunuch entered to announce her eagerly awaited visitor. "Prince 'Izz al-Din Aybak awaits your Ladyship in the Great Hall." Tree of Pearls rose and dressed. On this morning, she took great care with her toilette in order to appear as magnificent as possible before her lover. (If this is the way of all women without exception, then what of those few who attach momentous political ambition to their love-affairs?) She wore a dark-hued gown of striped silk and wove her luxurious hair into a few soft plaits, leaving two of these to frame her fine, oval face. On her head she knotted a scarf embroidered with silver and gold thread and adorned with precious stones that hung glittering on her brow, and left its long train to trail freely down her back. Around her slender throat she wore two chains, one of pearls and one of carnelian, and she wound a heavy belt of beaten gold around her waist and hips. Though Tree of Pearls was on the threshold of middle-age, the waters of youth still coursed through her veins. Her eyes still shot their spells at men's hearts and filled them, not with a sense of yielding feminine charm and grace like Shwaykar, but rather with a feeling of awe and dark, discordant passion.

'Izz al-Din Aybak keenly felt the might of this woman and her dominion over his heart. His love was born of respect and fear rather than tender longing. Her rank and influence in Al-Salih's household had fanned the flames of his desire to possess her. Thus it had come to pass that he had sought her favor, and she had freely bestowed it. The liaison suited Tree of Pearls, for she well knew the impossibility of pursuing her vast ambitions unaided. She was, after all, a woman, and could never hope to command an army. She saw the benefit that might accrue to her in the promotion of 'Izz al-Din to the rank of Commander-in-Chief of the Mamluk princes, and she had aided him in this suit during Al-Salih's reign. He was, of course, deeply grateful for this boon. When the chance to serve her by assassinating Turan Shah arose, he had not let it slip through his fingers, though he had also most certainly thereby served his own interests.

He had arrived at the palace that morning on his steed with a small company of officers and horsemen, and had rested only briefly from his long journey before hastening to the Great Hall for he keenly looked forward to the pleasure of receiving the elaborate expressions of praise and abundant gratitude that were sure to pour forth from his lady's lips.

Good Tidings

HE WAS NOT KEPT WAITING FOR LONG. The eunuch appeared and announced his mistress, and 'Izz al-Din rose to greet her. Tree of Pearls now stood before him, and 'Izz al-Din fell upon her hands as though to kiss them. She started and drew back from him in a graceful gesture of modesty. He motioned to her to take her seat upon the couch and seated himself by her side. She bade the servant to withdraw, and once alone with the Prince, she spoke. "Welcome, 'Izz al-Din. We have been informed of your bravery in ridding the country of that feckless child. May God reward you. You have done a great service to the Community of Muslims."

"I undertook this deed to serve my heart's sovereign, Tree of Pearls," he fervently replied.

His words affected her greatly—she, who loved him well—but they also rekindled her dormant suspicions. "I fully acknowledge this favor, 'Izz al-Din. It is not the first time that you have proved the sincerity of your affection, and I am but the prisoner of your grace."

"The merest token of your approval suffices me, my Lady," he replied. "Especially now that you shall be enthroned Queen of Muslims!"

Tree of Pearls flushed deeply and feigned astonishment. "Queen of Muslims? What can you possibly mean by this?"

"You are already my Queen and the possessor of my heart, and shall soon become Queen of Egypt and Guardian of the State and of Religion."

"How has this come to pass?" she demanded. "I beg you to explain yourself."

"When the Exalted King was slain yesterday, the princes convened a council to discuss the succession. At first there was much dissension between them, until I intervened to propose a happy solution. 'We would be ill-advised,' said I, 'to bestow the succession on a member of the Ayyubid Dynasty after having suffered such insult at their hands. Let us then choose a compromise. The Good

King—may God rest his soul—was the only Ayyubid that deserved our respect. We can trust no one else of his line. We well know that the mother of his son, Khalil, was the closest person to his heart. She is intelligent and capable, and she is our countrywoman, in addition. She will defend and uphold our honor. It is my opinion that we should invest her with crown and scepter.' While some amongst them continued to advocate the Ayyubid succession, the princes finished by accepting my counsel and have resolved to elect you Queen over Egypt. Should I not by rights then bend to kiss your hand and beg your grace?"

"God forbid such a thing! You are my beloved and to you I owe all. Without you I should never have attained to this rank. If I am truly invested Queen of Egypt, you shall be my scepter and I shall bestow upon you the post of First Minister, for who should deserve it more than you?"

'Izz al-Din secretly rejoiced at this promise. He had hoped that it would be so, and he anticipated yet greater honors to result from this propitious beginning. He poured forth his gratitude lavishly, subtly alternating between expressions of modesty and of flattery, while Tree of Pearls continued to insist on her great debt to him and to praise his zeal and valor. "I trust no one but you," she said, "and cannot do without you in managing the affairs of the state."

"Truly, you have no need of my poor assistance," 'Izz al-Din replied, "but I am nonetheless at your slightest command."

They spent an hour conversing in this manner, both elated by the great prize they had won. Finally, Tree of Pearls turned to more concrete matters. "We must work to cement the loyalty of our supporters in the army," she mused. "How, then, do you propose to distribute the posts and sinecures at our disposal?"

"My darling Tree of Pearls has thought of everything," he smiled. "She of course knows that our army is composed of diverse nations—Circassians, Byzantines, Kurds, and Turks—and that most of these are Mamluk slaves. The Turks are our own men, the base and might of our army. We must therefore strengthen them and promote them, according to their rank and precedence, to state office. There are, for example, the Commanders of the Hundred and the Commanders of the Thousand, and they are all, as you know, mighty warriors, the backbone of the army and its puissance. We should immediately confer the honor of royal sinecures on the great princes that aided us in this affair. The administrative posts of the state are many, the most important being the Chief of the Royal Arsenal, who bears the Sultan's arms at great assemblies and congregations, and the *Dawadar*, the Sultan's Executive Secretary, his messenger and postmaster, who recites his proclamations to those who attend upon him and receives his signature on state documents. The Royal Chamberlain stands between the princes and the soldiers; the *Jandar,* Wardrobe Keeper of the Imperial Court, also acts as the Sultan's Assassin, while the Majordomo is charged with management of the Sultan's household, and so forth. How does Tree of Pearls wish to dispense these posts?"

"I leave these matters to you," she replied gravely. "You shall distribute these posts among the most trustworthy of your men: those whom you know to be loyal to us. I have one request to make of you, however, and that is that you should take up the matter of Rukn al-Din Baybars—the young man with whom you sent your letter yesterday. He is a fine prince. I wish you to bestow upon him an office that will keep him close to us."

In spite of his confidence in the young prince, a quick stab of jealousy brought a spate of malicious words to the tip of 'Izz al-Din's tongue at this unexpected request—for jealousy, as we well know, both deafens and blinds its victim—but he quickly retrieved his calm and his native shrewdness and replied, "You speak truly, my Lady. Rukn al-Din is indeed one of the most brilliant of our young champions. I suggest you honor him with the post of Dawadar if you would keep him close by."

Tree of Pearls detected the subtle current of resentment in this reply—women being infinitely more sensitive in these matters than men—but she pretended to take no notice, for she would not be fettered in her actions by the love of any man. Rank and power were her true heart's desire and she would stop at nothing to acquire them. She now changed the subject. "When do the princes arrive from Mansura?" she lightly inquired.

"I expect them tomorrow, to attend the ceremony by which Tree of Pearls shall be crowned Queen of these lands. How sweet is that name on my lips, and how dear to my heart! Does she too thrill to the sound of my own, I wonder?" The glance that he directed at her was full of playful reproach, and she understood its meaning perfectly.

"You shall see for yourself the extent of my trust and my love. My deeds, and not mere words, shall be your proof. Your skillful insinuations suggest that you suspect the sincerity of my affections, 'Izz al-Din." She glanced at him reproachfully in her turn. "May God forgive you."

"God forbid that I should suspect you, my Lady—" but she hastened to interrupt him before he could say another word.

"Call me 'my Lady' no more. You are my love, my advocate and my confidant. You may be sure of me."

"I am sure of you, my love. And yet I would—"

"Leave this subject, I beg you," she commanded. "I believe we understand each other well, you and I. Let us now attend to our present affairs. I hear a clamor rising in the palace."

"It is the Commanders of the Army," 'Izz al-Din declared. "They have arrived from Mansura and seek an audience with you."

"Do you see fit that I should receive them, then?" The question was meant to flatter his vanity.

"I see no reason why you should not, if they wish it. You are henceforth beholden to them and to the great enthusiasm they have shown on your behalf, my dear," he added wryly. "You must of course draw the screen between them and yourself, for you are now Queen of Muslims."

She glanced at him sideways with an inscrutable smile. "'Izz al-Din offers further tokens of his jealousy: an auspicious sign indeed, for jealousy is proof of love. Nevertheless, I have no need of his warning. You know that I reveal my face to no man but you." She said this while signaling to the eunuch who attended her to draw the screen. No sooner had he done so than the Chamberlain entered. "The mighty Commanders of the Army seek the honor of an audience with our noble Lady." He then recited their names: Bilbay, Al-Rashidi, Faris al-Din Iqtay, Baybars al-Din al-Bunduqari, and Sanqar the Byzantine.

"Let them enter," 'Izz al-Din replied on her behalf.

He received them graciously and they returned the greeting, then Faris Iqtay delivered their message. "We have come to offer our condolences to her Ladyship, Mother of Khalil, for the loss of Turan Shah, and to inform her that our choice has fallen upon her as successor to the throne and Queen of Muslims. May this decision be deemed acceptable by her."

'Izz al-Din again spoke on behalf of Tree of Pearls. "My Princes, our noble Lady has been informed of the brave deeds you have undertaken for the good of the state. She grieves for the death of the young King, and yet knows his doom was prepared by his own hand. May God have mercy on his soul."

Prince Sanqar the Byzantine now spoke. "It was he who forced our hand, for he excluded us from the government of these lands. But he is no longer of concern to us. Her Ladyship, consort of our departed Sovereign, the Good King, is most deserving of this honor."

Tree of Pearls now replied to this speech from behind the screen. "I thank you for the great zeal and valor with which you have defended this state, and for the faith you have chosen to place in me. Know that I have no choice but to accept your decision, you, the flower of our sword-wielding princes. Know also that in accepting this great honor, I acknowledge my full debt to our noble Commanders and offer them in return my fullest confidence and my utmost devotion."

"We place ourselves at the command of our Queen, and our lives are her ransom," declared the princes in unison, "and tomorrow we celebrate her coronation in the Citadel, God willing."

As they prepared to withdraw, 'Izz al-Din added, "Our Queen, Tree of Pearls, has notified me in private that she has prepared rich gifts for you and your men as tokens of recognition for your noble courage and daring. She has, moreover, informed me that she accepts the scepter for the sole reason that you have deemed her worthy of it." Tree of Pearls had indeed portioned out a king's ransom in gifts to the princes in honor of her impending coronation—an event that she had not only expected, but carefully planned for in the weeks preceding. She was wise to exercise her generosity thus, for she was well aware of the difficulties that must beset the first woman to accede to the throne in Muslim lands. The princes, meanwhile, were exceedingly pleased at this news.

'Izz al-Din now escorted them out, all the while praising their devotion and flattering their hopes. He presently returned to the Great Hall to discuss with Tree of Pearls the matter of the royal gifts that would be distributed on the morrow.

Sallafa and Sahban

BY SUNRISE OF THE FOLLOWING DAY, the inhabitants of the Garden Island had all heard the news of Tree of Pearls's impending coronation as Egypt's Queen. Many were those who wondered at this news, while her fellow royal concubines received it with no small measure of envy—most particularly a Kurdish concubine by the name of Sallafa, who was often wont to boast of belonging to the same clan as the Good King himself. The late King had shown his favor by appointing her Custodian of the Royal Harem, but unlike Tree of Pearls, she had given him no sons. Sallafa was renowned for her beauty at the court but she lacked the refinement essential to a Queen. She was spiteful, moreover, and possessed a violently jealous disposition.

Most people among the inhabitants of the Garden Island and the city of Cairo had only ever heard tell of this legendary beauty, having never actually set eyes on her. A certain Baghdadi cloth merchant by the name of Sahban was one of the privileged few who had seen her. This merchant travelled to Egypt now and again to trade his rich Persian silks and Indian muslins, and the Good King would often summon him to the Palace to purchase the choicest bolts of fine cloth for the women of his house. On one of these visits, Sallafa was present, commissioned by the King to choose her heart's desire, and a frightful passion had seized the poor merchant's heart as soon as he had set eyes on her. Though the unlucky fellow had done his best to maintain the impassive and dignified air that befits a man of his station in such imposing circumstances, she had immediately sensed his confusion, and judiciously ignored it. From that moment on, Sahban availed himself of the slightest opportunity to convey his passion with valuable gifts of choicest cloth that he caused to be delivered to her through the palace eunuchs. In this way he appeared to be merely paying tribute to the Custodian of the Good King's Palaces.

Al-Salih's harem inevitably fell into neglect upon his death, and Sahban began to watch closely for an opportunity to seek Sallafa's favor more directly. His first efforts had met with complete failure, for it was the Steward who had come forth to bargain with him, and Sallafa had not even deigned to inspect his merchandise in person. He had lately arrived in Cairo once again, and on the very eve of Tree of Pearls's coronation he determined to try his luck a second time.

The news that Tree of Pearls was to be crowned Queen on the morrow had lit the raging fires of jealousy in Sallafa's heart. She well knew that the would-be Queen owed all to the efforts of her paramour, 'Izz al-Din Aybak, and she was determined at all costs to inflict the greatest harm possible on her rival. Her rancor was blind, and her only desire was to see the woman brutally stripped of the great prize that she had won. Such is the sole cure for chronic envy, those who suffer from it preferring self-destruction to the sight of another's happiness.

Sallafa finally grew weary of brooding over the matter in her close chambers. She veiled her face, wrapped herself in a loose silken cloak, and quit the women's quarters by a narrow passage that led to an adjoining garden artfully planted with all manner of trees and aromatic herbs and flowers. It had been Al-Salih's favorite retreat of a bright, breezy morning, and Sallafa now took refuge there from her dark thoughts.

A palace eunuch disturbed her reverie to announce the arrival of the Iraqi merchant with a new consignment of fine fabrics. Sallafa started at the sound of his name. A strange feeling of relief filled her, she knew not why, a feminine intuition that whispered, 'here is assistance' to her burning heart, for women are wont to set the pudding before the proof. She turned to the boy. "Where is he?" she demanded.

"In the palace courtyard, my Lady. He insists on meeting with you in person, for he would show you a number of articles that he claims shall especially please you."

"I do not wish to return to the palace yet. Tell him to come to me here in the garden by the main gate." She adjusted her robes, and covered her face with a corner of her cloak as she said this. She suddenly felt the hot blood coursing through her veins and warming her throbbing heart. She was surprised at this sensation, for the merchant had never before impressed her in any way. She took it as a portent of great things to come.

The eunuch ushered the merchant into the garden by the gate Sallafa had indicated. "Shaykh Sahban, my Lady," he announced, and promptly withdrew.

Sallafa was seated on a stone bench surrounded by myriad clusters of delicate flowers in full bloom. She turned her absent gaze towards the gate and saw Sahban standing there humbly in his Persian cap and his voluminous black cloak. He still wore the same short, fine beard and his eyes glittered strangely. She examined him more closely than she had done before and she perceived a marked change in his habitual expression. He approached her and they exchanged the customary greetings. She motioned to him to come closer. "Where are your goods?" she lazily inquired.

"I left them in the palace courtyard with the camels, my Lady. If you permit me, I shall have them brought here to the garden."

"Never mind," she replied. "Leave them where they are for now. You may take a seat," she added, pointing to a bench next to her own. He sat down gingerly while fiddling with his robes. "It has never before been your custom to request Sallafa by name when you come to the palace to exhibit your goods," she remarked.

"Have I offended you, my Lady?" he anxiously inquired.

"No. But I wish to understand the reason for this change."

Sahban rubbed his nose nervously as he considered his response. "I have altered my habit in conformance with the sweeping changes that have come upon the people of this palace."

This unexpected parry intrigued Sallafa, and her cheeks flushed with anger as she recalled the ill-starred events to which he referred. "You speak truly. The changes to which you allude have been great indeed. May God have mercy on the Good King, for he was the jewel of this state, and his passing has disturbed the balance of things."

"Too true, my Lady, may God rest his soul. But what is to be done? It seems fate must have its way."

"You have heard the news then?" she demanded sharply.

"If you mean the great honor conferred on Tree of Pearls, then yes, I have heard."

"This is indeed my meaning. And what are your thoughts on this subject, Sahban?"

This direct use of his first name delighted Sahban. "My thoughts? I think. . . . At the very least I think that such a thing has never yet occurred in the history of our Empire."

Sallafa smiled and her face took on a gay expression. "Well said. Such shocking heresy is unheard of."

"Yes," he replied, "but . . ." He gulped as though afraid to continue.

Sallafa pounced upon his hesitation. "Speak! But what? Speak, I say."

"But . . . I only wonder how a concubine has managed to attain such an unthinkable honor."

"How has she attained it? Have you not heard of 'Izz al-Din Aybak the Turcoman, Commander of the Army?"

"Yes, I have heard of him. I understand your meaning, my Lady. And I appreciate the difference between Sallafa the Kurd and the fortunate Tree of Pearls, the Turk."

Sallafa saw in these words an opportunity to broach the subject that plagued her. "And what is that difference?" she asked.

"The difference is that the former has remained true to her master's troth, while the latter has betrayed it."

Sallafa pretended to object. "You must not say such things. She is the mother of Al-Salih's son, Khalil!"

Sahban immediately sensed the dissimulation behind this protest and he warmed to the subject. "I only speak the truth, my Lady. I have been in the habit of frequenting this palace for a number of years now and have beheld Sallafa countless times. My eyes have constantly sought hers but have never as of yet won the boon of her regard. She stands aloof and proud like no other woman. I beg your pardon, my Lady, at this admission. As for Tree of Pearls, her relations with 'Izz al-Din Aybak are common knowledge, though she is the mother of the departed King's son. And yet she shall now become Queen of Muslims, and we shall all be obliged to bow to her will."

"She shall never be Queen!" Sallafa vehemently cried. "And even if she does, her reign shall not endure." Realizing that she had perhaps too boldly revealed her thoughts, she drew back and anxiously glanced around her, then she plucked a flower from a branch close by and busied herself over it, the hot blood burning her face.

Sahban seized the opportunity that this little scene afforded him. He lowered his voice confidentially. "My Lady, we need not prolong this senseless conversation. If a woman of this palace must rule, then you are certainly the most deserving of the honor, for you hold the highest rank in the King's harem and you are, moreover, of his own clan."

"No, Sahban," Sallafa interrupted, "I have no wish to rule. Women were not made to wield crown and scepter. This is why I believe that Tree of Pearls's reign cannot last. It must not!" she cried, and her eyes spit sparks of anger.

Sahban realized at once that this outburst masked an invitation of sorts. "If you would deign to place your confidence in me, my Lady, I shall be the instrument of your will. Reveal your thoughts to me."

Sallafa hesitated. A momentary confusion, a sudden reticence overcame her. She unconsciously twisted and tore at the petals of the flower in her hand. Before she could gather her thoughts together, Sahban quickly murmured, "If you have yet to understand my heart's purpose, I shall declare it openly to you, most beautiful of women. I have been a prisoner of your love from the moment I first saw you. Your reserve—your coldness even—towards me in the lifetime of the Good King only made me admire and respect your great virtue the more. But now that the King has departed this world forever, I beseech you: could you find in Sahban a creature that would deserve your confidence and esteem?"

Sallafa flushed and remained silent. She looked about while she struggled to put her thoughts together, but found nothing but the trees and the flowers to distract her from the answer she must now give to this direct appeal. Sahban noted her uneasiness and, taking it as a rebuke, made as if to rise, but Sallafa motioned for him to wait.

"I see that my presence weighs heavily on you, my Lady," Sahban finally said. "Allow me to take my leave. We should not wish to give fuel to the tongues of gossips and slanderers."

Sallafa threw him a burning glance that penetrated to his very bowels. "Gossips and slanderers? I fear no one. As for your presence here, I am in need of it."

This sudden retort delighted Sahban and he laughed out loud in frank surprise. "If my presence is indeed necessary to you, then I am truly at your command."

Sallafa sat up and her eyes grew grave. Underneath her veil, her mouth was now set in firm determination. "Do you speak seriously?" she asked Sahban.

"Put me to the test, my Lady—after you have bestowed upon me a word to set my heart at ease. Can I aspire to be the man who deserves your favor?"

She nodded slowly in the affirmative. "And to prove it," she whispered, "I shall confide a perilous secret to you; a secret that you must never tell to another living soul."

"Speak, my Lady, I pray you."

"I shall charge you, moreover, with a task that is not lacking in danger."

"My life is your ransom," he replied passionately. "I would gladly die if only to please you."

"You are from Baghdad, is that not so? You travel there every year?"

"I travel there when it pleases me to do so," Sahban replied.

"And why do you not prefer to remain in your own country?" Sallafa pursued.

"Am I obliged to answer this question?" he said.

"You are."

Sahban sighed. "Though this meeting that fate has granted us be ever so brief, I yet feel that our hearts have known each other for many a year. Allow me then to be perfectly frank with you."

"That is what I desire of you," Sallafa replied.

"Know then that I am a Shi'ite. The Abbasid Caliphs hate the Shi'a and persecute them brutally. The Shi'a of Baghdad are especially ill-used. This is why I prefer to live in exile rather than suffer all manner of extortion and plunder yearly instigated by the House of 'Abbas. I am a wealthy man, and am in no need of the money I earn as a merchant. I only took up trade for pleasure and as an excuse to see the wide world. When I do go to Baghdad, I never stay longer than the time it takes to purchase my stock."

"And the present Caliph, Al-Musta'sim?"

Sahban clenched his jaw and his eyes lit up with anger at the mention of this name. "Al-Musta'sim is the vilest scoundrel of the House of 'Abbas. His reign has been bitter indeed."

Sallafa gazed at him doubtfully and she bowed her head in silence.

"Why do you hesitate, my Lady? Speak your thoughts, I beg you."

"I do not wish to place you in harm's way."

"Danger is love's most delicate condiment," Sahban was quick to reply.

Sallafa still hesitated. "Will you then serve me in the name of love, Sahban?"

"If you permit me, my Lady."

Sallafa sighed. "Listen closely then. Our Turkish concubine shall remain Queen only as long as it takes you to depart for Baghdad and return from there."

Sahban understood her purpose perfectly. "I shall do as you bid. Do you wish me to undertake this mission in my own name or as your messenger?"

"You shall be my messenger," Sallafa replied. "I shall give you a letter to take to Baghdad. I am certain that she shall be dethroned by decree of the Caliph as soon as the reply to my letter arrives in Cairo."

"To whom do you wish me to deliver the letter?"

"To the Custodian of the Caliph's Harem. She is my friend and she is beholden to me. Will you do this?"

Sahban rose. "I shall go immediately. Give me the letter." He reached into his girdle and pulled out a pen and inkpot, and from his pocket a blank sheet, and he gave these to Sallafa, who took them from him, fixing his eyes all the while in a look of fierce questioning. They remained locked in this gaze for a space, as though closely negotiating in some silent, private language, until Sallafa finally spoke.

"I am aware, Sahban, that I have entrusted you with a matter of the utmost gravity on the sole basis of an hour's interview. Do you not think me overly impulsive? Shall I escape from this danger unscathed?"

"Listen to your heart. It speaks the truth. If you still doubt the sincerity of my service, I shall take any oath you please. I am your slave."

"Shall you swear then?"

The merchant prepared to take the oath she seemed to require of him, but Sallafa suddenly seized his hand with her own hot fingers and said, "No, I have no need of this oath." She took the paper and began to write. She possessed splendid handwriting and diction, for the sultans spare no pains in teaching their concubines the arts of grammar, rhetoric, and poetry. When she had finished, she folded the letter and gave it to Sahban.

"Here is my secret. I place it in your hands. If you succeed in executing my design, you will have proved your fine words."

He took it from her and only replied "God be with you" as he turned to go, looking back at her longingly every few paces until he had crossed through the gate of the garden. She remained behind after he had left, lost in thought and fretting over the wisdom of the impulsive course she had taken. The memory of his words and gestures, and his long years of trade at the Palace, all tended to reassure her. Moreover, the envy and spite she harbored against Tree of Pearls was such that she would have stopped at nothing to bring her to her knees.

The Coronation

THE NEXT DAY, Cairo was abuzz with excitement. The townsfolk, mounted and on foot, men and women, crowded round the Citadel, and the Ramliyya square that spread out at its foot bustled with people of all classes. Hawkers selling pastry, fruit, sweets, and all manner of preserved foods and freshly prepared dishes mingled with the crowds, as did all kinds of fortune-tellers with their diverse instruments of divination, be they seashells, mirrors, or pebbles. Peddlers and fortune-tellers hawked their wares and services in a variety of tones and melodies, while the braying of donkeys, the neighing of horses, and the barking of dogs punctuated the din of the multitude.

If you were to have looked down upon this square from the ramparts of the Citadel, you would have seen scattered across it groups of people dressed in gay colors, sitting cross legged on the ground and occupied in chewing on some morsel, or tracing forms in the dust with a stick, or exercising their fingers with some nimble device. Others crowded round a performing bear or monkey who passed the hat around at the end of the spectacle, while still others strained their necks in silent astonishment as they listened to a preacher who did his best to delight their ears and win their hearts by narrating Prophetic traditions of dubious provenance.

These popular recitations and the extreme naiveté of the audience who hung upon every word would not fail to astound you. You might for example hear a *hadith* with which you are perfectly well acquainted, but twisted and turned into something entirely unfamiliar, or mixed up haphazardly with an altogether different story. This tendency to muddle up and exaggerate the stories and sayings of the Prophet becomes even more pronounced the farther the subject in question is from people's daily experience, such as the one that was now on everyone's lips: the coronation of a woman as Queen of Muslims—an event they had certainly never seen the like of in their lives. Opinions differed on the subject. Explanations were invented, conspiracies were hinted at, and predictions were made. Some even claimed that the Day of Judgment was at hand, this certainly being, in the general opinion, one of its most manifest signs.

Finally, the trumpets sounded and the beating of the drums made itself heard over the general clamor. The procession of Mamluk princes, preceded by the magnificent horsemen to whom we have already made allusion, could be seen making its way towards the Citadel. They wore golden coats of mail that glittered in the sun and dazzled the eyes of the crowd. There followed the litter in which sat Tree of Pearls, borne by stout mules and draped in finest silk brocade. The litter was accompanied by stalwart Mamluk riders in gaily colored garments, who bore aloft the royal banners. Behind these rode a company of javelin-wielding horsemen and another of archers. The tumultuous, sea-like multitude of the people followed this great procession on foot. There were many amongst them who had abandoned their labor or shut up their shops for the day in order to see the Queen's procession pass. They hoped for no particular recompense for the losses they thereby incurred, for the common people are easily led into indolence by their primitive simplicity and their natural love of spectacle, and they readily follow any charlatan that comes along, being too easily impressed by appearances. For this reason, their opinions on a given matter often tend to be far from judicious.

The procession reached the great Madraj Gate of the Citadel, which faced out onto the city of Cairo. A group of armed soldiers stood at the Gate to prevent the crowds from following the procession into the fortress. In order to prevent the obstruction of the Citadel's courtyard, its other gate—the one facing the necropolis—had been kept closed for the day. At the farthest end of this vast courtyard stood an interior gate that led to the private quarters of the Sultan, the princes, and their soldiers. This area also boasted a mosque, as well as the Great Hall where the Sultan received his ministers and princes.

The crowds that remained outside the Citadel were obliged to content themselves with the receding echo of trumpets and drums. Having crossed the courtyard, the procession now reached the interior gate already mentioned. Only the very noblest of those present—princes, senior officers, and so forth—were allowed to pass this gate. Those who remained behind were nonetheless content to have been honored—unlike the common folk—with the privilege of being allowed to enter the precincts of the Citadel.

Past the gate and through a wide corridor on either side of which stood the buildings in which the great fortress's inhabitants resided, the horsemen dismounted. A group of them attended to Tree of Pearls and helped her to descend from her stately litter. A number of corridors and doors still remained to be crossed before the procession—now on foot—would arrive at the Sultan's Great Hall. These had been laid with carpets and hung with banners and all manner of fragrant green wreaths. 'Izz al-Din Aybak and the other princes, dressed in their best finery, accompanied Tree of Pearls, who was on this day adorned in the most exquisite fashion. A canopy of embroidered silk supported by four poles and carried by four officers had been especially designed for her. Flanked by a number of eunuchs and accompanied by Shwaykar, she now proceeded to the Royal Hall under cover of its billowing curtains.

Only the noblest of the company were permitted to enter here: those ambitious and power-hungry men who are accustomed to bending the common people to their will like rude cattle by dispensing a meal here, a sermon there, or perhaps a fine eulogy to some governor or saint adored by the crowd.

The canopy that hid Tree of Pearls from sight proceeded onto the raised dais on which the golden Royal Couch had been placed, and the structure with its ample drapes was placed so as to cover the Couch entirely. Tree of Pearls seated herself in such a manner as to be completely invisible to the assembled company, with Shwaykar at her side and the eunuchs standing at attention. The Chief Justice now entered and took his place to the right of the canopy, and behind him stood the Intendant of the Royal Treasury and the Controller of the Office of Market Inspector. To the left of the canopy stood the Secretary of the Chancellery, next to a number of ministers and other senior officials. 'Izz al-Din Aybak, General of the Army, and the chiefs of the Mamluk officers—amongst them Rukn al-Din Baybars—sat at the center of the dais, directly in front of the canopy, while two rows comprising the Chiefs of the Royal Arsenal, the Royal Wardrobe, and the Sultan's Personal Retinue were ranged behind, followed by the Chamberlains and other minor officials. A number of Frankish prisoners completed the assembly in an extravagant display of royal might and pride.

'Izz al-Din Aybak now rose and addressed his speech to the assembly. "Princes and Officers, you are all aware of the fate that has befallen the Exalted King, Turan Shah. He disgraced himself by gravely mistreating this country's Bahri princes, whose bravery under the leadership of Al-Salih and in the Frankish Wars is legend. For his crimes, he has paid with his life. We have deemed none other than our Lady, Tree of Pearls, Mother of Khalil and Consort of the Good King, worthy of the vacant throne, for she was ever the repository of his trust and she is the mother of his son. Our princes, judges, and magistrates have unanimously chosen to crown her Queen and Custodian of the State. Our officers have solemnly sworn to obey her by upholding the rule of justice and zealously defending the One Faith. We hereby celebrate her coronation. We shall invoke God's blessings upon her at pulpits throughout the land, immediately on the heels of the blessings we seek for our imperial sovereign, Commander of the Faithful, He Who Seeks Refuge in God, Al-Musta'sim Billah, and we shall engrave her image upon our coins. Peace and blessings upon the Commander of the Faithful."

The entire assembly rose and echoed 'Izz al-Din's last invocation. Then the Chief Justice came forth and invoked God's blessings upon Tree of Pearls. "May You, Lord God, protect the Sound Authority, Queen of Muslims, Guardian of Life and Faith, Mother of Khalil, Seeker of Refuge, Consort of our departed Sovereign the Good King."

'Izz al-Din Aybak then said, "Let it be known that our Queen has deigned to entrust me with the office of First Minister, and Prince Rukn al-Din Baybars with that of Executive Secretary of the Royal Court, and she has moreover commanded me to confirm those officers and scribes who have been loyal to us in their present posts." He then pointed to the page standing by the canopy to pull aside the curtain. The interior was quilted in yellow satin embroidered with gold and silver thread. Tree of Pearls sat erect on the golden couch and regarded the assembly with a proud expression on her noble face. She had lowered her veil, and she wore the royal headbands, which were also of yellow satin and on which her name and titles had been embroidered in gold thread.

The assembly once again invoked God's blessings upon her, and then the curtain was drawn. 'Izz al-Din resumed his speech. "We shall soon have occasion to celebrate the official reading of the decree in which the Commander of the Faithful, Al-Musta'sim Billah, shall approve the reign of our Queen, may God protect her."

Throughout these proceedings, the entire assembly held its breath, as though a quivering sparrow had suddenly perched on the heads of each and every person in attendance. The ascension of a woman to the throne had astonished them—such a thing had never been heard of. There were those who were furious at this perceived outrage; some were merely skeptical, while quiet disappointment was the attitude of many others. Not one of them, however, dared utter a single word against their new Queen, knowing as they did that behind her throne lay the swords of the Bahri Mamluks, the real masters of Egypt in those days.

Before bringing the ceremony to a close, 'Izz al-Din signaled to one of the Undersecretaries of the Court standing at attention. At this sign, the official promptly quit the Great Hall and returned with a number of attendants bearing large trays on which hefty purses had been placed, each bearing its recipient's name, and these were accordingly distributed amongst the assembly.

Once this task had been completed, the company prepared to disperse and 'Izz al-Din Aybak rose once more to speak: "Princes, we hereby inform you that our Sovereign, Queen of Muslims, has seen fit to move her royal seat from the Garden Island to this Citadel. Her reasons for so doing accord with the country's changed political circumstances. Henceforth, the Citadel will replace the Good King's Garden Fortress as the official residence of the administration."

This news was well received by some and with no little resentment by others, but no one dared venture his opinion on the matter. The assembly now broke up and each went his way. Tree of Pearls proceeded to occupy the palace that had been readied for her in the Citadel, and in the weeks that followed, the furnishings of the royal household at the Garden Island were gradually transferred to their new home. From that remarkable day onwards, the Island ceased to house the Royal Residence. Its ornaments and sculptures were removed piece by piece, a process which was further accelerated when 'Izz al-Din Aybak later acceded to the throne, for he commanded that the Good King's Garden Fortress be torn down altogether and that its columns, casements, ceilings, and woodwork be removed and used in the construction of a mosque-school in Cairo that bears his name to this day.

Shwaykar had closely followed the coronation proceedings from her corner of the canopy. When the curtain was raised, she had shrunk back even farther into her corner so as to see without being seen. Her eyes feverishly sought out the figure of Rukn al-Din—resplendent in his vigorous youth and in his *cidaris* and dazzling brocaded state robes—and never once left it. A thrill of pleasure ran through her when she heard the decree by which he was appointed her mistress's Executive Secretary, for she knew that the duties of the office would bring him often to the Queen's palace and hence into close daily proximity to herself. Her heart beat with joy, and she dared to entertain the hope that happiness was finally now within her reach, for she would soon be the wife of the Queen's Dawadar.

The Engagement

ONCE ALONE IN HER CHAMBERS, Tree of Pearls gave herself up to the ministrations of the slaves and eunuchs who proceeded to carefully remove her heavy ceremonial robes and ornaments and to dress her in more comfortable loose-fitting garments. After they had completed this task she ordered them to leave her, and now quite alone she sank into a deep reverie. She considered her new situation and the great prize that she had won—a prize she would never have dared to even dream of in her youth, when she had been but a naïve girl at court, as distant from the state of kings and sultans as the earth is from the moon. Now she herself had become Queen of Muslims, and all heads bowed in her presence. A sudden wave of wild joy swept over her, and then just as suddenly passed away as she recalled the many great hurdles ahead and the numerous grave political and military crises that beset the land of Egypt. The war against the Crusaders was the most pressing of these, but internal strife between competing and variously hostile factions in the administration and the ranks of the army were no less serious. She was somewhat comforted by her conviction that 'Izz al-Din and his allies in the army would support her to the last, be it for gain or from a sense of tribal solidarity—she cared little which—, and yet the deep frown that creased her brow as she pondered upon these matters would not leave her face.

While she was thus occupied, Shwaykar entered the chambers. The girl's lovely features glowed with delight. She fell upon the hand of her mistress and kissed it affectionately. "God be praised for his blessings, my Lady. You are crowned Queen of Muslims. Did I not remark to you, when I saw you stretched out upon the royal couch yesterday, that it suited you well?" Suddenly she noticed the expression on the Queen's face.

"Why do you look so troubled, my Lady? Does my presence displease you? Do you wish me to withdraw?"

Tree of Pearls drew Shwaykar to her bosom and tenderly kissed her brow. "Quit my presence? Never, my dearest Shwaykar. I am not in the least troubled. I feel my good fortune most keenly. My thoughts run to the many duties that I am now obliged to shoulder. I used to wish for nothing else but this very moment, and now that it has arrived, the thrill has passed away and the realities of statecraft crowd in upon my mind."

"If you have now come to detest your position, I should be glad to assume it in your place!" Shwaykar teased.

Tree of Pearls smiled, and kissed Shwaykar a second time. "How can I detest kingship, my dear, when I have yet to taste its pleasures? But neither must I discount the many trials and hardships that it must bring in its wake."

"The trials of which you speak are indeed unavoidable, my Queen," replied Shwaykar. "And yet our First Minister, 'Izz al-Din, shall carry the heaviest burden of it for you. And our Rukn al-Din is . . . a great hero." She blushed and bowed her head as she spoke his name.

Tree of Pearls laughed merrily and reached out to stroke Shwaykar's hair. "Rukn al-Din is indeed a great hero, and to show you the proof of it, I shall charge him with a mission of utmost importance that I dare entrust to no other. Will you permit me to do so?"

Shwaykar blushed again at this gracious deference. "Who am I to give my consent to such a matter, my Lady? Are we not your slaves, bound to obey your every command?"

A quick surge of elation filled Tree of Pearls at this ceremonial response—it was the first time she had heard it addressed to her royal person—but she was a sensible and discerning woman who cared nothing for pretty phrases in the end. "We are all God's slaves, my dear child," she replied. "I requested your permission because Rukn al-Din's affairs are no longer indifferent to you. Destiny has united his fate to your own. Is it not so?"

"Even if it be so," she ventured shyly, "the destiny of which you speak was guided by your own hand."

"That is of no importance. I only wish him to accomplish a truly valiant deed that will bring him renown amongst his peers before he weds you. You shall then have even more reason to be proud of your husband."

"Let it be as you wish, my Queen," Shwaykar obediently replied, though in reality she was far from content with her mistress's proposal. Rukn al-Din's prowess was already famed at court, and she saw no reason why additional proofs of it could not be put off until after her wedding. Shwaykar's wonder at her own good fortune had made her chary of the future. She had no choice but to submit, however, and submit she did.

Tree of Pearls took note of her handmaiden's misgivings. She sighed and, rising from her seat, paced restlessly around the chamber and then threw herself onto her bed. "Oh Shwaykar! I am weary of all this thinking! Give me some music. Let me hear that exquisite voice of yours—perhaps it will lift my spirits."

Shwaykar promptly complied. She ordered a page to bring her oud, and taking it into her practiced hands began to pluck it with expert skill and to sing her mistress's favorite ballads. Tree of Pearls gave herself up to the delightfully soothing sound of the girl's voice, but it was now Shwaykar's turn to brood. As she sang, her thoughts once again turned to Rukn al-Din. How she wished him to appear before her at that very moment, so that she could read his eyes and sound his heart. He had not yet declared his love to her. She, on the other hand, had fallen deeply in love with him, and she feared that her love would remain unrequited. Her heart's turmoil played upon her face and stole into her voice as she sang.

Tree of Pearls suddenly interrupted the girl's reverie. "What ails you, Shwaykar?" she gently pressed her.

"Nothing, my Lady," she replied quietly.

"Do not attempt to deceive me. Your look speaks worlds."

Shwaykar smiled wanly to hide her discomfiture. "Never, my Queen. I have every reason to be happy, and I praise God for his blessings," she broke off awkwardly.

Tree of Pearls guessed the thoughts that were passing through Shwaykar's mind. "I have no doubt that you are glad of your mistress's good fortune, but something disquiets you. Does the thought of Rukn al-Din's imminent departure from the court displease you, then?"

"Indeed no, my Lady!" Shwaykar quickly replied. "To obey your command is my only joy and solace. But . . ." and she lowered her head shyly.

"But what, child? You will not speak, then? This modesty pleases me," she smiled. "It appears that you would wish to see Rukn al-Din before his departure. Perhaps you would also know the state of his heart? I shall send for him this very moment to join us. I too have matters which I would discuss with him," and she clapped her hands to summon a page.

The page retired with his mistress's message and Tree of Pearls bade Shwaykar resume her singing while they waited for the noble Prince. She obligingly bent over her oud once more, but her heart raced with anticipation.

The page returned to announce the Dawadar's presence. "Prince Rukn al-Din awaits your command, my Lady."

"Let him enter," Tree of Pearls said, and she motioned to Shwaykar to fall silent.

Rukn al-Din strode in and bent to greet the Queen, who bestowed upon him a royal smile in reply. She had secured her veil in such a way as to reveal her dark, piercing eyes, and Shwaykar had done the same. "Welcome to our champion, Rukn al-Din," she said. "Pray be seated," and she pointed to a nearby chair. He sat down with marked circumspection and wondered at the reason for this summons.

Tree of Pearls read his thoughts. "Do you know why I have summoned you, Rukn al-Din?"

"No, my Lady. I am but a sturdy sword in my Queen's arsenal, a sword that she directs as she pleases," he replied.

"God reward you. But do you wield this sword in my name alone?"

He understood that she was teasing him, and that she alluded to Shwaykar with this pleasantry. He was pleased that she had raised the subject. "Indeed, my Lady, for it is you, and you alone, who commands and forbids." He glanced at Shwaykar and smiled as he said this.

"I see that we have embarrassed Shwaykar," Tree of Pearls remarked, and indeed, the girl had turned as red as a wild rose. "Give us a song to delight our Prince's ears, my dear. What say you, Shwaykar?"

"I am at your command, my Lady," she replied, and once again took up her oud. She sang and played upon her instrument, till Rukn al-Din's heart overflowed with sweet emotion. The music filled him with strange wonder and melancholy passion. He had heard tell of Shwaykar's peerless voice, but had never before experienced its exquisite resonance and spiritual depth. Falling in love with the voice, he fell in love with the possessor of the voice, and only now did he began to realize the great value of the jewel that Tree of Pearls had bestowed upon him.

She, meanwhile, had watched him closely as he sat listening to her music. She saw that it had moved him greatly and she wished that they could but be alone for a few moments, for she was certain that once unburdened by the commanding presence of Tree of Pearls he would finally speak out. Tree of Pearls, too, had seen that the Prince was much taken by her handmaiden's powerfully sweet voice, and she was well pleased. She had her own reasons for wishing to rule his heart and thereby shape him to her design. Her accession to the throne had made her fearful of intrigue and treachery, both within the Palace and beyond. Vague suspicions haunted her. Even her lover and First Minister was not exempt from the dark thoughts that crowded her mind, for she knew him to be ruthless in his ambition. In Rukn al-Din, she divined great courage and resolve, and she determined to make the utmost use of these qualities for her own ends.

"Does our Shwaykar's voice please you, Rukn al-Din?" she inquired coolly.

"Is it not enough that it pleases the Queen of Muslims, your Grace?" he replied. "And who, I wonder, may resist the power of such a voice?" he added warmly.

Tree of Pearls laughed. "I hope nonetheless that it is not the voice alone that pleases you."

Rukn al-Din did not directly reply to this sally, but he glanced furtively at Shwaykar.

"I see that you consult her own opinion first. Are you unconvinced that your person is agreeable to Shwaykar?"

"I would that it were so. And if she deigns to regard me with satisfaction, it is only because my Queen, Tree of Pearls, has seen fit to smile upon me."

"I do not deny that it was I who first brought you two together. Shwaykar has long heard tell of the daring exploits of the valiant Rukn al-Din, and I have ever been the first to recount them to her. It pleases me well that she particularly admires those brave princes who valiantly take up arms in defense of this state. This is why I asked you, when you first arrived, whether you had guessed at the reason for my summons. You answered well—did he not, Shwaykar? And now, tell me: do you know why I wish to speak to you? You are informed of the Frankish attacks on Damietta and its environs?"

"My Lady, allow me to speak. You wish me to rid you of the Frankish menace in our lands to the North. It is a simple matter, I assure you."

"Prince 'Izz al-Din will charge you with your commission tomorrow. Know that Shwaykar is well pleased with your undertaking, and that she is ever partial to men of courage and valor. There is one more thing. It has come to my attention that Shwaykar—" she laughed merrily as she glanced at her—"that Shwaykar would wish to ascertain Rukn al-Din's opinion of her."

Rukn al-Din's face glowed with feeling at these words. "Can Rukn al-Din have an opinion other than that of his Queen?"

"Nevertheless, I suppose she would not like to receive your love as an act of submission to the royal will," Tree of Pearls smiled.

"The Queen's will has but unlocked the doors that kept us apart. My love for Shwaykar submits to no other will but her own. I will be satisfied if her heart be only half as full as my own." He gazed directly at her as he spoke these words, and her shy eyes said to him what her lips dared not.

Once sure of the couple, Tree of Pearls sought to terminate the interview. "Neither of you, I believe, requires further proof of the other's affection. And now, Rukn al-Din, be the man I know you to be. Your success in this venture will assure your promotion to great office. Go, in God's grace, but before you depart, take Shwaykar's hand in your own. I give you my permission."

Rukn al-Din rose and did as the Queen bade, taking Shwaykar's delicate hand in his for the first time, and in this clasp there was a trembling vow. Bowing deeply before Tree of Pearls, Rukn al-Din turned to withdraw, and to Shwaykar, it was as though he had plucked her beating heart from her breast and taken it with him.

Tree of Pearls was the first to speak into the ensuing silence. "You see, my child? He loves you, and be sure that your love for him will flame even brighter when he has returned victorious from the fields of war. He shall fight and triumph in your name! I congratulate you, my dear, on your fine champion." She regarded her blushing handmaiden with kindly bemusement. "And now I am afraid you must leave me, for pressing matters of state require my attention."

No sooner had Shwaykar taken leave of her mistress than the Chamberlain came to announce that Prince 'Izz al-Din Aybak sought permission for an interview with her. "Tell him to await me in the Great Hall," she replied.

'Izz al-Din had come to congratulate his mistress in private on her triumph. As was his wont, he looked forward to a warm reception full of effusive expressions of praise and gratitude, for was he not the sole architect of her ascension to the throne of Egypt? He had gone first to the Great Hall, hoping to find her there alone, but being informed that she was closeted in her private chambers he made his way there directly. To his great surprise, as he approached the hall that led to the Queen's apartments he saw Rukn al-Din emerging with the dazed air of a pining lover. Rukn al-Din greeted him innocently enough, for truth be told, he had nothing to hide, but creeping suspicion nonetheless whispered in 'Izz al-Din's ear and the claws of jealousy dug at his heart. He returned Rukn al-Din's greeting curtly and resolved to discover the reason for his unseemly presence in the Queen's apartments as soon as he should enter them.

He was not to have his wish, however, for the Chamberlain emerged to inform him that the Queen would meet him in the Great Hall. This reception only inflamed 'Izz al-Din's jealousy the more, and he felt the slight deeply. He nevertheless struggled to master his doubts, and quickly assuming the mantle of his self-possession, he returned to the Great Hall to wait for her. He was obliged to wait longer than usual, for Tree of Pearls had lingered over her toilette and once again dressed in her rich robes of state. She finally made her entrance, followed by a pair of eunuchs who solemnly bore the magnificent train of her royal gown in their outstretched hands. 'Izz al-Din rose to greet her. She returned his greeting and urged him to be seated; then she dismissed her attendants and turned a radiant smile upon him.

This charming reception drove the gloom from 'Izz al-Din's heart and he put aside his misgivings. "I have come to congratulate the Queen on her ascension and to express my hope that she will ever be the mainstay of our government."

She smiled graciously, and replied, "I shall not forget your service to me, 'Izz al-Din, and I will most certainly have further need of your aid in untangling the many knots that bind the affairs of this state."

"I wait upon your will, my Lady," he bowed.

"You are aware that we are surrounded by envious eyes and dangerous enemies, most especially the Franks, who do not cease to plague us."

"Fear not on this count, Tree of Pearls. They shall be dealt with by my own hand."

"May God reward you," she replied. "I have nonetheless seen fit to charge Rukn al-Din with this task, for I have often heard you praise his valor. It so happens that I saw him today, and having mentioned this matter of the Franks I perceived that he was most anxious to meet them in battle. I would have your approval of this mission, however."

'Izz al-Din's apprehensions returned at this mention of Rukn al-Din. Why had she received him in her private chamber instead of the Great Hall? And how had this unusual meeting come to pass, if not by prior arrangement between the pair? But he suppressed these persistent questions and merely replied, "Rukn al-Din is worthy of your esteem, and you have acted wisely in trusting him with the Damietta campaign."

Tree of Pearls reached into the folds of her gown and drew out a paper scroll. "Read, then, what I have caused to be written here."

He took the scroll from her and unrolled it. It was a royal letter of commission.

From the Queen of Muslims, Guardian of Life and Faith, She of the Noble Veil, Mother of the Departed Khalil, Consort of Al-Salih—May God have mercy on his soul—to the brave commander, Prince Rukn al-Din Baybars al-Bunduqari.

In view of our utmost confidence in your valor and fortitude and in light of the proofs of these that you have shown by fearlessly repulsing the Franks from our lands, and in view of the continuing encroachments of the accursed foreigners in the area of Damietta, and having taken due counsel from the General of our Armies and First Minister, Prince 'Izz al-Din Aybak, we hereby charge you and your men with the defense of said city and the destruction of our enemies. God's peace and blessings upon you.

Mother of Khalil

It pleased 'Izz al-Din that Tree of Pearls had expressly invoked his counsel in her commission to Prince Baybars. He rolled up the scroll and ordered it to be delivered to Rukn al-Din directly, then he turned the conversation to other pressing matters of state. Tree of Pearls noted the restrained manner in which he addressed her. She guessed at his lurking suspicions—for lovers are ever suspicious—and wishing to soothe them away, she exerted herself in order to flatter him. She succeeded in this, for 'Izz al-Din was indeed appeased by her artful words of praise and the many marks of affection she showered upon him, but the truce did not last long, for no sooner had he left her than his misgivings returned to haunt him.

Rukn al-Din meanwhile hastened to put the Queen's commission into execution as soon as he received it. His greatest hopes had thereby been fired and he dreamed that this enterprise would be the means by which he should attain high office, and—why not?—the very highest office, even, for he was a mightily ambitious and determined young man and the realm was in sorry disarray. It had of course occurred to him that a royal throne which would so easily receive a woman could just as well be his for the taking. But he was also aware of the insurmountable obstacles that blocked his path to the Sultanate whilst 'Izz al-Din's influence reigned supreme in the army and in Tree of Pearls's heart. Though the great favor that the Queen had shown to him that very day encouraged his new-born aspirations, he breathed not a word of them to a living soul for fear of the many treacherous tongues that surrounded him at court. Like other young men, he was content to delight in his blossoming love-affair for the moment, and his vanity was well satisfied with the rich alliance promised him by the Queen.

An Important Visitor

AFTER TAKING HIS LEAVE OF TREE OF PEARLS, 'Izz al-Din returned to his
quarters in the Citadel. The chamber he now entered looked out over the grand
vista of Cairo. He often came here when he had need of solitude in which to
think, and he accordingly gave himself up to reflections on the events of the
day and his mistress's strange comportment. From his seat by the window,
he contemplated the royal city and the land spread out behind it, from Fustat
to the Nile. When his gaze fell upon the Garden Island, his mind wandered
back to the time when Al-Salih had strolled through its gardens and arbors
with his favorite young consort at his side. He now carefully reviewed the history of his own relations with Tree of Pearls and could find there no reason for
the nagging doubts that beset him. He was disposed to take comfort in this
accounting.

While he was thus lost in thought, a servant entered to announce the presence of a lady who urgently requested a private interview with him.

"Who is this lady?" 'Izz al-Din inquired.

"I know not, your Excellency, for her face is closely veiled," the boy replied.

Wondering who his mysterious visitor might be, 'Izz al-Din proceeded to the
chamber where he was wont to receive his numerous petitioners. The woman was
waiting for him there, wrapped from head to toe in a thick cloak of exceedingly
rich fabric. From this he surmised that she had not come to seek charity, as he had
at first supposed. She rose as he greeted her, but he motioned for her to resume
her place and took a seat by her side. "Permit me to inquire your name, my Lady,
and the nature of the errand which brings you here," he began.

Without a word, she drew the veil from her face. It was Sallafa.

'Izz al-Din had always been much taken with Sallafa's beauty, and had, moreover, on more than one occasion exchanged flirtatious pleasantries with her—a

lighthearted battle of wits from which she inevitably emerged unscathed, thanks, no doubt, to her close connection to Al-Salih. 'Izz al-Din had always held her in high esteem as a result, and was consequently rather taken aback by this precipitous visit. He now hastened to apologize for having received her in these rooms, but she assured him that she took no offence.

"I have not come to you today as a guest," she gravely declared, "but have indeed come as a petitioner regarding a matter which it is in your power—and yours alone—to resolve."

"And what might this matter be, my Lady?" he earnestly inquired.

"I have learnt today that your friend, Tree of Pearls, has been crowned Queen of Muslims. I, as you well know, am Custodian of the Good King's Harem. The King has now passed away, his palaces have been looted, his furnishings moved to this Citadel, and the succession has been bestowed upon one of his concubines. Do not blame me for speaking thus—concubine or no, she is the paramour of 'Izz al-Din Aybak, who has single-handedly raised her to her present state. You have done so because she is your mistress. This is your right, and I pray that God may bless her reign. But I have come to beg you to release me from my office, as there is no reason why I should now remain in it. The royal harem has lost all reason for its existence, now that a woman sits on the throne of Egypt, a woman who herself once belonged to this harem. Release me! Or is it impossible for you to do so without first consulting your sovereign?"

In his present state of mind, these words hit their intended mark. They pierced him to the heart. A number of disturbing emotions now struggled for possession of him, first and foremost amongst them a feeling of self-loathing that he—the great 'Izz al-Din Aybak—had effectively submitted to the will of a woman, while a mere female and slave refused to bend to this same will. At the same time, his besieged pride rekindled the embers of his dormant desire for this formidable woman, and it sparked and flared in his jealous heart once again. He nonetheless felt compelled to speak in his own defense. "You know that Tree of Pearls was offered the throne only because she is mother of the Sultan's son," he grimly explained.

"I know it," replied Sallafa haughtily. "May God bless our brave princes! You only invested her with crown and scepter because she is mother of the Sultan's son—wonder of wonders! And where is this child, I ask you? Dead! If your purpose were truly to preserve the lineage of the Ayyubid Sultans, would it not have been proper to elect one of their line to the throne, if only a child, and appoint the General of the Armies, 'Izz al-Din Aybak, as his Regent? Or is 'Izz al-Din powerless in this regard? I am a woman, and know well women's wiles. They honor not the bonds of friendship. I do not accuse Tree of Pearls of treachery," she added as she remarked 'Izz al-Din's darkening look, "but frailty is nevertheless central to our nature, as has been documented by our books of religion." She fell silent for a moment. "In any case, this reign cannot be confirmed without imperial decree of the Abbasid Commander of the Faithful."

'Izz al-Din leaned forward anxiously. "Do you then believe that he will reject our choice?"

"I am certain of it!" she cried.

He drew back and sighed. "You are mistaken, Sallafa. Tree of Pearls is as clever as she is prudent. She has been chosen by the Turcoman commanders of the armies of Egypt. The Caliph shall not oppose them."

"I assure you that not only the Caliph, but the people of Baghdad themselves shall rise up as one in anger against this unholy act. You shall see for yourself, 'Izz al-Din. But this is not why I have come to you. I beg you once more to release me—but by your own hand and none other's."

"And where shall you go if I grant your request?"

"I shall wander these lands aimlessly." She choked on her words, and tears began to stream down her cheeks. She slowly wiped them away and called forth a false blush of mortification.

'Izz al-Din was moved by the sight. "As you have nowhere else to go, you must stay here amongst your friends," he pressed her.

"Where shall I stay?" she demanded. "Our palaces and harems are a thing of the past, and if I remain, I shall be a prisoner of the Queen's favor. I could never bear such a condition—unlike yourselves, brave princes and great men that you are! I am only a puny woman, after all."

He perceived the mockery in her words and could not help but feel their bitter truth, yet he was amazed at her daring in speaking so to him. "Enough of these insinuations and reproaches, Sallafa! It is too late to turn back the hands of time. I, of all men, know your true worth, and would not wish you to fall from your high rank. You must stay here with me."

"Stay with you?" she brusquely replied. "How deluded you are to even propose such a thing! And what if Tree of Pearls were to learn of it?"

He was secretly forced to acknowledge the truth of her words, but his pride rose to the occasion. "And what if she should learn of it? She is not my master, or I hers."

"What, then, is the distinction between kings and their subjects? Are we to be permitted the same prerogatives as our rulers? Do you imagine that you would have the right to object to another man's place in the affections of Tree of Pearls, even though you are her paramour and her benefactor? She, however, would be well within her royal rights to question and censure your every step."

'Izz al-Din recalled his glimpse of Rukn al-Din leaving the Queen's chambers that very morning, and his torment now returned. He lost himself in his gloomy thoughts for a space, but not wishing to expose himself further to Sallafa's taunts, he hastened to reply. "You seem to think that Tree of Pearls's elevation to the throne has caused a rift between us. But if she has ever been free to do as she chooses, what then should prevent me from following my own inclinations without consulting her pleasure or fearing her anger?"

"Nay, I do not counsel you to act so. I would not be the cause of discord betwixt you."

"And even if your presence in my household should offend her, what of it?" He broke off moodily, then resumed. "Besides, I am not obliged to inform her of my private affairs."

Sallafa shook her head. "A bold move on your part, my Lord. But if you truly wish me to remain under your protection, I insist that you lodge me elsewhere than in your own residence. I should always court your affection and your trust, even were I to become Queen of Muslims," she laughed lightly, "though in truth, I cannot swear by it, for we daughters of Adam are inconstant creatures!"

'Izz al-Din frowned in displeasure. "Pray, speak your thoughts clearly."

"Women were not made to rule, my Lord. The Crown belongs to you and you alone, by rights. You are Commander of the Army, and it was you who valiantly met the Franks in battle and vanquished them. You have ever been the mighty arm that supports the throne of this land. Of this I am convinced, and I shall not soon change my opinion."

'Izz al-Din was pacified by this flattery, for a man is easily deceived by his own inclinations so that black turns to white and illusion to reality. He readily believes in the devotion and sincerity of his flatterer, and gladly opens his ears and heart to him in consequence. This is a truth universally known and practiced by all courtiers and men of affairs; likewise the rake, who wins his mistress's heart by praising her unparalleled beauty and unconquerable virtue:

They deceived her who called her a beauty
For beauties are dazzled by praise.

The truth, however, is that praise does not dazzle beauties alone. It blinds one and all, and rarely does a reasonable man escape its snares.

'Izz al-Din believed Sallafa and did not in any way suspect her motives in offering him this honest counsel. His heart now began to grow cold towards Tree of Pearls, though he barely perceived the spell that the woman before him had wrought upon it. They parted, having agreed that Sallafa should soon remove to a palace that 'Izz al-Din would put at her disposal, and thereby come under his protection.

Alone again, 'Izz al-Din thought long upon what had passed between them. Was she not right to insist that a child of the Ayubbid line should inherit the throne, and that he, 'Izz al-Din, be made Regent? Was she not right to point out the unseemliness of a female head of state? He now began to see that he had erred in his judgment, but he was nonetheless greatly pleased that the lovely Custodian of the Righteous King's Harem had so precipitously come into his possession.

Meanwhile, in the days that followed Rukn al-Din's departure for Damietta, Shwaykar constantly pined for news of him and of the distant war there, while he in his turn seized every opportunity to seek word of her from messengers or officers freshly arrived from Cairo. Three months passed in this way, Rukn al-Din returning from the battlefield only twice, and each time eagerly seizing the opportunity to see Shwaykar—after having received permission from Tree of Pearls—and to hear her sing. At their last parting, the lovers fixed the date of their nuptials immediately the war in Damietta should be over, and Shwaykar once again remained behind to breathlessly await the promised day, while countless evil omens plagued her young and innocent heart.

The Caliph's Messenger

ONE FINE MORNING not long thereafter, the people of Cairo woke to whispered news of the arrival of a messenger from the Caliph in Baghdad. It was said that this messenger had caused his magnificent pavilions to be raised on the outskirts of the city, and the entire population now eagerly engaged in diverse attempts to divine the contents of the letter he had brought with him from the imperial capital. The arrival of such a letter was a rare occurrence indeed, and could only contain an imperial decree either confirming or deposing the new Sultan of Egypt.

The messenger had immediately sent an attendant with news of his arrival to the princes and officers of the court, and they in turn dispatched a high-ranking emissary to receive him, in keeping with the rules of imperial protocol. The streets of the city soon filled up with noisy, boisterous crowds, particularly in the thoroughfare leading from the Nasr Gate to the Citadel, along which the messenger would pass with his delegation. The officers and princes meanwhile prepared to receive the messenger in the Citadel and to hear the contents of his letter read out. They suspected that it touched upon Tree of Pearls's investiture, and that it would confirm, as was usually the case, the choice they had made in raising her to the throne. They accordingly prepared to proceed to the Great Hall along with the other great Bahri princes, excepting Rukn al-Din, who was still absent in Damietta. Tree of Pearls meanwhile arranged herself on the royal couch to await the messenger's arrival. She wore the same magnificent robes of state that had graced her figure at her coronation three months since, and her lovely face bore the expression of calm and noble pride befitting a Queen. Shwaykar, who occupied her usual place at her mistress's side, secretly lamented her beloved Rukn al-Din's absence from the assembly.

Sallafa alone of all the inhabitants of Cairo was already aware of the exact contents of the momentous letter. Her confidant, the Custodian of the Caliph's

Harem, had sent her own messenger with the imperial delegation, and the private note he had placed into her hands had brought her the news that Tree of Pearls was to be deposed this very morning by decree of the Commander of the Faithful himself. Sallafa was of course overjoyed by this turn of events that she herself had so artfully engineered. Her first wish was to inform 'Izz al-Din of it. She therefore hastened to send for him, and when he finally stood before her, she carefully skirted the subject that threatened to burst her heart open with joy. "I believe a letter has arrived at court from the Commander of the Faithful—? What news does it bring, I wonder?"

'Izz al-Din appeared intrigued by her mysterious manner. "Indeed, I know not, Sallafa."

"And if you were to attempt a guess?" she persisted.

"I have already told you that I know nothing of it. Am I to suppose then that you might somehow be acquainted with its contents?" he added doubtfully.

She laughed merrily at this. "I am, my Prince, and what is more, I myself predicted its contents to you three months ago. Do you not remember?"

'Izz al-Din considered this reply briefly as his mind flew back in time. "You speak of our first meeting, and our first discussion of Tree of Pearls?"

"Queen of Muslims, indeed!" she mocked.

"You predicted that the Caliph would refuse to approve her investiture. Can this be the purport of the Caliph's letter?"

"It is!" she cried triumphantly. "He has decreed that the woman be deposed!"

'Izz al-Din was astonished by this news, for little did he expect it, and he wondered how Sallafa could possibly know of it before anyone else, before even the imperial messenger's arrival at the Citadel. He stared at her incredulously. "How do you know this, Sallafa?" he demanded. "Is it sorcery?"

She laughed again, and replied, "I knew full well that the Caliph would never approve this reign! And now, you must gather your resolve and recall the counsel I gave you three months ago. Do you remember it?"

'Izz al-Din's astonishment only grew at these words, and as he stood gazing at his mistress, a sudden sense of awe and of helplessness powerfully laid hold of him. "Yes, I remember," he finally replied steadily. "But how shall we proceed? Who is the Ayyubid child that we might raise to the throne?"

"You may leave this matter to me."

"Disclose your thoughts to me now, for the assembly gathers as we speak and we may not be allowed another opportunity to decide the matter."

"Perhaps you are right," she coolly replied. "Do you know Musa, son of Salah al-Din, son of Mas'ud Ibn al-Kamil?"

"I know him. He is a mere boy of eight."

"Were he but a lad of five he would suit our purposes all the more. This boy is the legitimate successor of Al-Salih in the Ayyubid line, and you shall be his all-powerful Regent!"

"But how shall I secure the Regency?" 'Izz al-Din feverishly demanded.

"I shall secure it for you. You must summon all your resolve, my love. You yourself shall propose the boy's investiture, and you may leave the rest to me."

'Izz al-Din surrendered to Sallafa's formidable will. His heart pounded with excitement. "Shall you attend the assembly?"

"I shall view it from behind the curtains of the women's alcove." He nodded and, bidding her farewell, took his leave.

Upon his return to the Citadel, he found the assembled princes waiting impatiently for him. Of all those present, his absence had disturbed Tree of Pearls the most and it augured ill to her, for she was conscious of the widening breach that had opened between them these past months, and she knew that Sallafa now held sway in 'Izz al-Din's heart. She watched him take his place amongst the assembled princes from behind her screen and steeled herself to hear what fate held in store for her.

The Caliph's Decree

TOWARDS MIDDAY, the courtyard of the Citadel overflowed with people and news of the messenger's arrival spread like wildfire. The Chamberlain had solemnly come forth to conduct him into the Great Hall where the princes waited, ranged in twin rows that led all the way up to the raised dais on which sat Tree of Pearls and Shwaykar behind their screen. Shwaykar, who had taken note of the deep marks of anxiety on her mistress's face, was all the while engaged in attempting to comfort her with soothing words, while the Queen sat like a statue chiseled in marble and listened closely to the invisible dialogue taking place beyond her screen. She now heard 'Izz al-Din raise his voice to speak. "My Princes, we hereby present to you the messenger of our Lord the Caliph, Commander of the Faithful, Al-Musta'sim Billah—may God preserve him. He brings us a letter from his master, which he shall now proceed to read out to us. Hark ye, and prepare to bow to his will, for he is the Successor of our Prophet, peace and blessings upon him."

"We submit to the Prophet and his Caliph!" the princes cried in unison.

The messenger now advanced onto a small platform that had been raised for this purpose. He unrolled the scroll he carried and began to read, while those in attendance waited breathlessly upon his words.

The Commander of the Faithful, Abi Ahmad Abdallah Al-Musta'sim Billah Ibn Al-Mustansir Billah, salutes the Commanders of the Army and the Ministers of Egypt. It has come to our attention that you have crowned Tree of Pearls, Concubine of the departed Righteous King, Queen of Egypt, and given her the reins of state. We hereby let it be known that if you have no men amongst you capable of assuming the throne of Egypt, then verily, we shall take it upon ourselves to provide you with one. Have you not heard the Prophet's saying—peace and blessings upon him—"Those who entrust their affairs to a woman will never know prosperity"?

No sooner had the messenger finished reading the letter than a great din rose from the assembly. You may imagine how these words affected Tree of Pearls, but she was a sensible and determined woman, and when she heard the Caliph's decree and realized that she had no choice but to bend to his will, she resolved to bear it stoically and motioned to the Chamberlain to pull aside the screen. The assembly immediately fell silent at the commanding sight of the deposed Queen seated upon her couch, and they breathlessly waited to hear how she would respond.

"Oh ye Princes!" she began, "You have heard the will of the Commander of the Faithful, which it is the duty of all Muslims to obey. He has spoken wisely—may God preserve him—, for a woman is not fit to sit upon the throne. I remind you that I accepted this sacred trust at your own insistence, and in the hope of putting an end to the many crises that beset our realm. Now that stability has once more come to the land of Egypt, and having heard the opinion of our lord and master, the Commander of the Faithful, I hereby submit my abdication. I beg you to choose at once whomsoever you feel to be an appropriate successor to the throne of Egypt, and I myself shall be the first to bend before him."

This speech was received with great approbation by Tree of Pearls's supporters, for it was proof of her judiciousness and her noble pride. Not so Sallafa, who would have preferred the Queen to cling to her throne to the very last and thus be forced to abdicate against her will before one and all. She was nonetheless content that her rival had fallen. Suddenly, a voice rang out from amongst the assembly. "We shall accept no sultan to rule over us other than a descendant of the line of Ayyub!"

Now, it is well known that a political proposal in the public interest strategically cast forth into the civic arena can only meet with approval if there be already a substantial consensus on its principal points. In such cases, it matters little who first gives voice to the scheme in question, for the people, already confirmed in their opinions, shall duly take up and echo the cry for the good of the community at large. The princes knew not from whence this voice had come, but it expressed the silent opinion of many of those present. It was therefore resoundingly seconded, and not one of those in attendance was much pressed to inquire who had been its instigator.

Most Egyptians had disapproved of Tree of Pearls's investiture, and would have much preferred the election of a male member of the Ayyubid line to the throne. They had only submitted to the fait accompli in fear of the all-powerful

Mamluk army. Now that she had been deposed by official decree of the Caliph, they were all eager to second the invisible voice that rang out so propitiously. A great din rose in support of the anonymous proposal, and all eyes turned to the most powerful of the princes present, 'Izz al-Din Aybak, as though to consult him on the matter. 'Izz al-Din accordingly rose to address the assembly. His deep voice was clear and unwavering. "Our Lady, Tree of Pearls, has abdicated her throne as proof of her obedience to the wishes of the Commander of the Faithful and to the obligations laid upon her by the Muslim community. Her rank as mother of the departed Khalil, descendent of the Ayyubids, had constrained us, the Commanders of the great army of Egypt, to place her on the empty throne, but we are now obliged to choose a prince of this line as our king. I hereby propose our Lord Musa Bin Salah al-Din Bin Mas'ud to the assembly, though he is yet a child."

The Caliph's messenger interrupted 'Izz al-Din. "His age is of no consequence, for you shall be his Regent, the commander of his armies and his First Minister. What think you of this proposal, Princes?"

"Hear, hear!" cried the assembled princes in unison.

'Izz al-Din was taken aback by this declaration, and he wondered how it came about that the Caliph's messenger—a stranger to the court—should single him out of all the great princes and commanders of the army as a suitable Prince Regent for Egypt. He therefore remained silent and somewhat perplexed before the loud acclamations of the assembly. The messenger now spoke again. "Hear ye, Princes of Egypt! As you have consented to place Musa Bin Salah al-Din on the throne, let him be brought forth and crowned immediately. The Commander of the Faithful has seen fit to provide me with the royal emblems for the occasion of this coronation." Upon signaling to a member of his retinue standing by, he was ceremoniously presented with a large emblazoned chest. The messenger ordered that it be opened and its contents laid out upon a rich carpet placed on the ground before it, while the company craned their necks to catch a glimpse of the royal objects. The page first withdrew a black cloak richly embroidered with the Abbasid crest. This was followed by a black turban and a collar and anklet of solid gold. "These are the royal insignia," declared the messenger. "Now bring me the Sultan Musa Bin Salah al-Din so that we may place them upon him, for the Commander of the Faithful has charged me not to quit Egypt without having first raised an Ayyubid king to its throne."

'Izz al-Din duly caused the boy to be sent for. They were not kept waiting long. The new King of Egypt was a mere child of eight years. They dressed him in the royal insignia as much as this was possible, given his age and size, and declared him Sultan, and 'Izz al-Din Aybak his Regent and First Minister.

Throughout these proceedings, Tree of Pearls remained immobile as a statue, watching and listening in stony silence. Once the coronation had drawn to its conclusion, and the screen was lowered again, she took a deep breath of relief and burst out into bitter tears upon Shwaykar's shoulder. "Come, my Lady," the girl whispered tenderly into the weeping Queen's ear, "Let us withdraw at once to your apartments."

Tree of Pearls willingly submitted to her handmaiden's care. Now, in the privacy of her chambers, Shwaykar did her best to comfort her grieving mistress and to stem her sighs. Finally, Tree of Pearls spoke. "I know not the reason for this sudden change of affairs, but I am content to have abdicated of my own free will. Do not suppose, Shwaykar, that I lament the loss of the throne. It is a heavy burden indeed, and you have often heard my complaints on this count. I am content to be the first woman to have been crowned Queen in the history of our Empire. Now you are the only consolation left me," she broke off wretchedly.

These last words made Shwaykar somewhat uneasy, but she held her peace, for if she was to be someone's consolation she preferred to fulfill that role for Rukn al-Din and for him alone. Tree of Pearls resumed, as though reading her thoughts, "I am only sorry that having lost the throne I am now no longer in a position to raise Rukn al-Din to the rank he so well deserves. But he shall win it through his own high merit, no doubt. If he had been here today, he should have certainly secured some honor or other from the Caliph's emissary—who knows, perhaps the Regency itself."

Shwaykar's spirits fell at this thought, and she regretted the lost opportunity, but she resolutely directed her attention once again to her mistress. "I care only for your present happiness, my Lady."

"You are my delight, dear Shwaykar, as you well know. I thank God that I have rid myself of the burdensome cares of state. Having once tasted them, never again shall I aspire to such responsibility."

"Well said, my Lady, for you have had nothing but care and anxiety as your constant companions these last months. When shall Rukn al-Din return, I wonder?"

"Soon, my dear," Tree of Pearls replied. "He shall surely come to us the minute he hears of this turn of events. And when he comes, I shall fulfill my promise to you both." And lowering her tearstained eyes, she fell silent.

An Unexpected Demand

AS WE HAVE SEEN in the course of this narration, by nightfall of that momentous day Tree of Pearls had been precipitously toppled from the throne of Egypt, Musa Bin Salah al-Din invested in her place with the title of Al-Ashraf, the Most Honorable King, and 'Izz al-Din Aybak installed as his Regent. 'Izz al-Din, whom this turn of events had not a little taken by surprise, was now more than ever convinced that he owed his present position to none other than Sallafa. His first act after the coronation was consequently to betake himself immediately to the palace in which he had installed her. He found her there, proud as a victorious queen and chuckling to herself at the success of her plans. "What think you of this day's events, my Prince?" she slyly inquired in reply to his greeting. "Is not your Sallafa well versed in the secrets of statecraft?"

"Indeed, my Lady, for you have accomplished miracles. Will you not enlighten me as to your divinatory methods?"

"Now that I have convinced you of the sincerity of my affection, I see no reason to hide from you that it was I—through my connections to the Custodian of the Caliph Al-Musta'sim Billah's Harem—who effected the great changes that took place today. It was I who sent her the letter which produced the desired results. In return, she has demanded a small service which I have had no choice but to promise her. I did not think to inform you of it before now, as I was sure that you would not refuse."

"And what is this service?"

"Do you then promise that you shall undertake it?"

'Izz al-Din was silent for a moment as he wondered to himself what this request might be, for he feared that some lurking harm to his interests might therein lie. He felt, however, that he had no choice but to comply. "I shall do as you ask," he replied.

"The Custodian of the Caliph's Palaces informs me in her letter that the Commander of the Faithful has heard tell of a girl of wondrous voice in Tree of Pearls's possession. He requests that this slave be immediately sent to him, for the Commander of the Faithful is passionately enamored of music and song, as you well know. I have promised to present her as a gift to the Caliph, and she must presently leave for Baghdad with the royal messenger."

"Do you mean the singing-girl, Shwaykar?"

"Indeed, it is her I mean. What say you?"

"A simple request. It shall even please the girl no doubt to leave the service of a deposed Queen and enter into that of a great Caliph."

The words "a deposed Queen" rang pleasantly in Sallafa's ears. She smiled and replied, "You know full well that you are now bound to satisfy the Caliph's whims. You shall have need of his support when your plans to seize the throne for yourself come to full fruition. I think you understand me."

He nodded in reply and quickly rose to take his leave. "I shall take care of the matter at once."

"Go in God's keeping. Shwaykar shall depart with the messenger on the morrow . . . shall she not?"

"She shall," he replied, and he turned his steps back to the Citadel, his cloak wrapped well around him so as to proceed unrecognized through the streets of Cairo. Sallafa and the great debt he now owed to her prodigious energy and cunning occupied his thoughts on the way home. Though his heart misgave him his betrayal of Tree of Pearls, he excused himself on the grounds of her suspicious liaison with Rukn al-Din. He knew that in all decency, he should postpone this visit to her so that she should have an opportunity to calm her grief, but he was obliged to undertake the evil errand in haste at Sallafa's insistence.

'Izz al-Din entered the Citadel and directed his steps to Tree of Pearls's palace. He found her secluded in her chambers with Shwaykar, who had taken up her oud and now sang to soothe her mistress. The strains of her melancholy voice wafted forth from behind the closed door. He stopped for a moment to listen pensively, then signaled to the Chamberlain to announce his presence.

'Izz al-Din did not wait for the Chamberlain's return. He entered the room as had been his habit of old, and found Tree of Pearls in her dressing-gown. She had tied a plain cloth around her head to prevent the full onslaught of the headache that had afflicted her since the trials of that morning, and she now rose heavily to greet him. The headache was but a trifle compared to the pain she felt at the clear change in 'Izz al-Din's affections. His relations with Sallafa, and in particular, the frequency of their meetings in the days leading up to her overthrow, had hardly escaped her. She was now certain of the breach between herself and the Prince, for she had been informed by her spies that 'Izz al-Din had gone to Sallafa immediately after the assembly had broken up, rather than coming to her in her great affliction. She presaged ill from this belated visit, but she stifled the bitter resentment that caused her heart to beat violently at the sight of him and rose with difficulty from her couch.

'Izz al-Din hastened towards her. "I beg you to remain seated, my Lady. We have no need of formalities. I see you are in poor health. What ails you, pray tell?"

Tree of Pearls sank back and pulled her shawl tight around her. She shivered as though an icy wind had suddenly swept through her veins.

'Izz al-Din took note of her continued silence. He drew a chair near to her couch. "It is the headache that afflicts you from time to time, is it not?"

"The worst I have ever experienced. May God preserve you from such pain, 'Izz al-Din, and shield you from the devastation it brings in its wake."

Her words made him uneasy, for he guessed at the hidden meaning behind them. "We are all prey to such bouts, my Lady. It is but a small malady that will soon pass."

"I am unused to its sudden violence . . . and any change in habit goes hard on a body, do you not agree?" she replied with a trace of melancholy and reproach in her voice.

'Izz al-Din ignored this remark. "If I had known that you were unwell, I would have come to you sooner."

"There is no need to trouble yourself over a deposed Queen, particularly now that you are occupied with even greater responsibilities than heretofore."

"Is it possible that my duties should make me forget Tree of Pearls? I have come to congratulate you on your escape from these very burdens of government and to tell you how I admired the great fortitude and self-possession that you displayed this morning. You were wise to act so. Let not the Caliph's command distress you." He fidgeted in his seat and coughed uncomfortably. "If truth be told, it is we princes—or rather, myself in particular—who bear the most responsibility in this matter, since it is we who pressed you to accept the throne. We did not suspect that our choice would contradict the will of the Commander of the Faithful."

Tree of Pearls keenly felt the patronizing formality of his excuses. "You erred in your judgment, as I erred in mine. But the loss of the throne has not distressed me as much as . . ." She fell silent and her lustrous eyes met his.

"I fear that you have come to doubt my friendship, but you may rest assured, Madam, that—"

Tree of Pearls quickly interrupted him. "I harbor no resentment," she proudly declared. "But I have learned that one must not always trust to appearances. And now let us leave reproof aside and amuse ourselves with a song from Shwaykar's lips." She turned to the girl, who took up her oud once again at a sign from her mistress. "My dear child, you are the last solace left to me now. You at least will not change. Give us a sad song," she murmured, and her eyes shone with tears.

'Izz al-Din's sympathies were struck by the mournful tenderness in Tree of Pearls's voice. He lowered his eyes and attempted to lose himself in the music, but was too troubled by the mission on which he had come, and which he had not the luxury of postponing. He now racked his mind for a way to broach the subject. As soon as the girl had come to the end of her song, he smiled approvingly and turned to Tree of Pearls. "It appears that you abandon all society but Shwaykar's. Is there not some other songstress of equal merit in all your palace?"

"It is not only her musical talent that endears her to me," she replied. "She is my boon companion and I know that she loves me well and that her heart shall never change."

'Izz al-Din once again ignored this remark, for he was determined to pursue his object. "But it is unwise for you to place all your affections in one slave. I shall provide you with a much better singing-girl, if you like."

"I thank you, but I want none other," she replied simply.

"It would go better with you to request another."

Tree of Pearls looked up. She divined some hidden purpose behind this ominous counsel. Then its meaning slowly dawned upon her. "Surely, you do not mean to deprive me of even this small joy?" she demanded in a choking voice.

'Izz al-Din frowned imperceptibly. "I did not know that you valued her so highly. Were it not for this, I would not have agreed to take her from you."

"Take her?" she cried. "Who would dare such a thing? Never! She is my slave, and moreover, I love her as I would my own child. I will not permit such a thing!"

'Izz al-Din rubbed his nose anxiously as he considered how to reply to this outburst. "You are within your rights to say so of course. And yet we cannot always have our way in such matters—especially if the request comes from one whom it is impossible to refuse."

She rose abruptly and regarded him with astonishment. "Who makes this demand? Speak, 'Izz al-Din!"

"Do not be angry, my Lady. The demand comes from the greatest man among Muslims."

Tree of Pearls fell back confounded onto her couch. "Al-Musta'sim Billah . . . Commander of the Faithful," she murmured. Anger now came into her voice. "Is it not enough that he has deprived me of the throne? Now he would deprive me of my slave and companion?"

"Truly, I am sorry, Tree of Pearls, but I see no way to refuse his request. We are his subjects all, and he is the successor of our Prophet, peace and blessings upon him."

"How comes he to make this request, then? And who shall take her to him?"

'Izz al-Din studiously ignored the first part of this question. "The Caliph's emissary shall take her to him. He informed me of his master's will yesterday."

Tree of Pearls was thunderstruck by this unwelcome news, and she wept openly in spite of herself. She turned to Shwaykar and found her silently bent over her instrument, tears streaming down her cheeks. This sight affected her greatly, and fanned her rising anger. "Am I then to understand that you acquiesce in this grave injustice, 'Izz al-Din?" she demanded.

"Can I do otherwise? His will must be obeyed in matters of much greater importance."

She rose again and dried her eyes with her handkerchief as she struggled to calm her mounting fury. Then she raised her head and met his eyes. "But the girl is betrothed," she said.

"It matters but little. I am bound to honor the request of the Commander of the Faithful. The concerned party may petition the Caliph himself if he so wills." He rose, and his face was set with somber determination. "She must be ready to depart tomorrow morning. You may rest assured that she will travel safely and will be given every possible comfort on her journey. Fear not for her, for she has been summoned by the Commander of the Faithful." And with that, he swiftly took his leave.

As the doors closed behind him, the sound of Tree of Pearls's renewed sobs echoed in his ears but he resolutely ignored them, and before quitting the palace, he instructed the guards to keep close watch over Shwaykar in case she attempted to escape in the night.

Rukn al-Din and Tree of Pearls

'IZZ AL-DIN was justified in taking this precaution, for Tree of Pearls had determined to encourage Shwaykar to fly and to aid her in the undertaking. Quickly realizing that all avenues of escape had been barred, however, she waxed furious at 'Izz al-Din's foresight. She now resigned herself to the inevitable and set about doing her best to comfort the wretched girl. She summoned her resolve and tried, with a variety of arguments, to convince her favorite that there was nothing to be done; that go to Baghdad she must, but that she, Tree of Pearls, would nonetheless move heaven and earth to have her returned as soon as possible. At the same time, she did her utmost to assure her that there was nothing to fear from the Caliph.

As for Shwaykar, her greatest worry was how Rukn al-Din would receive this catastrophic news and whether it would fire his jealousy or leave him indifferent. It was impossible to know this while he remained far away on the battlefields of Damietta, however, and time was too short to summon him before the morrow and her imminent departure. She finally realized that she had no choice but to resign herself to her fate and to put her trust in God. Her lot was a common one in those days of absolute royal privilege, for these slave-girls were property like any other, to be disposed of by a prince or a sultan as he pleased. Girls like Shwaykar were regularly transferred from master to master, and indeed, had it not been for Rukn al-Din, Shwaykar may have counted herself lucky in being chosen for the Caliph's harem, for this was the greatest of honors for such as her. In either case, a concubine was powerless to choose, and must bend to the will of another.

The next morning, after a long and mournful farewell between the two women, a company of eunuchs bore Shwaykar to the encampment of the Caliph's emissary. Tree of Pearls had renewed her promise to come to her aid and to do all in her power to conclude her marriage to Rukn al-Din. Shwaykar departed for Baghdad the same day, but she left her heart behind in Egypt.

Tree of Pearls too suffered greatly from the separation. She was convinced that Sallafa was behind all her misfortunes and she bitterly blamed 'Izz al-Din for his double treachery—first as a lover, and second as an ally. She saw how easily he had replaced her on both counts, and despite the rancor that now burned in her heart, she could do nothing but submit to her lot.

She spent the rest of the morning brooding alone in her apartments, now railing against her lover's betrayal, now grieving over the smoldering ashes of her dreams. Her thoughts then turned to Rukn al-Din, whom she expected shortly in Cairo. How would she receive him when he returned from Damietta, she wondered. And what should she say to him?

As luck would have it, he arrived on the very afternoon of Shwaykar's departure for Baghdad, for when news of the coup that had taken place in Cairo reached him, he had immediately resolved to return to the Citadel and seek an audience with Tree of Pearls. Consequently, no sooner had he passed through the gates and dismounted from his sweating steed than he proceeded directly to the deposed Queen's quarters, in his dusty cloak and before even having reported to his Commander, 'Izz al-Din Aybak. Tree of Pearls received him warmly and she informed him of all that had come to pass, most particularly of the wretched fate that had befallen Shwaykar. She averred that she had done everything in her power to deflect 'Izz al-Din from his purpose, but to no avail, and she exaggerated his arrogance and insolence in order to arouse Rukn al-Din's anger against him.

As he listened to her pour out her grievances, Rukn al-Din, freshly arrived and exhausted by the great haste he had made on his journey, was overcome with conflicting feelings. At first he imagined—thanks to the artful picture she painted—that 'Izz al-Din had meant to spite him personally by depriving him of Shwaykar, but he was by nature highly self-possessed, broad-minded, and circumspect, and he accordingly held his tongue, though his eyes flared with the anger she had roused in his heart. Tree of Pearls watched him closely as she embroidered her complaint, for she wished he would say some word to cool the fires burning in her breast. She hoped above all that Rukn al-Din would be moved to declare 'Izz al-Din his mortal enemy, if only secretly and in the privacy of her chambers. Thus would she have her desired revenge, and a powerful accomplice through whom to work it.

She finally grew weary of his stubborn silence and resolved to attempt a change of strategy. "Why do you remain silent, Rukn al-Din? You are perchance content that we have been deprived of Shwaykar and the throne at one fell swoop, both acts accomplished by the will of that profligate Caliph?"

Rukn al-Din frowned at this remark. "Of which Caliph do you speak, Madam?"

"I speak of Al-Musta'sim, ruler of Baghdad, who is too proud to see a woman placed on the throne but none too proud to occupy it himself—a cowardly, spineless man whose occupations are confined to the harem and the disgraceful pursuit of pleasure," she angrily replied. She paused to mark the effect of these words on Rukn al-Din, but he remained as still and silent as the grave.

If it had been given to her to read his thoughts, she would have discovered that this gloomy silence effectively concealed his smoldering anger while his mind, sharp as a fine steel blade, worked furiously to make sense of the whirlpool of clashing interests, ambitions, and intrigues which now closed in on him. What could Tree of Pearls mean by speaking so of the Caliph before him? And what had the state of affairs at the Imperial Court to do with Shwaykar's unfortunate but not uncommon lot?

Tree of Pearls could perceive nothing but weakness and cowardly equivocation in his continued silence, however. She pressed him irritably. "Speak, Rukn al-Din, I entreat you! I have had enough of this silence. Perhaps you do not believe me? Patience! I shall prove my words. I shall present to you a man who knows our miserable Caliph well. He arrived from Baghdad only yesterday. Question him, and he shall speak to you of the man's true character. Pray be seated and I shall summon him before you immediately."

Rukn al-Din accepted her invitation and sat down distractedly, his fingers nervously tugging at his beard as though he would pull out its fine hairs one by one. The Baghdadi entered shortly and Rukn al-Din recognized him at once. "It is Sahban!" he exclaimed.

"God be praised—He has finally forced your tongue! I suppose we must thank Sahban for this grace, God preserve him. Speak, Sahban. Tell Rukn al-Din what you know of Al-Musta'sim, Ruler of Baghdad. Do not be afraid to tell the truth, for Rukn al-Din is our friend. Tell him what you told me yesterday."

Sahban had just returned from the mission with which Sallafa had charged him. Upon his arrival in Cairo, he had immediately sought to meet with her to inform her of the success of his errand, but she had received him coldly, as had 'Izz al-Din, her new master. Sahban was quick to realize that he had been sorely used, and his heart swelled with hatred against the new lovers and against the entire Ayyubid State. His recently disappointed hopes of winning Sallafa now mingled with his deep resentment of Sunni power in the Empire, and he resolved to strike a blow against both through the medium of the deposed Queen. If he succeeded in provoking her against the Abbasids, he might eventually succeed in securing the conditions necessary for a Shi'ite restoration in Egypt.

In the course of his frequent travels to Egypt Sahban had founded a Shi'ite secret society that met to discuss the affairs of the Empire and complain of Shi'ite political fortunes. Together they dreamed and they plotted an Alawite Restoration in Egypt and a return to the days of the glorious Fatimid Dynasty. He hoped that enlisting Tree of Pearls in this project would be an easy task, for she was no doubt already furious at having been deposed by order of the Caliph, and at 'Izz al-Din's inconstancy. He had accordingly sought an audience with her on the usual pretext of exhibiting his wares, and had subtly turned the conversation to the miscreant Caliph and to 'Izz al-Din's relations with Sallafa. Tree of Pearls had listened in rising anger, but had kept her silence and waited to sound Rukn al-Din upon his return from Damietta.

Rukn al-Din now received Sahban warmly and invited him to be seated. Tree of Pearls then spoke. "What news of the Commander of the Faithful, Sahban?" she prompted, and let out an acid little peal of laughter.

"If you so permit me my Lady. The Caliph is a slothful glutton who cares for nothing but wine, food, and song."

"And what is your opinion of his government?" she continued, with a glance at Rukn al-Din.

"I fear for the Empire, from the discontent of its own people as much as from the ambitions of the Mongols. They are preparing an invasion as we speak, and the population of Baghdad lives in daily fear. The Caliph is otherwise occupied, however. If he does not change his ways and shoulder his responsibilities, the Empire will surely be destroyed."

Rukn al-Din laughed and said, "The Abbasid Empire destroyed? The experts who are wont to pronounce on such matters never cease to repeat that it shall last forever!"

"They may say what they will. The end approaches," Sahban grimly replied.

Rukn al-Din leaned forward in his seat. "Surely you do not mean to say that the Caliphate itself is doomed?"

"By no means, my Lord."

"But if what you say be true, where shall we find a new Caliph, and who shall secure his dominion over Egypt?"

Sahban glanced around and nervously licked his lips. "There is no reason why the future Caliph need be of the Abbasid line. Why should he not be from the land of Egypt? Was not Egypt the seat of a brilliant Caliphate less than one hundred years ago? Was not the country then all the more prosperous and magnificent?"

Rukn al-Din interrupted him impatiently. "I believe you speak of the 'Abidi State? But these were Shi'a!"

"What difference does it make whether they were Shi'a or Sunnis? Are we not all the descendants of Qurayshi Muslims? The real difference would be an Egyptian Caliphate. Think upon it! Egypt's commerce would thereby prosper, its fleets expand, its cities flourish, and its conquests multiply, while Iraq would become one of its many provinces rather than its imperial master."

Rukn al-Din listened carefully to Sahban's words while his sharp mind plumbed their hidden purpose. He was not unaware of the longstanding Shi'ite grievance against the Sunni Caliphate, and he did not propose to be used as a pawn of some fledgling Shi'ite conspiracy. He therefore refrained from comment and proceeded to politely dismiss his eager interlocutor. He rose from his seat. "You have enlightened us, Sahban, may God recompense you well."

Sahban immediately rose in his turn and, bowing deeply, requested permission to withdraw. Rukn al-Din's utter silence had bewildered him. "Here is a man who trusts no one!" he thought to himself as he left.

Tree of Pearls was no less surprised than Sahban. As soon as he had left, she turned to Rukn al-Din and clenched her teeth in frustration. "The time has come for you to speak! I shall refrain from adding anything to what you have already heard of the decline of the Abbasids in Baghdad, or of the state of the Egyptian Sultanate—for its King is a boy of eight years and the entire government is in the hands of his Regent, 'Izz al-Din!"

"Methinks you wax exceedingly angry with my Lord 'Izz al-Din, my Lady. Is it because he has permitted Shwaykar to be taken from you?"

"Indeed, this is the main cause of my vexation—though I may well have other, more personal grievances against him," she added grimly.

"Permit me to inquire whether Shwaykar went to Baghdad of her own free will?"

"Upon my word, Rukn al-Din! Her tears overflowed like fountains as she took her leave of me, and she repeatedly begged to be remembered to you. You may be sure that she shall remain true to her troth and never accept another, though it be the Caliph himself. I assured her that you would not abandon her and that the valiant Rukn al-Din would be our zealous champion until the end—both hers and mine, for I too am quite alone now since the infamous 'Izz al-Din saw fit to turn his attentions elsewhere. He has forgotten our friendship . . ." she trailed off plaintively, but the fire quickly returned to her eyes. "But what of it?" she cried as she gazed squarely at Rukn al-Din. "God is with those who are patient!"

Rukn al-Din chose to ignore this last exclamation. "Shwaykar still loves me, then?" he demanded. "Do you suspect that I may be any less true to her?"

"I have no doubt that you shall do all that is within your power to rescue and avenge her. And now," she continued, changing the subject, "what think you of Sahban's views on the Fatimid Caliphate?"

"I do not like it," he testily replied. "A Shi'ite restoration in Egypt would neither serve our interests nor suit our present conditions. There is, however, a time and a place for everything," he added. "Let us wait for the appropriate moment in which to act, if act we must. I must now beg permission to withdraw, my Lady," and he rose to go.

Tree of Pearls gave a bitter little smile. "In God's keeping," she replied.

A Secret Conversation

RUKN AL-DIN returned immediately to his quarters in the Citadel. He informed no one of his arrival and he postponed his meeting with 'Izz al-Din to the morrow. He dismissed the servants and shut the door to his bedchamber fast behind him; then he undressed while mulling over all the extraordinary things he had heard that day.

Despite his great bravery and his martial prowess, Rukn al-Din was still an inexperienced youth. Only now, after hearing of the upheaval that had taken place at the heart of the Egyptian State and being informed of the condition of the Caliphate in Baghdad, was he beginning to understand the true meaning of ambition. Sahban's purpose in disparaging the Abbasid Caliphate and praising the Fatimids had not escaped him. Neither was he deceived by Tree of Pearls's exaggerated account of Al-Musta'sim's faults, and her incitements against him. Likewise, he had taken careful stock of her rancor against 'Izz al-Din, and he well perceived that if she wished him—Rukn al-Din—success in his endeavors, it was only to be revenged on her enemies. All these thoughts passed through his mind as he changed into his dressing gown and nightcap and stretched out onto his bed.

One thought now became fixed in his mind: that Tree of Pearls and Sahban had attempted to incite him to seize power, not out of the high regard or affection in which they held him, but simply for their own various ends. He saw no perfidy or injury to himself in this, nor did he find it strange that it should be so, for he was sensible and astute and saw straight into the heart of a matter. He was not the sort of man to believe in the selflessness of even his closest friend, for he knew full well that men never embark on an action without having a secret purpose and an expected profit to themselves in mind. Those who claim to do good without recompense and for the sole benefit of others are either mistaken, or deluded, or outright liars: those who will but acknowledge this simple fact would be in a much better position to treat their friends justly, neither expecting the impossible from them, nor blaming them for their natural selfishness.

Rukn al-Din was grateful to his two friends for revealing the outlines of their blossoming intrigue and he resolved to profit from it when the time was ripe, but for now he preferred to conceal his own intentions for as long as possible. In the close privacy of his rooms he considered his situation aloud. "They have taken Shwaykar from me. The Caliph has summoned her to Baghdad so that he might delight in her unparalleled voice, a rare treasure even amongst the loveliest and most accomplished of singing-girls. Tree of Pearls attempts to provoke my anger against Al-Musta'sim because of this. But is it right to resent him for an act by which both Shwaykar's worth and her good fortune have been multiplied? I have no right to feel myself injured on this score, for he did not deliberately deprive me of her. Perhaps it is true that this Caliph is weak, or extravagant and licentious, and that he consequently deserves to die or be deposed, as some would say. But who shall guarantee that his successor would be any better? And who would undertake such a perilous mission, unless himself a hardy aspirant to the throne? Truly, our Shi'ite friend's delusions of reviving the 'Abidi State or some like Alawite dynasty in Egypt were quite amusing! What possible benefit could Egypt thereby derive? Were the Caliphate to be transferred to Egypt, there would be no more Sultanate! The Abbasid Caliphate in Baghdad is the guarantor of the might and independence of the Egyptian Sultans, after all. I would do well, nonetheless, to keep myself apprised of the man's intentions, and even to encourage his fancies, for some good might come of it. There is no harm in it for the present, at least."

The thought of the Sultanate made the blood run quick in Rukn al-Din's veins and enflamed his burgeoning ambitions. He jumped up from the bed and paced restlessly about the room. "Egypt's throne!" he whispered to himself. "It is better by far than the Baghdad Caliphate. Do I then aspire to it? Yes! I desire it. But were I to speak openly of such a lofty hope I would be taken for a fool. Perhaps I am a fool after all. So be it then! From today on, I shall keep my own counsel and watch and wait."

The passing sound of a horse's hoofs below his window interrupted his reverie, and he now recalled Shwaykar's plight. "And what of Shwaykar," he asked himself. "Can I simply leave her to her fate? I love her! Even though this love was first born at the command of another, it has taken possession of my heart. In any case, it is quite enough that she loves me and expects me to come to her aid—if she remains true to this love once ensconced in the Caliph's palace!"

The sun had just set, and Rukn al-Din resolved to rest for the remainder of the evening and to rise early for his meeting with 'Izz al-Din. His duty also bound him to wait upon the new Sultan and to congratulate him on his ascension to the throne. He settled down to his dinner and then stretched out upon his bed once more, but the turbulence of his thoughts drove all sleep from his eyes.

When night had lowered its inky veil, Rukn al-Din rose and, putting on a flowing black cloak, walked out of the precincts of the Citadel towards the vast solitude of the Muqattam Plateau. The sky was cloudless, the moon had risen to its zenith, and nature revealed itself in all her awesome splendor. On such a perfect night as this, the wanderer, perched atop some summit or lingering in a verdant garden, takes keen pleasure in quiet contemplation, as though he would confide his deepest secrets to the moon or hold nature herself in tranquil converse.

Rukn al-Din's thoughts were full of his plans and ambitions. He walked on, unmolested by the guards, and climbed the plateau in the moonlight until he had reached its summit. He turned his thoughtful gaze upon the great city spread out before him. His eyes wandered over its lush gardens and graceful minarets, and behind them all, the Nile rippling silver in the moonlight. Further on in the distance stood the mighty pyramids, their sharp points piercing the sky, and all around, the palm and sycamore orchards veiled in the purple dark. He sat down on a rock behind a pile of stones that had once been a mosque or a small fortress of some kind, and silently contemplated the view before him. His thoughts wandered aimlessly from one thing to another. Shwaykar's face appeared before him and he wondered where she might be at this very moment. Then the thought of the throne and whether it would one day be his stole upon him. By the light of the moon, the shadows of his fancies grew and grew until they took on the shape of reality.

Suddenly he heard a light rustle, like the sound a snake makes as it slithers through the dust. Though he was not in the least afraid, the solitude of the place and his own fretful distraction reminded him of the comforts of his waiting bed. As he rose to go, the nearby sound of a man's throaty chuckle met his ears. He looked about in an attempt to locate its source but could see nothing. He was almost inclined to believe that the laughter had issued from the mouth of a mischievous *jinni*—such superstitions being quite common in those days—but he now distinctly heard the sound of footsteps on the other side of the ruined structure by which he stood. He held his breath and waited.

Now he began to make out the sound of a group of people talking. His curiosity caused him to draw closer, and to his great surprise he distinctly heard the voice of him who had been so much in his thoughts all this evening. It was Sahban. "That Sallafa is a real sorceress—more cunning than a pack of ministers," he said.

Another voice replied, "You mean the Custodian of the Righteous King's Harem? It's true what they say about her, then?"

Sahban gave a short, hard laugh. "Try as hard as you may, you'll never be able to do justice to her wiliness. I have experienced it first-hand. You have surely heard of the tumult that befell the government yesterday? She is the sole cause of it all."

"You exaggerate, Sahban! How could she have possibly managed all this from Cairo? She may well have come between Tree of Pearls and 'Izz al-Din Aybak, but . . . this?" a third voice demanded.

"I am sure of what I say. Sallafa engineered a coup and a transfer of the throne from her own palace here in Cairo."

"And how did she accomplish such a feat?"

"It seems that her influence in Baghdad is great, and that her opinion is highly regarded in the Caliph's palaces."

The second voice now spoke up. "Perhaps you're right. She used to belong to the Caliph before he presented her to Al-Salih as a gift. But still, you surely inflate her power."

"I know of what I speak," Sahban insisted. He lowered his voice. "I myself took a letter from her to Baghdad. The official decree deposing Tree of Pearls came immediately on its heels."

The third man laughed heartily at this. "And what compelled you to stick your nose into such goings-on in the first place, my friend? What business do you have to undertake such errands for these Turks?"

"My personal reasons are unimportant," Sahban sniffed. "Nevertheless, I did hope that Sallafa's plot might aid us in our enterprise. The forced abdication of Tree of Pearls may eventually lead to an uprising that would serve our ends."

Rukn al-Din's interest was powerfully aroused by this last statement, and so he put aside his misgivings and continued to eavesdrop on the conversation. A fourth man now broke in. "You made a mistake, sir, in agreeing to this mission, for you thereby caused the throne to pass from the hands of a chit of a woman to those of a powerful man—I mean ʿIzz al-Din Aybak. He will certainly contrive to depose the child-Sultan and to rule with an iron fist in his stead. I suppose you undertook this service for no other reason than to please Sallafa—in truth, she is a heavenly creature."

"It is true that she is beautiful," Sahban mumbled, "and the thought of seeking to please her may have crossed my mind. But I undertook the mission only to serve our declared ends."

"Did she reward your efforts, then?" the voice archly inquired.

Sahban ignored the raillery in this question. "The woman is surely one of the Caliph's spies," he muttered. "At the very least, she is an impenetrable riddle. It would seem she has no heart, or at least that she belongs to a different order of beings. I admit that I almost won her favor and that she gave me many indications of her confidence and her partiality to my person. Then she changed towards me quite suddenly. When I returned from Baghdad yesterday, I found that she had passed into the house of the Regent ʿIzz al-Din and that she seemed to have conquered him completely. Tree of Pearls herself is bitterly aware of this coup but is powerless to challenge it."

"Sallafa has always been jealous of Tree of Pearls," the third speaker broke in, "and especially after she was crowned Queen, for she no doubt felt that as a Kurd and distant relative of Al-Salih she herself would have been more deserving of the throne. Revenge, rather than political intrigue, must be her only motive, for she has merely caused the Sultanate to change hands with no perceivable benefit to herself. There is one thing that puzzles me though. I don't see how the Caliph came to hear of Shwaykar, the singing-girl, so as to request her by name in the first place."

"It was no doubt Sallafa who caused news of her to reach the Caliph's ears," Sahban replied. "She meant to spite Tree of Pearls a second time. The girl is her slave and handmaiden."

Rukn al-Din's heart beat faster at this reference to Shwaykar. He listened closely as the fourth man now spoke up. "I see no great cunning in this little maneuver," he said lightly. "Tree of Pearls can easily do without Shwaykar—there are scores like her in the Palace. The real secret of Sallafa's success is her friendship with the Custodian of Al-Mustaʿsim's Harem. The woman owes her many favors. But let us speak no more of Sallafa, for she's nothing but a deceitful and jealous slave."

Sahban laughed and said, "Too true, my friend. She deceived me and I see no reason why she would not serve another from the same dish. The moon has begun to set," he added as he glanced up at the sky. "It's high time we each went our way before the sentries chance upon us in this place."

Rukn al-Din crouched back in the dark as he waited for the sound of their receding steps to fade away. His thoughts were full of Sallafa and 'Izz al-Din, and of the coup that had taken place at court. The conversation he had just overheard had shed light on much that had been obscure to him. He returned by and by to his rooms, terribly fatigued by his long journey from Damietta and by his lack of sleep in the past two days. The next morning, he dressed and went directly to the Great Hall to meet with 'Izz al-Din. He tendered his excuses to the Regent, informing him that he had only arrived in Cairo the previous day and had been too tired to present himself at court. 'Izz al-Din in turn presented him to Al-Ashraf, and Rukn al-Din submitted to them a report of his mission in Damietta, the result of which had been the withdrawal of the Franks from that city under favorable terms.

'Izz al-Din lengthily praised his officer's zeal and courage, and promised to reward him well for his efforts on behalf of the Egyptian state. Rukn al-Din thanked him gracefully for his generous solicitude, but he felt that something imperceptible had changed in 'Izz al-Din's manner. He reflected on this subtle shift as he left the Great Hall and wondered whether, after all, it was his own perception of the Regent that had changed. Perhaps his mounting ambitions or perhaps all the rumors that he had recently heard had altered his relation to 'Izz al-Din. This thought stayed with him in the days that followed, but he kept his own council and waited patiently for the opportunity to put it to the test.

Shwaykar

THE DAYS AND WEEKS PASSED and Rukn al-Din was greatly occupied by the duties of his office, for 'Izz al-Din had kept him in the post of Dawadar to the new King. He was haunted by thoughts of Shwaykar, however, and he pined for news of her in Baghdad. He could not make up his mind whether to follow her there or to wait until he had received some proof of her continued devotion to him, for he was apprehensive, knowing the honors that would be heaped upon her and the particular admiration that she was sure to inspire at the Caliph's Palace. His nature was not of the impetuous, passionate kind that hastens to sacrifice its own interests in the name of love. He was steady and rational in his actions, and was guided in all he thought and did by utility and, above all, ambition. In his heart, he did not believe that Shwaykar would remain true to his love, once installed at Baghdad. His love for her was strong and he suffered at her absence, but he was partly consoled in the knowledge that she was surely now living in great comfort and luxury. Was this not the greatest aspiration of such as her?

One morning, however, he woke from a dream in which she had appeared to him in a state of wild terror. His heart grew anxious in the wake of this troubling vision, and he immediately resolved to act. His heavy duties still obliged him to remain at court for the time being, but it occurred to him that he might send Sahban in his place. Such a mission, he reasoned, would also be a means of further drawing the man into his confidence.

Sahban eagerly responded to the Prince's summons, and Rukn al-Din immediately broached the subject that troubled his mind. "God's peace, Sahban. You spoke truly of the state of the Empire when we last met. I have since thought long upon it. The Abbasids are unfit for the Caliphate so long as they wallow in corruption."

"Did I not say so, my Lord?" the merchant fervently replied.

"You did. I myself have felt the yoke of their oppression. Perhaps you have heard that they have taken Shwaykar, Tree of Pearls's handmaiden?"

"Indeed my Lord, I have heard."

"She is my betrothed."

"Your betrothed?" Sahban exclaimed in astonishment. "And Al-Musta'sim dared to take her from you? The tyrant! The 'Alawi Caliphs would never have been guilty of such a deed," he added slyly.

"He did not knowingly do so. But that is not my point—what I wish now is to know how Shwaykar fares there. I cannot travel to Baghdad myself for the present. You, however, go there often in the course of your business. Would you then undertake this service for your friend Rukn al-Din?"

Sahban was flattered by this noble recognition. "I am at your service, my Lord. I shall depart as soon as possible—tomorrow. May God blight them! They shall soon be the ruin of this Empire," and he shook his head in bitter wonder.

"I thank you for your devotion, Sahban. The days to come shall show you my gratitude."

"It is my duty to serve you, my Lord. I shall depart tomorrow." He rose to take his leave. "Say no more, and rest assured. I know perfectly well what you require." He bowed deeply and withdrew.

Rukn al-Din took up his affairs once more with a heart less troubled than before, and he did his best to patiently wait out the month or so that it would take for Sahban to make the journey to Baghdad and back.

But one night, before two weeks had passed, an unexpected messenger arrived from Baghdad and would not wait till the following morning to deliver his urgent letter to the Prince. On the evening in question, Rukn al-Din was visiting privately with Tree of Pearls. He often went to see her now in order to while away her solitude and to cheer her spirits as best as he could. The Usher entered and solemnly made his announcement. "A messenger waits at the gate with a letter for Prince Rukn al-Din. He says that he will deliver it into none but his own hand."

"Let him enter," replied the Prince calmly, but his heart jumped in his breast, and after a moment's reflection he hastened to meet the messenger at the door. "What news?" he cried.

"Do I speak to Prince Rukn al-Din Baybars?"

"I am he."

"I bring a letter to the Prince from a lady who wishes her communication to him to remain secret."

"Give it to me," he brusquely replied.

The man withdrew a scroll from his pocket and handed it to Rukn al-Din, who took it and read it eagerly as he walked back into the hall where he had been sitting with Tree of Pearls. She meanwhile studied his face closely as he read, and she shivered slightly at the mounting disquiet she saw there. "What news, Prince? What has happened?" she cried as soon as he had finished.

He handed the letter to her. She took it and read the following:

From the wretched Shwaykar to her Lord and love, Prince Rukn al-Din. I have been snatched from the arms of Tree of Pearls in your absence. My Lady was unable to discover the means of detaining me until your return, and so I was forced to quit Cairo with a heavy heart. I have done nothing but grieve since leaving it, and I take solace in nothing, in spite of the comfort and respect showered upon me by the master of that caravan. My companions marveled at the copious tears of a slave whom the Commander of the Faithful has seen fit to honor. It seems my tears were but an evil portent of things to come, however, for no sooner had we arrived at the outskirts of Baghdad than my situation changed for the worse. I was transferred to a company come from the Caliph's palace to receive me, as I then supposed, and I resolved to beg them to return me immediately to Egypt or at least to send a representative to the Caliph who would tell him my story and seek his grace. But from the moment they laid hands on me they commenced to treat me as a prisoner, and even as I write these lines they prepare to take me away, I know not where.

There was, in the caravan that brought me from Egypt, a good eunuch—'Abid of Basra. He is the bearer of this letter to you. I found refuge in the great kindness he showed me on this wretched journey. I have seized an opportunity to hastily compose this letter and I have begged him to deliver it into your hands. Pray reward him as you should see fit, and may God bless you, for I fear we shall meet no more in this world. I seal this letter with my tears.

While Tree of Pearls was engaged in reading this letter, Rukn al-Din impatiently questioned the eunuch about the mysterious circumstances of which Shwaykar had written.

"I know nothing, my Lord," the man replied. "I was but a servant in the caravan that brought the Caliph's decree to Cairo, and when the girl joined our company on the return voyage to Baghdad, I was ordered to wait upon her. We only knew that she was destined for the Caliph's harem, and I did my best to serve her well and to provide her with every comfort, for she was generous and kind to me. Upon reaching the outskirts of Baghdad, a company of soldiers came out to meet us, and having informed us that they had been sent by the Caliph, they demanded that we hand her over to them. We had no choice but to obey, but we soon realized that they were not whom they pretended to be and surmised that they had no intention of conducting her to the royal palaces as they claimed. I took pity on the poor child, and when I attempted to comfort her she replied, 'My only wish is that you will take this letter to Prince Rukn al-Din at the Citadel of Cairo and deliver it into his own hands,' and this I have now done."

"And where is she now?" he demanded. "And what shall these scoundrels do with her, think you? What can be their purpose in seizing her in this manner?"

"I know not, my Lord. We were all astonished by this turn of events."

Rukn al-Din stopped to consider. What could the cause of all this be? He could see no reason in it. He turned once again to the messenger. "And now, 'Abid, if I give you a letter will you take it to her? Do you think you can find her?"

"I shall do my utmost to find her, and shall not rest until I succeed. I shall be her faithful servant and my life shall be her ransom, for she is truly a generous and affectionate child."

Rukn al-Din praised the eunuch's devotion. "Come to me tomorrow morning," he said. "You shall find me in my chambers at the Citadel."

'Abid bowed in submission and took his leave.

Revenge

RUKN AL-DIN stood nailed to the spot, lost in thought. Then he became once again conscious of Tree of Pearls, who had finished reading the letter, her face flushed with mounting fury. She met his look fiercely. "Such are the actions of caliphs who disdain to place a woman on the throne! Here is your Musta'sim, Commander of the Faithful. Upon my word, if a bold woman were to take up his scepter, she would wield it a thousand times more effectively than he! He busies himself with wine and slaves, he seizes our womenfolk, and we meekly submit."

Rukn al-Din would not be so easily provoked. "Al-Musta'sim is surely innocent of Shwaykar's current distress," he retorted.

"Who, then, is responsible for it?" she demanded. "Was it not he who sent that band of villains to seize her? And even if they acted without his knowledge, does this not yet prove the man's weakness and the little respect in which he is so generally held that thieves and bandits would dare to abduct a singing-girl coming to him in a great retinue from the court of the Egyptian Sultan?" She wrung her hands in despair, and suddenly added, "But it is my fault after all, for letting her go!"

For once, Rukn al-Din's self-possession failed him. "If it is anyone's fault, it is 'Izz al-Din's," he interrupted brusquely. "If he had wished it, he would have found a ruse by which to retain Shwaykar."

Tree of Pearls eagerly seized on this unexpected declaration. "You speak too truly, my friend! I know not what has wrought this change in our great Prince," she said derisively. "It seems that ambition disfigures its lovers. In aspiring to the Sultanate, 'Izz al-Din discarded his conscience and those who were once dear to his heart." The words stuck in her throat, and she fell silent.

Rukn al-Din was struck by the force of Tree of Pearls's resentment against her arrogant paramour. He realized that he had made a mistake in so openly speaking his mind, and he resolved to temper his accusations and to carefully draw out her true intentions towards the Regent. "I do not believe that his actions were guided by ambition, for his position has not greatly changed since you sat upon the throne. On the contrary, he wielded even greater power during your brief reign, my Lady," he added meaningfully. "Perhaps after all he had no choice but to obey the Caliph's command regarding Shwaykar."

She gave a forced laugh and her face grew pale with indignation. "Perhaps he obeyed the command of someone other than the Caliph." She swallowed her bile and set to wiping the perspiration from her mouth and forehead with her handkerchief.

Rukn al-Din understood that she referred to Sallafa. "Do you blame him then for seeking his own interest? There is no one in the world who—"

"Nay! I blame him not for this," she interrupted him forcefully. "I blame those who fail to seek it! This Prince has sacrificed us all—Shwaykar, Rukn al-Din, and Tree of Pearls—to his ambition. He shows us nothing but contempt, while we continue to honor him and seek his favor." She shifted in her seat and fell silent.

Rukn al-Din took note of her evident discomfort. Wishing to provoke her further, he continued. "I feel the insult to myself keenly, as you well know, but I see no reason why he should deserve this fury from you. He was not the author of the fate that has befallen you; neither has he substantially gained from it."

She waved her hand impatiently. "You constrain me to speak, Rukn al-Din. Allow me therefore to reveal my mind to you. You perhaps suspect that I have grown to hate 'Izz al-Din because of his attachment to that Kurdish slave. She is the one who has aided him in his treachery. She is but a poor fool, however, for he has betrayed her, as he betrayed me, and shall surely abandon her entirely once he has achieved his ends."

"And what may these ends be?" he inquired.

"'Izz al-Din has resolved to seize the throne!" she exclaimed.

He laughed at the folly of this claim. "Does he not already possess it? Al-Ashraf is after all nothing but a pretty picture with no substance."

"True, but he shall nonetheless depose the boy and have himself crowned Sultan in his stead, with the full support of the Turcoman Commanders," she darkly predicted.

Rukn al-Din shook his head doubtfully. "How can such a thing be? The people have declared that they shall be ruled by none other than a scion of the House of Ayyub."

Tree of Pearls laughed scornfully in her turn. "You are still inexperienced, my Lord, but you shall soon understand that what you call the people have neither voice nor opinion. They are ever wont to change their minds with each passing wind of political authority. 'Izz al-Din has taken advantage of your lengthy absence from the court to win the support of the princes closest to him. I have heard that they have already chosen the title of the first Fatimid Caliph for him, that of Al-Mu'iz. Do you still doubt it then? Think! Do you not feel that he has changed towards you?"

Rukn al-Din was stunned by this news, but he made a supreme effort to remain composed and reveal nothing to Tree of Pearls's watchful gaze. Was not the throne of Egypt destined for a scion of the Ayyubid line? Tree of Pearls's short-lived and ill-fated reign had only proved this politic rule. And yet here was 'Izz al-Din Aybak plotting to assume the Sultanate by force of arms. And if 'Izz al-Din could succeed in this endeavor, why not himself? He now coveted the throne even more, but determined to continue his policy of dissimulation. He was more than ever convinced that 'Izz al-Din owed all to the cunning efforts of Sallafa, and resolved to question Tree of Pearls directly on the subject. "My Lady, I do believe that Sallafa has played a momentous role in these events."

"I do not doubt it," she stonily replied, "considering her Kurdish lineage and the good relations she maintains with a number of the most influential princes at court, Ayyubid and others. I am convinced that she has acted most treacherously, first by stealing 'Izz al-Din away from Tree of Pearls, and second by subverting the will of the Caliph she pretends to serve. But mark you my words, she shall be sorely disappointed, for our new Sultan shall yet spurn her, as he spurned me." She smiled triumphantly and her eyes flashed with malice.

"Explain yourself, I beg you, my Lady," Rukn al-Din replied.

"Do you wish then that I should tell you all I know of the intimate affairs of that traitor?" she hissed. "You ask me to whom he shall belong. I shall answer you. He claims a third woman."

"And who is this third woman, pray tell."

"She is not of this country."

"Surely you jest?" he said in wonder.

"Nay, I speak the truth. 'Izz al-Din seeks the hand of the daughter of Badr al-Din Lu'lu', Governor of Mosul."

"The Caliph holds the Governor of Mosul in high esteem," he mused aloud. "Do you then think that he will succeed in his suit?"

Tree of Pearls sprang furiously from her seat. "Never! He shall never have her! His destiny lies elsewhere, for there is a fourth lover who awaits him," and she executed the swift motion of a dagger slicing through the air.

From this gesture, and from the bloodshot fury in her eyes, Rukn al-Din perceived that Tree of Pearls meant to assassinate her former lover. He laughed to hide his alarm at this extravagant design and rose to take his leave. "Your passion carries you away, my Lady. I am inclined to doubt the sagacity of such a plan. You yourself will agree with me if you think well upon it. It is midnight and I must take my leave of you. May God preserve you."

"Woe unto you, Rukn al-Din!" she cried, as he turned to depart. "How dare you quit me so precipitously after I have bared my heart to you?"

"What would you have of me, my Lady?"

"Your indifference astounds me! We have spoken of many things, and I have confided much to you that I have jealously guarded from all other ears, yet you remain as silent and unmovable as a rock. If it be subtlety and cunning that make you act so, then I commend you, but if not, it is clear that you are truly a cold and unfeeling man. So be it! I yet expect you to say a word regarding that wretched girl who accepted your love, and who suffers the more for it. Her letter has broken my heart. If I were in your place, I would have mounted my steed and sped off to Baghdad this very hour, and would never return until I had wrought my vengeance on the debauched tyrant who stole her away!"

Her words fell like arrows upon the Prince's heart, and he was sorely tempted to confide in her, but he held back from such rashness with great effort and hid his perplexity with a short, sharp laugh. "By God, you are indeed a zealous and brave champion, my Lady! I suppose myself to have similar qualities, but I shall hold my tongue at present, for I am certain that my deeds shall do infinitely more to gratify you than anything I could possibly say." His eyes glittered as he said this, and an expression of gravity and determination darkened his face.

She walked towards him and placed her hands on his shoulders. "This is the Rukn al-Din I know well!" she said. "Your words reassure me. Know that I shall do my utmost to aid you in your endeavor." She lowered her voice significantly. "Once at Baghdad, you shall slay Al-Musta'sim and I shall take care of 'Izz al-Din here in Cairo! The Sultanate shall then be yours!"

Rukn al-Din's face turned pale at this deadly compact now openly prof-fered. They searched each other's eyes for a moment then he bowed deeply to the deposed Queen. "Shall you now give me permission to withdraw, my Lady?"

She motioned her consent to him, and he took his leave, while his mind spun with the echo of her words and the utter folly of such a perilous undertaking.

Another Messenger

RUKN AL-DIN sorely wished to gain the peace and solitude of his rooms in order to ponder his remarkable conference with Tree of Pearls. He pressed on but could barely make out his way in the dark, so disturbed was he by the evening's events. He was not to have his wish, however, for the sentry hurried towards him as he reached the door to his quarters. "A servant waits here to speak with my Lord," and he pointed to a man standing next to him.

"Who is he?" Rukn al-Din inquired as he turned to peer at a figure that stood back in the shadows. It was not Shwaykar's messenger come to receive his reply to her letter, as he first supposed, but someone he had never seen before.

The man approached and wordlessly placed a sealed letter in the Prince's hand. Rukn al-Din commanded his servant to hasten to his chamber and light the lamps there as he examined the paper and the unfamiliar seal.

He mounted to his chamber and opened the letter. A cloud of perfume rose to meet his nostrils; from this, he surmised that it had been composed by a feminine hand. He began to read by the light of the lamp and was greatly surprised to discover that it was from the mysterious woman who had been so much in his thoughts of late.

> *Sallafa, Slave of the Good King and Custodian of his Harem, requests an audience with Prince Rukn al-Din Baybars the moment he should receive this letter. Her messenger shall guide him to the appointed meeting-place.*

Rukn al-Din pondered this strange note. He wondered what possible reason Sallafa could have for wishing to see him so urgently, for they barely knew each other. Curiosity triumphed over caution and fatigue, however, for he powerfully desired to discover the cause of this summons and whether he might somehow benefit from the interview.

He summoned the messenger. "Is the place far from here?" he demanded.

"No, my Lord, it is close by."

"And have you been waiting long?"

"I have waited two hours, my Lord, for my mistress forbade me to return empty-handed."

This reply only increased his wonder. "Take me to her, then," he commanded.

"If you please, my Lord."

They passed through the gates of the Citadel unmolested by the sentinels on duty. As they walked on in silence, a strange feeling of disquiet slowly crept over Rukn al-Din, and he was powerless to discover the cause of it.

They moved quietly through the darkened streets of Cairo, with nothing but the scattered lamps that hung over an occasional doorway to light their gloomy way. Finally, Rukn al-Din's guide stopped and knocked at an imposing door. A small aperture was opened and a servant thrust his head through to peer at them. The guide nodded to him, whereupon the door slowly swung open and Rukn al-Din was invited to step inside. He entered into a dark garden. The dim candle-light that emanated from a balcony above barely sufficed to dispel the murkiness of his surroundings. Rather, it gave the place an eerie air, casting ghostly shadows around the densely planted trees that seemed to crouch in waiting for the unsus-pecting guest.

Strange fancies beset him as he looked about, and he almost began to regret having come, but he steeled himself and walked on with a firm step, for he was a stranger to fear—except perhaps the fear of scandal. Rukn al-Din was well apprised of the relations that bound the mistress of this house to 'Izz al-Din Aybak.

The messenger had preceded him into the garden and disappeared to inform his mistress of the arrival of her guest. He presently returned and motioned for Rukn al-Din to follow him. They continued on into a candlelit hall where thick carpets and soft cushions had been carefully spread. He was surprised to note that many of the room's rich furnishings had heretofore decorated Al-Salih's pal-aces, and he surmised that 'Izz al-Din had presented these looted ornaments to Sallafa as valuable tokens of his esteem.

Sallafa herself stood at the entrance of the hall to receive him. She had dressed in her richest finery, leaving her lovely face unveiled, and her heady perfume filled the room. When Rukn al-Din's eyes fell upon her, he regretted even more having obeyed her summons, for he saw that a trap had indeed been laid for him.

Rukn al-Din and Sallafa

SALLAFA RECEIVED HIM WARMLY. "I fear I have disturbed your rest, brave Prince."

"By no means, my Lady. I am pleased at an opportunity by which I may perhaps have the occasion to render you some small service."

She extended her hand in greeting, and Rukn al-Din took it in his. Her fingers, which were cold as ice to his touch, made him shiver slightly. She led him by the hand to a seat in the very center of the candlelit room and gracefully arranged herself on a pile of cushions by his side. Once thus installed, she gazed at him in silence. Rukn al-Din politely waited for her to refer to the urgent subject that had caused her to summon him at this late hour, but she showed no signs of doing so and he was forced to speak again. "I have come at your command, my Lady, and would know if I may be of some service to you."

"On the contrary, it is I who place myself at your disposal, Rukn al-Din," she finally replied. "You have been perchance unaware of my existence until this very night. I, on the other hand, have followed your every step for years now from afar." Her eyes glittered and the glow that suffused her cheeks as she said this made her ravishing features even more comely.

This opening sally did not bode well for Rukn al-Din, for he was in no mood for flirtation, and particularly on this of all nights, when his mind was occupied with much graver matters. He had heard tell of this woman's great beauty, and occasional news of her doings had reached him in Al-Salih's lifetime but he had paid them no heed. Moreover, his knowledge of her most recent intrigues disposed him to treat this pleasantry with the utmost caution. He lowered his eyes. "You are too kind, my Lady. I have heard of the noble rank you occupied in the Good King's esteem, but circumstances were never such as to permit a mutual acquaintance."

Sallafa smiled. "I, however, have come to know you quite well, my Lord. I have often watched your comings and goings at the Garden Palace. I used to stay up late of a night and await your passage through the courtyard so that I might catch a glimpse of you through the curtains," she added as she gazed at him intently.

"I am honored, my Lady, and I am indeed sorry for having been ignorant of it."

"You are no longer ignorant of it," she whispered hotly. "I beg you to indulge my boldness, Rukn al-Din, and to refrain from judging me too severely."

He blinked at this clear hint and once again he sorely repented having come. "I beg your pardon, my Lady. I did not expect to hear such words, knowing as I do that our Lord Regent 'Izz al-Din often visits this place, and is, moreover, its master."

Sallafa sighed. "Your Lord does not deserve his good fortune. But of what concern is he to us? Let us speak no more of him."

Here was the trap that Rukn al-Din suspected! He resolved to refuse her advances and to extricate himself from the audience as quickly as possible. "Is this why you have summoned me tonight, Sallafa?"

Her languishing eyes spoke eloquently. "And is this such an insignificant matter in your opinion, my love?"

He stood up and firmly replied, "Far from it, my Lady, but I must beg your indulgence, for I am sorely occupied at present."

Sallafa rose to bar his way. "What can distract you from the love I offer you?" she demanded. "She who once claimed your interest is no more, cruel-hearted Prince! Baghdad is a long way away."

This malevolent allusion to Shwaykar repelled him all the more. "I must nonetheless beg your leave to withdraw, my Lady."

She seized both his hands in her own. "Tread carefully, Rukn al-Din, and do not rush to refuse me. Open your eyes! Know that Sallafa alone is capable of fulfilling your desires. What good can a mere songstress be to you? You are in need of a woman who shall clasp your hand and carefully nurture the fire of your ambitions until the time is ripe to enthrone them."

"By God, my Lady, allow me to withdraw, for pressing matters call me away."

"Do not attempt to deceive me, Prince. I am well informed of your affairs. Forget Shwaykar! You shall never find her!"

At these words, Rukn al-Din angrily withdrew his hands from her fierce clasp. "And what has she to do with you?" he demanded.

"Is she not my rival for your affections? But she is far off now. Let us speak of her no more."

"She shall be close by soon enough, God willing!"

"Whoever has told you so lies," Sallafa laughed. "Shwaykar is lost! I have warned you, and you would do well to take heed."

He shuddered at these words and stared, speechless, at the formidable woman who stood before him. Was she somehow responsible for Shwaykar's abduction? The letter that had arrived from her that very evening only added to his growing suspicions. He slowly resumed his seat and invited Sallafa to join him. "My Lady," he solemnly entreated, "I beg you to listen closely to what I shall say. I have often heard tell of the great esteem in which you are held in the palaces of the Commander of the Faithful at Baghdad. I therefore wish you to aid me in a matter of great import to me in those quarters."

"I am at your service, brave Prince," she replied. "I do not deny my influence with the Caliph. Perchance you are aware that it was I who engineered the recent coup d'état in Egypt."

Rukn al-Din indeed believed that she was capable of wonders. He was nonetheless taken aback by this naked admission, and he realized that in so openly speaking she offered him the chance to reach for the throne in his turn. He could not bring himself to trust her, however, and moreover, his sole concern for the moment was to rescue Shwaykar from the great peril that threatened her.

"I thank you profoundly for the great favor you show me, my Lady. I do not doubt the truth of what you say, and should I one day dare to engage in politics, I am convinced that your aid and advice will be invaluable to me. But I now beseech you to assist me in one matter alone. Shall you grant me this boon?"

"I shall do so with pleasure," Sallafa replied complacently.

"Shwaykar . . . I would have her returned from Baghdad."

Sallafa's smile turned to a deep frown and she glared at him. "You are not a judicious prince, I see. Do you yet hope to recover your poor songstress after all I have said? She is not at Baghdad!"

"Where is she to be found then?" he persisted. "Surely not in Egypt?"

"Neither is she in Egypt," Sallafa replied. "She is gone forever!"

Rukn al-Din started violently at this terrible declaration.

"She shall never be returned to you," Sallafa continued. "I shall never allow such a thing to happen. It was I who flung her to her fate in the first place!"

Rukn al-Din's suspicions were now confirmed by this frank admission. "You caused her to be sent to Baghdad? But she has never harmed you. You are her superior in every way and she can never compete with you for the favor of kings and princes."

Sallafa rose and pointed at him. "And what of you, Rukn al-Din? Does she not yet prevent me from gaining your love?" She sobbed with the bitter force of her frustrated passion.

Rukn al-Din could not bring himself to believe in the sincerity of this wild declaration. He suspected that she wished to use Shwaykar as a bargaining chip in the execution of some purpose known only to herself. "By God, Sallafa, do not continue to torment me. If you wish me to serve you in some way, then speak, and I shall do so from the bottom of my heart. But I only ask that you help me to bring back Shwaykar."

She glared at him fiercely. "Woe is me! How you test me, man! I throw myself at your feet and unburden my heart to you but your ears remain shut fast! Do you not know that the greatest of your princes aspires to the merest token of my favor?" She fell silent, for tears threatened to overcome her, and she turned her face away from him in shame.

Rukn al-Din took pity on her. "I am honored by your solicitousness and I thank you for it sincerely, Sallafa. But I must persist in begging this service of you."

"I would do anything for you but this," she replied. "I could easily make you Sultan of all of Egypt, but I cannot bring back the girl. Do you still not understand?"

Rukn al-Din was overcome by confusion. Sallafa's passionate confession and her frank offer troubled him deeply, and he was suddenly tempted to let go of his scruples and join forces with her. He was an ambitious young man, as we have already pointed out, and it would have been quite natural for him to submit to Sallafa and be guided by her towards the greatest prize of all. But her cruel animosity towards Shwaykar spoke to his honor and provoked his manly loyalty. He now knew himself to be the cause of her predicament, and he could not bring himself to sacrifice her to his ambition and to consort with her worst enemy.

Sallafa watched him closely as he sat thinking. Her hungry eyes followed his every expression as though she would devour him whole. Rukn al-Din keenly felt the difficulty of his present position. He was confounded by the conflicting influences that competed for mastery of his will, and he sorely needed a small delay in which to rest and to mull over his course of action. He therefore resolved to postpone the discussion to a more opportune time.

He accordingly rose and smiled courteously at Sallafa, though his eyes bespoke the turbulence of his thoughts. "I thank my Lady for her high opinion of me—an opinion which I surely do not deserve—and I beg leave to withdraw from her presence." He bowed and awaited her accord, but Sallafa only turned her back upon him and refused to speak. Baffled by this obstinacy, he took a step towards her. "By God, my Lady, permit me to leave instantly, for I am greatly fatigued and have need of rest," he pleaded.

"How wretched is my lot!" she finally cried. "I complain to you of my passion and you complain to me of your lack of sleep. A poignant token of the fires of love!" She had moved a few steps away from him as she said this. Now she turned back and pierced him with a contemptuous look. "Go in God's keeping," she said. "Go to your bed, oh Prince, and do not suppose that my disappointment tonight shall be without consequences," and with that, she rushed out of the room.

The Departure

RUKN AL-DIN breathed a sigh of relief as he hurried to quit the oppressive mansion. On the way back to the Citadel, he reviewed all that had passed between him and Sallafa on this inauspicious evening. Now that he had met her in person, he well understood her legendary reputation at court, and he was forced to admit that he was not a little in awe of her. Moreover, he greatly feared for Shwaykar on her account, and he realized that his betrothed's perilous situation had now become even more dangerous. Sallafa would surely seek to inflict yet greater harm on the defenseless girl. Perhaps she would even go so far as to. . . . Rukn al-Din dared not complete the thought that had half-formed in his mind. A shiver went through his body and the hairs on the back of his neck stood on end. He now began to regret having so undiplomatically rebuffed Sallafa's advances. What harm would it have done to play along with her, until he had managed to bring Shwaykar back to safety?

He entered the gates of the Citadel and gained his rooms. The servant let him in, silently lit the lamps, and withdrew. Rukn al-Din wearily began to undress.

Then his eyes fell upon Shwaykar's open letter. He snatched it up and re-read it eagerly. This second reading affected him even more powerfully than the first, and he was overcome with deep compassion for her. He would not rest until he had found her, and he resolved to travel to Baghdad in person, for Sallafa's threats were deadly and no one but him could be trusted to undertake such an uncertain mission.

The call to dawn prayers sounded and he retreated to his bed seeking much-needed rest, but the piteous image of Shwaykar filled his dreams and disturbed his sleep.

The next morning, the messenger arrived seeking the promised reply to her letter. Rukn al-Din received him warmly and questioned him about the journey to Baghdad. He had travelled to that city only once in his life, but was nonetheless familiar with its principal streets and quarters. He gave the letter for Shwaykar to the messenger and rewarded him generously in parting.

"Do you then intend to travel to Baghdad, my Lord?" the messenger inquired.

"God willing, my good man," he replied, and dismissed him after having first ascertained the place in which he should find him in the imperial city, should he have need of his services.

As for Sallafa, she was furious at Rukn al-Din's vacillation, for she desired him with all her heart, and she had supposed that her confession would be enough to make him her prisoner.

She had long sought an opportunity to declare her passion. She had marked how Tree of Pearls had deftly drawn him into her nets, once crowned Queen, and she had hated her all the more for it. She had also heard news of his engagement to Shwaykar. Her letter to Baghdad had thus been meant to kill two birds with one stone. News from Baghdad came to her regularly, and that very morning she too had been informed of Shwaykar's abduction. She armed herself with this news and waited to confront Rukn al-Din with it, for she was determined that he should give up all hope of ever seeing the girl again. She had expected that he would eagerly respond to her advances, and had flattered herself that he would soon belong to her alone. She had set her heart on serving him and seeing him crowned Sultan of Egypt, with herself at his side, but she had been sorely dis-appointed. All her plans had succeeded except for this one vital thing. She had failed utterly to ensnare al-Din in her nets. Now her love slowly turned to hate, and she resolved to oppose him tooth and nail if he did not come to his senses and attempt to conciliate her.

And now let us take leave of these Egyptian intrigues for the time being and move our story to Baghdad, Capital of the Abbasid Caliphs.

Baghdad

Baghdad had reached the zenith of its architectural glory in the days of Al-Ma'mun. Its numerous buildings and gardens extended over a vast area the size of which was estimated to be 53,750 juribs; 26,750 to the east and 27,000 to the west (a jurib being the equivalent of 3,600 square cubits, and its proportional relation to the feddan, about 100 to 333). The total area of Baghdad was thus about 16,000 feddans—a very large size indeed. We are told that the Abbasid capital was an agglomeration of contiguous towns: forty in all, according to the imperial chronicler Al-Khatib the Baghdadi, who, wishing to give an idea of the city's architectural splendor, states the following in his *History:* "In the days of Al-Ma'mun, Baghdad's public baths numbered 65,000. At least five persons were employed in each of these baths: a bath-attendant, a caretaker, a janitor, an oven-stoker and a water-carrier, making in all 300,000 souls. It is said that five mosques adjoined each one of these baths, a number totaling 300,000 mosques. Each mosque in turn employed at least five persons, making 1,500,000 employees in all." While these figures are no doubt exaggerated, they do give us some sense of the size of Baghdad at the time.

The famous traveler Al-Astakhri described it as he had himself seen it in the eleventh century: "The imperial palaces and gardens occupy two farsakhs between Baghdad and Nahrabin, so that they extend from Nahrabin to the banks of the Tigris. The city rises above the imperial complex about five miles to the north on the shores of this great river. Shamsiyya stands opposite Harbiyya in the western part of the city and descends towards the Tigris, to the extremities of Karkh. Between Baghdad and Kufa (or between the Tigris and the Euphrates) lies a vast and monotonous area of arable land intersected by tributaries of the Euphrates." The author then counts the tributaries that run from the Euphrates to the Tigris.

In those days, Baghdad lay towards the west and the circular capital built by Al-Mansur still stood in exactly the same spot, surrounded by the city's residential quarters, streets, and markets. Things had changed, however, by the time of our story in the thirteenth century. The city had moved eastwards, and the imperial complex had disappeared along with Al-Mansur's capital.

In the first centuries following its founding, Baghdad was the Mother of Cities: the center of imperial trade and of science and poetry, and a magnet for all those who sought wealth and distinction. When the Caliphate began to grow weak, conspiracies flourished and dissension grew amongst its people. The most devastating of these conflicts was the rift that opened up between Sunna and Shi'a: a deadly breach that was reproduced at the heart of the government. Not a year would go by without some violent confrontation taking place between the two communities. Though the imperial state usually strove to arbitrate these conflicts, pressure was most often brought to bear on the Shi'a, since the administration was dominated by Sunnis. Baghdad's Shi'a lived mostly in Karkh and Qadhimiyya, and while they patiently bore intermittent persecution, the government continued to entrust them with its interests and to delegate important posts to them.

The schism in question eventually brought about the fall of Baghdad and its occupation by the Tatars under the leadership of Hulagu—a typical chain of events in the history of empires. If you but consider the roots of the political upheavals that cause dominion to pass from one dynasty to another, you will note that they are most often nurtured in the soil of religious or political conflict between countrymen. Despair overtakes the weaker party once it is forced into submission, and it seeks the aid of a foreign people to champion its cause. These foreigners then bide their time and wait for the right moment to seize power. Most, if not all, political revolutions of the period of which we speak unfolded in this manner.

The Palaces of Baghdad

THE MIGHTY TIGRIS was traversed by two bridges that connected the eastern and western parts of the city and served a busy traffic of people and goods. These bridges were built of wooden planks fixed to round floats. The more important of the two lay between the quarter called 'Isa's Palace and al-Rusafa.

On the eastern banks of the Tigris stood the Caliph's palaces and Baghdad's most illustrious buildings, the most famous of which were the Palace of the Crown, the Husayni Palace, the Mustansiriyya School (built by Al-Mustansir Billah, father of Al-Musta'sim Billah), the Nidhamiyya School, the Rihaniyya Palace, and the Firdaws Palace. Mu'ayyid al-Din Ibn al-Alqami, Al-Musta'sim's First Minister, lived in the palace closest to the bridge on the eastern shore. He was a shrewd and capable politician and a loyal advisor who was quick to perceive the Empire's turbulent state of affairs and exerted himself to counsel the Caliph wisely. Al-Musta'sim was a weak-willed and indolent sovereign, but he trusted his First Minister and was usually disposed to heed his judicious advice.

The result was often less than satisfactory, however, for if the head is disturbed, the rest of the body's limbs are sure to come unhinged. It often transpires that a ruler is led by flatterers and favor-seeking courtiers or political men with sectarian interests. If he counts them among his favorites, they do not hesitate to pounce upon his weakness and sow corruption throughout the land. Such a ruler refuses to hear a word against his men, and he obstinately shuts his ears to any complaint, however loud.

So it was with Al-Musta'sim in those days. He had become a plaything of his courtiers and his chiefs of staff, for he loved nothing better than to submerge himself in pleasure of all kinds, gaming, wine, and song, and he was never out of their company for long. His boon-companions and cohorts were made of similar stuff. They too were sunk in luxury and vice, and paid not the least mind to his true well-being.

Even worse, Al-Musta'sim had taken a path traditionally shunned by his imperial predecessors, who had all without exception firmly reined in their off-spring and closest relatives. It had been so till the last days of Al-Mansur. But when Al-Musta'sim succeeded to the throne he let his children loose upon the land, and this was the cause of much evil. The oldest of his sons was Abu al-'Abbas Ahmad, known to the common folk as Abu Bakr. The youth was spoiled and over-proud of his father's dominion, and he exploited his position to serve his personal ends. He especially detested the Shi'a. He harassed and persecuted them bitterly and was wont to insult them openly in public. There were those in his entourage who encouraged this prejudice for undeclared reasons of their own. Mu'ayyid al-Din Ibn al-Alqami was forced to put up with the boy, and he often complained of him to his father.

In the meantime, Hulagu the Tatar, grandson of Genghis Khan, had founded the Ilkhanid dynasty, the Mongol dynasty of Persia. Once installed in Persia, Hulagu had begun to cast his eyes on Baghdad and to plan for a war of conquest. At the time of which we write, he was at war with the Isma'ilis in Persia. He laid siege to their fortresses and he wrote to Al-Musta'sim to request his aid. Al-Musta'sim was inclined to comply, but his generals forbade it for fear that the Khan's real intention was to strip Baghdad of its defending troops so that it might be the more easily taken. Hulagu succeeded in breaking the Isma'ili resistance, and he wrote again to Al-Musta'sim, this time to reprove him. Mu'ayyid al-Din Ibn al-Alqami then advised the Caliph to conciliate the Tatar with gold and precious gifts. The Caliph accepted his Minister's counsel and set about preparing a rich caravan of gold, jewels, and slaves, but the Dawadar, Commander in Chief of the Imperial Armies, protested fiercely and attempted to cast doubt on the Minister's loyalty. The Caliph again yielded, this time to his Dawadar, and caused a trifling sum to be sent to the Khan instead. The insult provoked Hulagu's wrath and produced further grave consequences, to which we shall soon have cause to return.

Al-Musta'sim was oblivious to the reality of his situation, and Mu'ayyid al-Din was at a loss as to how to awaken him to its gravity. The minister thought of nothing else. He alone was alive to the great danger that beset the Empire. His warnings and his profuse advice to the Caliph were useless. Hulagu meanwhile secretly dispatched messengers to the Abbasid minister with offers of alliance and promises of great rewards should he join the party of the Ilkhids, or tender his assistance in delivering the city to them. Mu'ayyid al-Din hesitated, for he still hoped that the Caliph would come to his senses. Al-Musta'sim listened to his Minister's counsel and promised to be guided by it, but as soon as Mu'ayyid al-Din turned his back, his enemies at court succeeded in changing the Caliph's mind by whispering poisonous charges against him. A Shi'ite, they claimed, was of necessity a traitor.

At the same time, the leading Shi'a of the city constantly hovered around Mu'ayyid al-Din. They complained to him of the outrages they suffered at the hands of the Caliph's son, so that they no longer felt secure of their wealth and property, nor of their honor. Mu'ayyid al-Din did his best to ease their minds and assure them that better days would surely come, but he avoided meeting with them in public for fear of the suspicion that might consequently fall upon his own person. He allowed them to visit him only in secret. He knew that Al-Musta'sim's spies surrounded him and marked his every breath.

Mu'ayyid al-Din Ibn al-Alqami

THE DAY FINALLY CAME when Mu'ayyid al-Din had had enough of this state of affairs. Of what use were all his efforts when in the end they served neither himself nor the Empire? On this day he decided to remain at home and while away the morning on the terrace that gave out onto the Tigris and the wide panorama of al-Rusafa and Karkh. He had caused the structure to be built with this very view in mind.

He dressed himself in a light cloak and turban, and having informed the servants that he was indisposed and must on no account be disturbed, he mounted to the second floor of his mansion. The terrace was furnished much like an intimate reception room. It was spread with carpets and cushions, and boasted a number of board-games for those of his guests who wished to amuse themselves. He sat down next to a chess-board that rested on a large cushion. The game of chess was widely favored in Baghdad in those days amongst men who enjoyed vigorous mental exercise, or whose interest in politics made them appreciate the intellectual brinksmanship that the practice of chess inevitably sharpens. He toyed restlessly with the pieces ranged on the board and moved them about in strategic combinations, but this idle play failed to soothe his troubled spirit.

He put the pieces aside and rose to take a seat on a high chair whose position commanded an uninterrupted view of Baghdad. The weather was fine and his eyes ranged unimpeded over the historic city intersected by the blessed Tigris, on whose banks stood the palaces and schools, hospitals and mosques, public baths and gardens famed throughout the Empire. His mind wandered and his thoughts turned to the history of the city's founding five and a half centuries earlier. The Caliphs who had ruled over it succeeded one another in his mind's eye, and he recalled their changing fortunes and the days of its great glory under Al-Rashid, when it was the indisputable capital of the entire Muslim world and the wealth of most of the civilized lands from Turkistan to the Atlantic Ocean poured into its overflowing coffers. In those days, the kings of the earth had humbly sought the favor of its great Sultan on bended knee.

Catastrophe then befell the Barakmids, the true founders of Abbasid glory, and their magnificence gave way to depravity. The great dissension between Al-Amin and Al-Ma'mun followed, and many souls perished in consequence. These and other political upheavals had taken place in quick succession, shaking the very foundations of the Abbasid State. Petty princelings now imposed their conditions upon the Empire and began to claim their independence. Fortune hunters hungered after its riches and, growing bold, they dared to invade the great city. These were the days of the upstart Buwayhids and the Seljuks. The influence of the Caliphs began to wane, their dominion was confined to Baghdad and its immediate environs, and they became mere instruments in the hands of their own administrations. Their dreams of glory faded away and their ambitions were increasingly confined to wine, song, and the pleasures of the flesh.

This sorrowful rumination turned Mu'ayyid al-Din's thoughts once more to the present Caliph. His gaze fell upon the Palace of the Crown across the river on the left bank of the Tigris. Lush gardens and great flowering trees circled its perimeter, and it boasted a fine marble pier along which a number of sturdy vessels were moored. He tried to imagine what this palace must have looked like a century earlier. Its façade had been built upon five arches, each arch made up of ten slabs of marble five cubits long. A great fire had reduced it to a blackened shell, and the gorgeous slabs of marble were replaced with baked brick. The marble with which it had been built at the end of the ninth century by order of the newly invested Caliph Al-Muktafi Billah had come from the ruins of the White Palace of the Sassanian Khosraus, of which nothing now stood but the Great Hall. Some of this precious material had also been used to pave the pier. This architectural history struck Ibn al-Alqami as offering a lesson of sorts. "And so the world turns," he sadly mused. "The Abbasids destroyed the palaces of the Persian kings and built their own with the rubble that remained. Now it is the turn of the Imperial Palaces to fall into ruin. All praise to He who alone endures!"

The daily hubbub made by the students of the Mustansiriyya School next door suddenly interrupted his reverie. In those days the school was at the height of its glory. It had been built by Al-Musta'sim's father, Al-Mustansir Billah, who had staffed it with professors of jurisprudence and hadith, mathematics and medicine, zoology and geography, and many other sciences. Mu'ayyid al-Din's restless gaze wandered over the public baths of Baghdad. The people of Baghdad were wont to paint their bath-houses with pitch from a famous spring located between Basra and Kufa, and their shiny blackness stood out darkly against the blue sky. Ibn al-Alqami had never before paid attention to this peculiar feature, and suddenly the black line of buildings on the horizon appeared to him to be an evil omen massed over the waiting city.

A sudden din rose from the courtyard below and he heard voices raised in dispute. He strained his ears and picked out the voice of a man demanding to see him, and the servant's shrill insistent reply: "His Excellency the Minister is indisposed and will receive no one, I say!"

Mu'ayyid al-Din was familiar with that other voice, and rather glad to hear it. He rang a nearby bell that communicated with the ground floor of the palace, and one of his pages immediately responded to the call. He demanded the cause of the hubbub, and the boy replied, "A stranger seeks an audience with your Excellency and refuses to take no for an answer."

"I know his voice. You may admit him."

The page withdrew and returned a moment later followed by the person in question. He wore Persian garb and his features were of Persian cast. Mu'ayyid al-Din greeted him warmly. "Sahban, welcome!"

Sahban fell upon the Minister's hand and kissed it, but Mu'ayyid al-Din quickly withdrew it and embraced him instead. He offered him a seat beside his own and ordered the servant to leave them. "How long have you been in Baghdad, my friend?"

"I arrived last night, my Lord."

"And from where do you come?"

"From Egypt."

"From Egypt? I recall having seen you here in this very city not long ago."

"Indeed. I was at Baghdad, then I left for Cairo and now I am returned," Sahban replied grinning.

"A speedy journey!"

"Am I not a travelling merchant who plies his trade between Baghdad and Cairo? When my goods are sold, I return to procure more. The discomforts of the journey are no matter to me."

Mu'ayyid al-Din smiled. "So now you devote your time to trade, Sahban?"

Sahban let out a brisk laugh. "Is there any occupation more profitable than trade, my Lord Minister?"

The irony of this sally was not lost on Mu'ayyid al-Din. "Perhaps you are right, my friend," he sighed. "Government service is futile—and woe to the minister, for his hard labors are all in vain. The days of true leadership are over and done with."

"The office of First Minister is the most noble of government posts, my Lord," Sahban declared, "for it is the Minister who commands and forbids." Sahban coughed meaningfully, then he took out his handkerchief and slowly wiped his mouth.

"Do you believe that the Minister is as indispensable today as he used to be in former times, Sahban?" Mu'ayyid al-Din absently wondered.

"Even more so in these black days of imperial impotence!" Sahban vehemently replied.

Mu'ayyid al-Din shook his head sadly. "The weak hearken not to advice, for their ears are given over to slaves and eunuchs."

"Have you no remedy for this weakness, my Lord?" His voice had grown deadly serious.

Mu'ayyid al-Din raised a brow. "What mean you, friend?"

Sahban stared deeply into Mu'ayyid al-Din's eyes. "The man of whom we speak is as a corrupt limb. The surgeon must order its amputation lest the disease invade the rest of the body."

Mu'ayyid al-Din was shocked by this audacity. He frowned at his guest as he prepared to reproach him, but Sahban hastened to resume. "You consider my speech reckless, insolent even. So be it. But I speak from my heart. We share common interests, you and I, and we hold the keys to victory. All we lack is resolve. You need only follow the example of the Abbasid Caliphs themselves."

Mu'ayyid al-Din looked about him nervously, then he turned once again to Sahban. "Your words please me not, nor do I understand their import."

"You only pretend not to understand out of excessive caution, my Lord. I refer to that which Al-Rashid did to Ja'far. Did he not murder him along with all the rest of the Barakmids because they were Shi'a, and because he feared their power? He disposed of them on the basis of a simple accusation, thereby dealing a terrible blow to his government and to himself. As for you, if you were to avenge the Shi'a with the same determination, you would be saving these lands from certain ruin."

Mu'ayyid al-Din was appalled by the import of this declaration. "Enough of this pointless talk," he frowned. "You are pained, it seems, by the misguided actions of the Prince of Believers and his family."

"I speak not in anger or rancor," Sahban passionately declared. "I have no personal grudge against these men. I speak on behalf of those who are being persecuted for no other reason than their love of the Imam Ali and the People of his House." Anger made him choke back the remaining words that rose to his lips.

These same thoughts had often occurred to Mu'ayyid al-Din as well, but he was above all a cautious and prudent politician. "Calm yourself, Sahban, and let us put aside this matter for now. There is a time and place for every action."

"The time is ripe now! Only ask me to explain myself and I shall readily comply."

"I am not ignorant of what passes through your mind, but I insist that the time for such talk is not yet upon us."

"You have not quite understood my purpose, my Lord," Sahban insisted. "I have a project other than the one you imagine. I speak not of Hulagu!"

Mu'ayyid al-Din shuddered when he heard this name spoken, for it had never once quit his thoughts for months past and had caused him much anxiety. "What is it then?" he demanded.

"I thank you for agreeing to hear me out, my Lord. The project of which I speak will lead us directly to our dearest object. I propose to revive the great 'Alawi Dynasty in the same country that once hosted it for over two hundred years!"

"You mean Egypt?" he replied incredulously. "Upon my word Sahban! This is indeed a farfetched scheme. The Turks are masters in Egypt now."

"I know very well where matters stand in Egypt, having only just returned from there yesterday. Trade is not the real purpose of my travels, my Lord," he officiously declared. "It is the wellbeing of my people and the victory of our persecuted Imams that motivates my constant journeying. I have studied Egypt and her secrets for years. She is mine to do with as I please."

Mu'ayyid al-Din laughed out loud at this ridiculous boast. "How vast your dreams are, and how deep your illusions! From whence comes this arrogance that permits you to believe that mighty Egypt is your plaything? Egypt is a Sunni country, its leaders all Sunni Turks."

"I know this, my Lord. But they are divided and at odds. There is a Prince amongst them who seeks the throne, a bold warrior with a personal grudge against the present Sultan. He will exert his powers in our cause. He hates this Caliph of yours for stealing his betrothed away, and he shall surely be avenged. If we help him to kill your Master and raise him to the throne of Egypt, he will serve us by establishing a Fatimid Caliphate there. Only then shall we be rid of our cursed oppressors and return to the days of our old glory." His eyes shone as he finished speaking, as though this fantasy had already come to pass.

The Reader will no doubt already have noticed that Sahban was one of those people who possess a vastly colorful imagination and a great capacity for self-delusion. If a person of this sort sets his heart on some goal, the flimsiest pretext will suffice to make him believe it possible. He will take not the slightest notice of obstacles, whether natural or man-made. Those with the character which I describe are plentiful, particularly in the countries of the East. To wit, the difference between a successful man and a failure depends on the degree to which he is able to evaluate the truth with a steady eye and prepare for events before they come to pass.

Uproar

MU'AYYID AL-DIN, on the other hand, was a fastidious and farsighted man who carefully considered all obstacles and patiently set out to overcome them. If not for this, he would never have risen to the post of First Minister in a government whose religious doctrine was different from his own, and especially amongst a clan that hated and persecuted the Shi'a. He had nothing but bemused contempt for Sahban's plans and projects regarding a Shi'ite restoration in Egypt. He knew full well that the Shi'a were too weak to win such a suit. He was favorably inclined, however, to the idea of replacing the present Caliph with another more competent one, but he did not wish to confess this to Sahban, and so he decided to put an end to the discussion. "We shall let this matter be for now," he firmly declared.

Sahban felt the edge of scorn in the Minister's voice. "It seems that my project excites not your interest, my Lord. Perhaps you find it improbable. If you knew my reasoning you would be more inclined to listen," he sulkily added.

Mu'ayyid al-Din sighed. "Indeed, my friend, your hopes strike me as being exceedingly difficult, if not impossible, to fulfill."

"If you find my reasoning to be weak, then let us hear your own proposals. Or do you believe that we should quietly accept this humiliation for the rest of our lives?"

"Certainly not. But we must deliberate carefully, and above all refrain from rambling on like this for any and all to hear."

"As you wish, my Lord. What, then, is our route to salvation?"

"You have put me in a delicate position, Sahban, for I would not have disclosed my mind to you just yet. We Shi'a must not allow ourselves to indulge in dreams of a restoration, for present conditions will simply not allow it. There will perhaps come a day when our sons will be in a position to realize this dream, but for now, it will suffice to replace this feeble voluptuary with a wise and steadfast Caliph who will give us justice. This is the plan on which we must fix our sights."

Sahban lowered his head in thought. He was suddenly ashamed of his own foolish schemes. In addition to being prey to all sorts of illusions, he was also very fickle and easily led. He now agreed wholeheartedly with Mu'ayyid al-Din. "True, my Lord. Upon my word, but you are a sensible and prudent minister! Tell me, what provisions have you laid for the execution of this plan?"

Mu'ayyid al-Din suddenly grew tired of the conversation, for he had no real intention of discussing his plans with Sahban. He rose pensively and his eyes were drawn to the floating bridge that crossed the Tigris. He suddenly noticed that it was unusually crowded with folk on foot, many running in panic as though flee-ing a battle. He was unable to make out any of the faces in the crowd, but he immediately assumed that an event of great import had taken place. He turned to Sahban, who had come to stand by him, and saw that the look of astonishment on his face was even greater than on his own. Sahban's eyes were sharper, as well. "Do you see, my Lord?" he cried. "Do you not see? These are the Caliph's soldiers returned from an expedition of plunder with their prisoners in tow."

"But from where do they come?" Mu'ayyid al-Din exclaimed.

"I know not, but I see imperial soldiers and those are their banners before them. If my vision fails me not, then that is the insignia of the Dawadar himself that precedes them. The scene puts me in mind of the recent military raids that were directed against our people in Karkh and Qadhimiyya."

Mu'ayyid al-Din stared at the crowds on the bridge but was unable to see clearly. Suddenly he heard a great tumult in the precincts of his own house. He put his head out of a window that opened onto the inner courtyard of the palace and saw a group of women weeping and wailing, their torn clothes covered in blood and dust. In their midst was an old man with bent back, leaning for sup-port on a cane. Like the women, he too wept and groaned. Mu'ayyid al-Din's heart went out to these wretched strangers. Sahban stood by his side and gazed down at the yard. After a few seconds of keen inspection, he let out a sharp cry. "Father!"

Mu'ayyid al-Din started. "Who is this? Can it be your father?"

"Yes! It is my father! I last saw him living peacefully in our house in Karkh. What has happened to him?" He excused himself and rushed downstairs, and Mu'ayyid al-Din followed.

As soon as Sahban set foot in the courtyard he heard his father cry, "Where is our Minister? Where is Mu'ayyid al-Din?" His eyes now fell on the person he sought. "How dare they act thus against us while you are First Minister in these lands?" he cried. "If our only sin is that we honor the noble House of 'Ali, then we gladly accept the punishment, and may God reward each soul for its actions in this world!"

Sahban rushed over to the old man. "Father—what has happened to you? What has induced you to leave home in this state?"

The old man turned to the younger, and when he saw that it was his son, he dropped his cane and threw himself into his arms, kissing him and sobbing. "My son, Sahban, is it you? Are you here? When did you come? Would you had come to us first! Or perhaps you did well in staying away and escaping your brothers' fate."

Sahban shuddered at these words. "My brothers? What has befallen them? Who has done this to you? Why? Tell me, father! Tell me everything!"

The old man struggled to catch his breath and regain his strength to speak. "You ask me who did this to us. Do you not know those who are responsible for our calamities?" He cast his tear-stained eyes about him fearfully. "You know who is responsible!"

"Did those soldiers we saw crossing the bridge come from Karkh?"

"We fled before them and came here to take refuge with his Excellency Mu'ayyid al-Din! My Lord," he cried, turning to the Minister, "deliver us from this torment! Lead us out of this country!" And turning once again to Sahban, he continued bitterly, "You! You escape these yearly raids. You save yourself while your brothers and sisters and I remain here to face this horror. Good God! When shall we be free of this affliction?"

Shaking with fury, Sahban replied, "Soon enough, God willing!"

Mu'ayyid al-Din had ordered the womenfolk to be taken to the women's quarters of the palace. He now listened to Sahban's father with grim composure. "Take a seat here, I beg you, uncle. Calm yourself and tell me exactly what happened," he gently prompted.

"You know our story well, your Excellency, how we labor in constant fear, how we are continuously persecuted and how we patiently wait for the day of deliverance. This time it is different, for the number of arrests and deaths have exceeded all earlier counts and have spared neither property nor honor!" He repeated this last word in a trembling voice, and confusedly cast about for his cane.

Mu'ayyid al-Din was greatly affected. He glanced at Sahban and saw that he struggled to hide the bitter tears that threatened to spill over. The Minister clung to his composure and set about comforting Sahban's father. "Everything comes to an end one day, uncle. Patience, for God is with the patient. Tell me what happened."

"Do not ask me what happened, my son, for it would break your heart. What you see around you is enough," he sobbed as he wiped his eyes with trembling fingers.

"We have grown used to their atrocities," Sahban muttered darkly.

"Never! I have grown old in this country, amongst these people, and I have seen many misfortunes unfold, none of which are comparable to this! They used to attack passers-by or accuse some men with false crimes in order to insult them and confiscate their property. This time they forced their way into people's homes without cause or reason. They violated the sanctity of the women's quarters and trampled upon their honor, and they murdered innocent children—enough! I can no longer speak, and I would be glad to die here and now. I only beg God to keep me alive in order to witness the annihilation of this dynasty." His breath came faster as he said this, and for a moment it seemed as though he would faint away. They sprinkled water upon his face and Sahban helped him to hobble inside to take some rest in the quiet of the palace. He then went immediately to the women's quarters and charged a eunuch with a message to his sister. She emerged in tears, sobbing aloud, her wild hair uncovered and torn. "What happened to you, Safiyya? Speak! Has harm befallen any of you? Where are your sisters?" he demanded.

She slapped her hands against her cheeks in despair and replied, "I know not where they are, or whether they be dead or alive! Good God! You were not there to see the slaughter, brother. They entered my chamber and were on the point of assaulting me. I take refuge in the Almighty!"

He shuddered deeply at these words, but forced himself to remain calm in front of her. "God is gracious, sister," he murmured. "He will surely wreak His revenge on the tyrants." He turned back towards the Palace and went in search of Mu'ayyid al-Din but did not find him there. The servants informed him that the Minister was dressing in his private chambers, and from this Sahban understood that he intended to go to the Imperial Palace and to speak to the Caliph on this momentous matter. The thought of the Minister's great anger filled Sahban with grim satisfaction and he hoped that his impending audience with the Caliph would lead to no good, so that Mu'ayyid al-Din might be persuaded to take his counsel and work towards the overthrow of the Abbasid State.

Sahban returned to his father's side and was relieved to see that he had recovered a portion of his strength. He sat by him to comfort him and to press him further on the day's events, growing more astonished by the moment as his father spoke. He promised the old man that revenge would be theirs, multiplied fourfold, that God was surely the scourge of tyrants, and other like expressions of condolence to which the Shi'a of Baghdad had become accustomed due to the many tribulations that never ceased to befall them.

Al-Musta'sim

MU'AYYID AL-DIN donned his cap and black cape and mounted his mule. Just as Sahban had guessed, he meant to see the Caliph to protest the unacceptable behavior of the imperial troops. He passed first the Mustansiriyya School, then the Husayni Palace before finally arriving at the Palace of the Crown. The servants respectfully made way for him as he rode grimly through the gardens. When he arrived at the main doors, he dismounted and hurried inside, anger writ large on his face. He did not return the greetings of the courtiers who crossed his path.

The palace guards accompanied him to the public gate, and there he inquired after the Caliph's whereabouts from the gatekeeper. "He is in the Grand Terrace overlooking the pier at present. Shall I request an audience for his Excellency the Minister?"

"Is he alone?" Mu'ayyid al-Din demanded.

"He is attended by the singers and a number of his courtiers."

Mu'ayyid al-Din was cast into yet deeper gloom by this all too habitual answer. "Pray seek permission for me to wait upon the Commander of the Faithful at his convenience."

The gatekeeper returned shortly. "The Commander of the Faithful requests that his Excellency the Minister proceed to the terrace." Mu'ayyid al-Din was again disappointed by this invitation, for he would have much preferred to see the Caliph alone. He saw no alternative but to obey, however, and he strode from hall to hall, the eunuchs making way for him, until he arrived at the terrace.

This terrace was artfully appointed like a bower. It was roofed in latticed woodwork ornamented with an exquisite gold-leaf motif and strewn with precious carpets woven with superb designs. Richly embroidered cushions lay everywhere. On the table in the middle of the terrace were dishes filled with a lush array of fruits and sweets. Al-Musta'sim reclined near the table on a raised couch. His elaborate dress was in the Turcoman style. He wore a flowing, long-sleeved white garment embroidered with gold thread. On his head he wore a golden cap ringed with rich black fur of the kind only used by the Turkish kings. Al-Mustaʿsim was of medium stature and dark-skinned, with a long shining beard. He was retiring, soft-spoken, and easy-mannered, but also timid and inexperienced in politics and in the business of Empire, and many were those who hoped to take advantage of him. The waters of the Tigris rippled gently before the terrace and rocked the boats moored to their marble pier that waited to receive the Caliph whenever he should so desire.

At sight of the assembled company, Muʾayyid al-Din's heart misgave him and he regretted having come at this hour. He had no choice now but to greet the Caliph with the appropriate marks of deference. Al-Mustaʿsim signaled for him to be seated on a cushion nearby. "Welcome to our energetic Minister!"

Muʾayyid al-Din returned the greeting politely. He turned to the men in attendance and saw none amongst them that merited either interest or esteem. They were a coterie of the Caliph's personal officers and dependents. The Palace Steward and the Majordomo were two of these. This last officer was known as "the Friend." He exercised great influence over the Caliph and his name was invoked and blessed immediately after that of the Caliph by Friday preachers in the mosques. Rarely did he appear in public, for he was almost constantly occupied with his vast management duties. Day and night, he watched over the obscure workings of palace life. The Palace of the Crown was home to a large number of women, seven hundred in all. He was responsible for them and their many children, and imagine how many more eunuchs these women required for their simple service! The young Abyssinians and Majabib amongst these eunuchs were the Caliph's particular pride. They had advanced mightily in the Abbasid State. They possessed gorgeous mansions and rich estates, and if one of them were to venture abroad in public, he would be surrounded by a company of valiant Turkish and Dalmatian horsemen and accompanied by fifty unsheathed swords.

There were a number of these eunuchs in the gathering, but no matter how great their station outside the palace, they were obliged to bow their heads humbly in the Caliph's presence. No voice but the Caliph's was permitted to be heard above a whisper, unless it be that of a petitioner who begged a royal favor.

Once Muʾayyid al-Din was seated, Al-Mustaʿsim signaled to the vocalist to repeat the piece he had just sung, and he immediately lost himself in public transports of ecstasy quite unbecoming the dignity of the Caliphate. His companions were used to this lack of decorum. Some considered it elegant and refined, while others thought it feeble and contemptible. Mu'ayyid al-Din was of the latter opinion. All agreed on the Caliph's artlessness, however, this being perhaps one of the main causes of the weakness that made him such easy prey for plotters.

Mu'ayyid al-Din listened to the song absently, his thoughts constantly returning to the mission on which he had come, and he waited for the Caliph to address him. When the vocalist had finally finished, Al-Musta'sim turned to his minister and said, "Have you ever heard a voice more pure and more plaintive than this? The piece itself moves us greatly. There is another composition, similar to this one, that no one in Baghdad is capable of performing. We have been told of a singer in the Sultan's palace in Egypt who executes it beautifully, and so we sent for her, but she never arrived here . . ." he trailed off, and a sudden frown crossed his brow. "We have been meaning to send for you for many days now to inform you of this mishap and to request your help in finding this singer. We are certain she reached Baghdad, but it seems that some thieves snatched her from the caravan in which she came from Egypt."

Mu'ayyid al-Din bowed his head obediently. "The thieves shall be pursued and punished, your Highness. It is unacceptable that any should dare to commit a crime in the dominion of our Lord and Master the Commander of the Faithful, may God sustain him." He now prepared to turn to the subject on which he had come, but the Majordomo spoke up first.

"The impudence of these thieves in stealing a singer destined for the Caliph is unheard of. It gives evidence of the failings of the government and the low regard in which it is held by the public. We had dared to hope that our First Minister—God preserve him—would never have allowed such goings-on in the city."

These words fell like an arrow on Mu'ayyid al-Din's heart and it was all he could do to control his anger and hold his tongue. He knew full well that the eunuch only wished to display his eager—and false—solicitude for the wellbeing of the State before his master. This was an insolence ill becoming the decorum of the royal assembly. He turned a cold look upon him. "True, Sir, brigandage is a capital offense and the Minister would be responsible if it be considered to fall under his jurisdiction. Our lives are ransom to the Commander of the Faithful and our common goal is to defend the state and do our utmost to obey its Caliph." He now addressed Al-Musta'sim. "All kinds of criminal offenses are duly dealt with by his Highness's officers without news of them ever troubling the ears of his Highness, the Commander of the Faithful. Even the imperial troops, it seems, are not above committing acts unbefitting their commissions," he added darkly, and the Caliph understood that his Minister wished to present a complaint.

"Such acts must not go unpunished," Al-Musta'sim vaguely replied, "unless they have our express permission or that of our Minister or our Majordomo. Has something occurred recently?"

Mu'ayyid al-Din assumed a formal tone. "I wish to inform his Highness, Commander of the Faithful, that a group of residents of Karkh—old men and women—have come to me this hour weeping and grieving. They have told me that a band of soldiers descended upon them, robbed their houses, killed those who stood in their way, and assaulted their women."

The Majordomo shook his head contemptuously. His voice was full of sarcasm. "The people of Karkh never cease to make such complaints. Not a month or a year goes by without word of such ridiculous accusations reaching us."

Mu'ayyid al-Din was greatly incensed by this insolent interruption, and he marveled at the man's objections. Turning to him directly, he said, "The people of Karkh continue to protest because the soldiers continue to harm them."

"Harm or no harm, they love to complain. This is the way of the Shi'a." He looked around at the company and laughed disdainfully.

Mu'ayyid al-Din grew red with rage. He turned away from the man and addressed the Caliph directly. "I did not suppose that anyone would dare to say such a thing in the presence of his Highness, the Commander of the Faithful."

Al-Musta'sim was now obliged to intervene. "This exchange displeases us," he said uneasily. "Our Majordomo is wrong to speak in this tone. If the people of Karkh—or any others for that matter—protest, we must look into their complaint and give them justice if they have been wronged or punish them if they have done wrong." He turned to Mu'ayyid al-Din and said, "Tell us, Minister, what happened?"

"I was told, your Highness, that a band of soldiers descended upon Karkh this morning and applied themselves to robbing and murdering the people. I myself saw a group of wounded composed of women and children and the elderly. I could do nothing, however, until I had consulted the opinion of my Lord and Master."

Al-Musta'sim showed signs of deep interest. "This matter surely concerns the Dawadar. We must question him about the affair. Perhaps he had some good reason for directing the troops to Karkh." He clapped and ordered the Chamberlain, who swiftly appeared, to summon the Dawadar immediately.

The Caliph now motioned to the vocalist to resume his song, a special composition for which he accompanied himself on the oud. The assembled men were all swept away by the music, except for Mu'ayyid al-Din, who did his best to control his seething anger.

After a short while, a page came to announce the arrival of the Dawadar. The Caliph ordered him to conduct the General to the Hall of Public Assembly and to await him there. He then rose and dismissed the company, except for Mu'ayyid al-Din, whom he summoned to attend him.

The Caliph first stopped at the Royal Wardrobe, where he was dressed in his official reception robes—the large turban, the cloak, and other items—, then he entered the Assembly Hall through a private communicating door. The Hall was spread with valuable drapery, couches, and sofas. Historians describe its splendor as an example of the overweening luxury that plagued the very heart of the Abbasid State in its last days.

Al-Musta'sim seated himself and nodded to Mu'ayyid al-Din to do the same. He then ordered the Chamberlain to summon the Dawadar. Mu'ayyid al-Din had by now regained his composure. The Dawadar entered and, after greeting the Caliph and the Minister, stood by in respectful silence.

The Caliph began. "Our Minister—may God preserve him—tells us that a band of soldiers have attacked Karkh and wrought great destruction there. Did you have knowledge of this?"

"Yes, your Highness," replied the Dawadar.

"Yes, you say? And why did you permit this violence to transpire?"

"I only executed the orders of his Excellency, Prince Abu Bakr, son of his Highness the Commander of the Faithful."

"If Ahmad tells you to murder people, you would do this without good reason?"

"I did not permit troops to be sent to Karkh without reason, your Highness. His Excellency Abu Bakr informed me that a group of Karkhis had kidnapped one of his slave-girls and hidden her in the area. We sought her there, but the people refused to let us enter the town and they turned their weapons upon us. The Prince commanded me to search the area and to preserve the lives of my men, and I undertook to do so."

"Scores of people dead because of an insignificant slave-girl? This is unacceptable. Where is Ahmad?"

"I believe he is at his palace, your Highness."

"Call him to me immediately," the Caliph commanded.

Muʾayyid al-Din took the Caliph's visible anger at his son's reckless actions as an auspicious sign. He dearly hoped that he might soon be relieved of the impudent youth's constant meddling in the business of the Empire. He glanced at Al-Mustaʿsim. The Caliph's head was bowed and his features contracted in a dark frown, but Muʾayyid al-Din could see no resolve or firmness there. This was the single great fault of the Caliph. He did not lack good intentions; he simply lacked determination.

Muʾayyid al-Din bowed his head in turn and kept his silence until the Chamberlain returned to announce Prince Ahmad's arrival and the Caliph ordered him to be introduced into the Hall.

Ahmad, Son of Al-Musta'sim

ABU BAKR, barely past his twentieth year, moved with the preening self-importance of vacuous youth. With every step his arrogant bearing declared his self-proclaimed perfection. At this age, young men sincerely believe their surpassing beauty and virility to be a magnet for all eyes and if they but speak, they expect their words to fall as revelation upon the ears of those around them. The boredom or contempt of others only serves to enrage them and to provoke unfounded accusations of envy and spite. If this is the way of common youth, then what of the progeny of kings and caliphs, upon whom sumptuous praise and the most poetical of eulogies are lavished all day long by professional flatterers?

And what if the youth in question be both innately frivolous and mean-spirited, as was this Ahmad, son of Al-Musta'sim? The fact that his father had released him from the prison of his minority—a highly unusual act in the annals of the Caliphate—had only increased his natural arrogance a hundredfold. He cared not a fig for the consequences of his actions, nor did he understand the simplest facts about the state of his father's Empire. He only cared that his outlandish orders be obeyed and his petty desires fulfilled, no matter the cost.

Abu Bakr greeted the company and his gaze carelessly wandered over the room. His eyes came to rest contemptuously upon Mu'ayyid al-Din, but the Minister did not betray the slightest reaction. Abu Bakr then seated himself without waiting for his father's permission.

"Ahmad," Al-Musta'sim began, "did you order the Dawadar to attack the people of Karkh?"

"I did, father," Abu Bakr replied with a spiteful little smile directed at Mu'ayyid al-Din.

"And why, pray, did you do so?"

"One of my slave-girls fled my palace and took refuge in a house there. I am certain that the Karkhis incited her to this treachery. I sent a courier to retrieve her, but they insulted and beat him. I then ordered the Dawadar to discipline the wretches for their scandalous defiance, but they resisted and our soldiers were obliged to defend themselves. What, pray tell, is your objection to this simple affair?"

"I object to an 'affair' in which a dozen men were killed because of a slave-girl. There are hundreds of choice slaves in our palaces. If you had asked me to give you ten in place of the one you lost, this would have been preferable to me than the news I now hear. They are all alike, after all."

Abu Bakr fiddled with his belt and simpered coyly at his father. "If all slaves are alike and if there are hundreds of them in our palaces, then why did the Commander of the Faithful feel obliged to demand a particular one from the Sultan of Egypt?"

Mu'ayyid al-Din watched Al-Musta'sim's face closely to gauge the effect of the boy's impertinent words. The father's stern demeanor crumpled in the face of this cunning objection and his voice suddenly grew conciliatory. "I only wished to hear her sing. They say she possesses a voice unparalleled in all the land of Egypt," he replied.

"And how do you know that this slave of mine has not similarly unique qualities?" the son insolently demanded. "Does it not behoove me to emulate my father, Commander of the Faithful and supreme model for all Muslims?"

The sarcastic tone of this question cut Al-Musta'sim to the quick, and he was ashamed to let it pass in front of his Minister and his Dawadar without comment. "Is this how you answer me, Ahmad? Are then the privileges of the Commander of the Faithful to be the common rights of all? This action of yours displeases me."

Ahmad shook his head in mock regret. "That it should please me is enough. Are the actions of my father agreeable to one and all? A man cannot be expected to satisfy everyone!"

Al-Musta'sim had at first made clear his disapproval of his son's unseemly disdain. Now he evaded the issue and ignored the evident sarcasm in this reply. "Have you found this unparalleled slave, then?" He smiled feebly.

"I have not," the boy petulantly replied. "And I shall have to keep looking for her."

"That will not be necessary. I shall ask our Minister Mu'ayyid al-Din to look into the matter. He will find her and have her returned to you."

Abu Bakr glanced suspiciously at Mu'ayyid al-Din, then turned to the Dawadar. "If he does not find her, we will dig her out of her hiding place though it be the Minister's own pocket." Rising to go, he addressed himself once again to his father. "I now beg my Lord's permission to withdraw, for I have a hunting appointment with a company of our officers." He nodded for the Dawadar to follow him and strode airily out of the hall. Al-Musta'sim watched him go with despair in his moist eyes, then sighing, he turned to Mu'ayyid al-Din. "He spoke truth who said, 'our beating hearts walk this earth in the shape of our sons.'"

Mu'ayyid al-Din only hung his head, amazed and disconsolate at the Caliph's infirmity. "You are our Minister and the repository of our trust, Mu'ayyid al-Din," Al-Musta'sim finally said. "You have seen the scorn with which Ahmad has met our rebuke. Perhaps we were wrong to diverge from the tradition of our grandfathers and to make our children their own masters. If Ahmad were still under guardianship as the sons of Caliphs have ever been, we would not be in the present situation." He broke off and began to fiddle with his beard.

Mu'ayyid al-Din preferred not to delve too deeply into this subject for fear that the father's helpless tenderness would get the better of him and his anger be transferred to the Minister who had witnessed the debacle. "We beseech God to restore the boy's reason," Al-Musta'sim continued heavily. "You are a father and you know a father's heart. Search for Ahmad's slave and recompense the people of Karkh for their losses. We deeply regret these events and hope they shall not be repeated." He shifted uncomfortably in his seat and prepared to rise. "And neglect not your charge to retrieve the other slave-girl, Shwaykar, the singer that we caused to be brought from Egypt."

Mu'ayyid al-Din rose and lowered his head obediently. "I am the slave of the Commander of the Faithful. May God aid me in his service." He cleared his throat and was on the point of speaking again, but the Caliph quickly intervened.

"We know that Ahmad should not have spoken as he did, but he is still an inexperienced youth and is sure to come to his senses in good time." With that he rose and, graciously taking his leave of his Minister, quit the Grand Hall by the door through which he had come.

Shwaykar

LOST IN THE WHIRL OF HIS BLACK THOUGHTS, Mu'ayyid al-Din al-Alqami quit the Palace of the Crown and mounted his mule for the return journey home.

As he approached his palace, he noticed two mules tethered to the post outside the gates. One of these he immediately recognized as belonging to Sahban. At his knock the gates were thrown open, and he entered the spacious courtyard. The page who rushed forward to help him dismount led the mule away to the stables. Mu'ayyid al-Din strode into the palace and the doorkeeper hurried alongside. "Who is the rider of the second mule that is tied up outside alongside Sahban's?" Mu'ayyid al-Din demanded.

"A woman that accompanies him, Master. Sahban awaits your Excellency on the terrace."

"Tell him to come to me in my chambers. And who is this woman?"

"I know not, my Lord. After you left this morning, Sahban took his father and sister back to Karkh and has only just returned this hour, accompanied by the woman. I suppose her to be a slave of some kind."

Mu'ayyid al-Din had gained his chambers, and the doorkeeper bowed respectfully and withdrew. The Minister's staff and domestics knew that no one was allowed access to these rooms without special permission. The head cook knocked at the door and begged to inquire whether Mu'ayyid al-Din would now dine. "Prepare a light meal and bring it hither. Sahban shall dine with me this evening."

Mu'ayyid al-Din began to change his heavy robes of state. He had barely finished dressing when Sahban was introduced into the anteroom with an expression of barely concealed delight on his face. Mu'ayyid al-Din wondered at this sudden change in the man's bearing. He had left him sunk in the depths of despair that very morning. He sincerely hoped that some happy event lay behind

Sahban's broad grin. His own weary smile of welcome did not go any further than his lips, however. "What news, my friend?"

Sahban immediately remarked on the telltale signs of fatigue and dejection that clung to his host. "It seems that your audience with the Caliph has vexed you, my Lord," he replied. "Wherever one turns, the news is bad," he sighed, and smiled mysteriously.

"Have you reason to celebrate, then, Sahban? If so, speak, by God, for I grow wearier of this life by the day! Come, let us eat first."

Sahban bowed and seated himself at the low table upon which their meal had been laid a few moments earlier. He helped himself to a portion of meat stewed in vinegar and busied himself in carving it up as he watched the Minister's face out of the corner of his eye. "I have news that shall please and astonish you," he finally said between mouthfuls.

"Out with it then!" he demanded impatiently. "I was told that you arrived in the company of a woman. Who is she?"

Sahban laughed again as he raised a morsel of meat to his mouth. "She is the one sought by Prince Ahmad; the one in whose name the people of Karkh were slaughtered."

"God be praised! We shall at last now be rid of Abu Bakr's latest mischief. How did you find her? Where was she hid?"

"In a neighbor's house, my Lord. My sister knew of her hiding place but she said nothing, thereby exposing herself to great danger for the poor girl's sake. The girl was terrified lest she be returned to her persecutors. My sister confided the story of this slave to me, and she took me to her. I have brought her to you."

"Well done. The Caliph seeks her everywhere and intends to return her to his son. It seems he will spare no madness to placate him. The man's weak-willed fondness continues to baffle me."

"But the girl does not wish to return," Sahban replied.

"That is unfortunate," Mu'ayyid al-Din shrugged, "but I must discharge my duty to the Caliph."

"She fears the Caliph even more than his son, and does not wish her presence here to be known."

"How so? I have never known a slave-girl to refuse the favor of a caliph!"

"This girl's circumstances are singular. No one in Baghdad save myself knows her story."

"By God, man, you seem to know all!"

"The traveler learns much on his travels."

"And what has this business to do with your travels, Sahban?"

"I shall tell you. I first heard the sad tale on my last trip to Egypt. Its twists and turns will astonish you, my Lord."

This mysterious statement only increased Mu'ayyid al-Din's curiosity. "Speak, Sahban. I have no patience for these vagaries."

"Have you not heard of the Egyptian slave-girl who was abducted from the Caliph's caravan just outside Baghdad a few weeks ago?"

"Indeed. He has spoken to me of her."

"This is the girl."

"The same who fled from his son to Karkh?" Mu'ayyid al-Din demanded in wonder.

"Exactly, my Lord. She is Shwaykar, the former slave of Tree of Pearls. The Caliph heard tell of her unparalleled voice and her musical genius, and he sent to the Sultan of Egypt to claim her. Before she entered Baghdad, a band of horsemen descended upon the caravan in which she travelled, saying that they came by order of the Caliph, and they abducted her. The people of Baghdad spoke of nothing else for many a day. The real reason for the assault was as follows: Upon hearing that this slave was to come into his father's possession, Prince Ahmad decided that he would have her for himself. He was the one who sent those brigands to abduct the girl. They then brought her to a safe house prepared for that very end. Meanwhile, the Palace of the Crown continued to await her arrival. They quickly discovered that she had disappeared, but continue to be entirely ignorant of her whereabouts."

Mu'ayyid al-Din was astounded by Abu Bakr's sheer impudence, and the evident contempt in which he held his father. "And what is the girl's objection to her new master? Does she not prefer the company of the youth to that of the father?"

"The girl refuses to reside anywhere but Egypt, for she is betrothed to one of its Mamluk princes."

"Betrothed?" Mu'ayyid al-Din repeated incredulously. "And the Caliph nonetheless sought to possess her?"

"The Caliph was unaware of her engagement. He only knew that she belonged to Tree of Pearls, the deposed Queen, and that she was an excellent vocalist. The Sultan's regent had no choice but to comply with the Caliph's request."

"Who then is her betrothed?" demanded Mu'ayyid al-Din.

"He is Rukn al-Din Baybars al-Bunduqari."

"Rukn al-Din Baybars," Mu'ayyid al-Din mused. "I met him once in Egypt and we have corresponded a few times since. I know him to be a brave warrior and an intelligent and noble-minded prince. What shall he do now, I wonder?"

"He is exceedingly angry, and I confess to my Lord that he entrusted the matter of this slave to me when I was last in Egypt. I hastened to return to Baghdad and discover some news of his future bride. She was able to inform him secretly of her abduction in a letter. At the time she did not know who the perpetrators were. My guess is that he may soon travel to Baghdad to search for her in person."

Mu'ayyid al-Din pushed his plate aside and bowed his head as he considered the unfortunate state of affairs that the Caliph and his son had brought to pass by their indecorous occupations. "Do you suppose that he will come?" he finally asked Sahban.

"It is not unlikely. If you would permit me to speak, my Lord: let us keep this Shwaykar with us until he does so, or at least until we can send him word of her recovery and await his instructions."

"How did she manage to escape from Abu Bakr's palace? She is, after all, a stranger in these lands."

"A eunuch in her service gave her succor. He knew the people of the house next to ours, and he carried her there in secret."

Mu'ayyid al-Din thought carefully about all that he had just heard. He feared that the girl's presence in his own house would provoke any number of suspicions, for he knew himself to be surrounded by spies. "See here, my friend," he began, "the girl's plight has moved me, and I am glad that she has escaped her prison. I shall not insist you return her to Abu Bakr, but I cannot keep her in my house."

"Indeed, my Lord, you are right to say so. I only wished to inform you and to consult you on the matter. I also wish Rukn al-Din to know that her liberation was your own doing. He is a great leader whose prudent views and discretion may benefit us in the project of which we have spoken. We must arrange a meeting. Rukn al-Din promised me in Cairo that he would consider aiding us in the overthrow of this government. He shall kill the Caliph and give us an Alawi State in Egypt. Once this is accomplished—"

Mu'ayyid al-Din silenced him with an impatient gesture. "Give not free reign to these extreme ideas, man! Let us set aside wanton illusion and deal in the possible."

Sahban was nonplussed by this rebuff, for he truly believed his plans to be within easy reach. He also believed that Rukn al-Din had indeed promised to aid him in their execution, even though the noble young man had remained resolutely silent in the face of Sahban's wild proposals. But Sahban lived on illusions, as we have already pointed out, and he tended to build mountains out of molehills. Fantasists of this stripe concoct schemes and shape them according to their own wishes. Thus silenced, Sahban was obliged to feign acquiescence. "Suppose, then, that my hopes are far-fetched," he said. "Do you see no benefit whatsoever to us from Rukn al-Din's presence in Baghdad?"

"His coming may be useful to us if we work to make it so. But this is neither the time nor the place to discuss such matters."

"There never seems to be a right time or place for such matters!" Sahban broke in. "Suppose that I agreed with you and was content to replace one Caliph with another. May we not at least discuss this?"

"Perhaps, my friend. I am of two minds about our Caliph. At times he seems reasonable enough, while at others he appears hopelessly irredeemable. We shall consider it."

"Assuming then that Al-Musta'sim is indeed irredeemable, who would you have replace him? Do you not think that the Imam Ahmad Ibn Al-Zahir would be an appropriate substitute?"

This abrupt proposal took Mu'ayyid al-Din by surprise. He had often considered it himself in private. He knew that the Imam Ahmad was indeed the only suitable candidate to replace Al-Musta'sim, but he had never openly discussed the possibility with a living soul. He hesitated as he pondered his response, and his eyes glittered darkly. "Yes. He would fulfill our requirements. But he is a prisoner in the Firdaws Palace, as you well know. It is impossible to communicate with him."

"Once we agree on a course of action, no prison can stand in our way," Sahban replied. "But I beg you to be candid with me. I have had enough of silence and mystery. Though they be inherently politic strategies, they may also confound him who practices them too liberally. I beg you to speak clearly, my Lord. Do you think the Imam Ahmad could take Al-Musta'sim's place as Caliph?"

"He descends from the most excellent branch of the House of 'Abbas," Mu'ayyid al-Din spoke slowly. "But we cannot reach him. We must scale back our ambitions for now and continue to hope that Al-Musta'sim can be reformed. This would spare us the need to depose him."

"So be it," Sahban sighed as he rose to withdraw. "I wish you luck in your endeavors, my Lord," he added ironically. "Do you not wish to see the slave Shwaykar and give her leave to kiss your hand before I return her to Karkh?"

"Very well, though I pray you to speed her departure from under my roof."

"She shall kiss your hand and leave immediately."

Sahban left the room and returned shortly with the girl. Shwaykar's appearance had changed dramatically, thanks to the many trials and tribulations that she had undergone since leaving Egypt. She had been kept a prisoner until that very day, when Sahban had brought her from Karkh to Baghdad. He had assured her that all was well with Rukn al-Din, and that it was Rukn al-Din himself who had sent him to search for her. Her dearest hope now was to be quickly returned to Egypt, or at least that Rukn al-Din would soon arrive in person at Baghdad. She bent to kiss Mu'ayyid al-Din's hand but the Minister quickly withdrew it, wet with her copious tears. "Have no fear, my child. The Commander of the Faithful is just, and God abandons not his creatures."

Shwaykar bowed her head shyly and, swallowing the lump in her throat, replied, "I thank God for sending this brave man to save me and bring me to you, my Lord. I ask for nothing but to be returned to Cairo."

Mu'ayyid al-Din rose from his seat. "You shall return safely, God willing."

Sahban now thanked Mu'ayyid al-Din and bade him farewell. He signaled to Shwaykar to follow him, and he took her to the house of one of his relatives in Qadhimiyya.

The Dervish

AS SOON AS MU'AYYID AL-DIN found himself alone again, he mounted to the terrace and stretched out on a couch. He thirsted for the quiet solitude in which to ponder his great dilemma. The sun was about to set and the Tigris glittered gold in the sun's mellow rays. Hearing the sunset call to prayer, he rose and set off on foot for a nearby mosque, for nothing offers more comfort to the believer in his hour of need than to pray and to entreat God to guide him on the true path, and to rescue him from dangers both real and imagined.

Mu'ayyid al-Din was in dire need of such comfort. As he prayed, however, he was distracted by an odd-looking Sufi sheikh kneeling behind him and mumbling his prayers. Suddenly, from the corner of his eye, he saw that the man had begun to creep slowly in his direction. The hairs on the back of Mu'ayyid al-Din's neck stood on end. He wondered whether the man was mentally disturbed. He turned to stare at him, but the Sufi had resumed his original position and seemed to be lost in prayer. Reassured, Mu'ayyid al-Din once again returned to his own pleas for divine guidance.

When he had finished, he rose and slowly made his way towards the door of the mosque. A group of people stood by, waiting to pay their respects to the Abbasid Minister, and he returned their greetings distractedly. When he reached home, he was startled to see the same Sufi that he had noticed in the mosque standing by the great wooden doors and muttering over a string of prayer beads. Mu'ayyid al-Din stopped and stared at him. The Sufi approached Mu'ayyid al-Din and greeted him with a cunning smile. "I reveal that which is hidden. Allow me to unveil the Way to you, Mu'ayyid al-Din."

Mu'ayyid al-Din blinked. In contrast to his shabby appearance, the man's voice rang out forcefully. His accent, moreover, was distinctly foreign. Clearly, this was no poor, wandering dervish and it was no small matter that had brought him to Mu'ayyid al-Din's door. He scrutinized the stranger's face and clothes. He wore the cap and gown of a Sufi and carried the prayer beads of a Sufi, but his expression was not that of a dervish, nor was his short, finely groomed beard. "Who are you?" Mu'ayyid al-Din sternly demanded.

"I am a seer into the hearts of men. I chase away all cares and reveal all secrets. I shall guide you on the Sound Path. If you do not believe me, then put me to the test."

After a moment's hesitation, Mu'ayyid al-Din signaled for him to follow, and he instructed the porter to introduce the dervish into his private chambers. Mu'ayyid al-Din preceded his strange guest, his mind teeming with unanswered questions. He was strongly inclined to consult the stranger's visions, for he believed in the saintly power of God's chosen ones and he dared to hope that this man was indeed one of them. A few moments later the dervish entered, one hand thrust deeply into the opposite sleeve of his garment while the other ceaselessly told a set of fine prayer beads. Mu'ayyid al-Din invited him to be seated and inquired if he would take some refreshment. The dervish declined, and Mu'ayyid al-Din dismissed his servant and ordered him to shut the door securely.

The Minister's restless gaze rested once again on his unlikely guest. He did not recall ever having seen this man before, and the thought again occurred to him that he looked nothing like a real Sufi. He decided to test him immediately. "Give us your saintly counsel, wise sheikh," he began.

"Show me your palm," the man replied. He took Mu'ayyid al-Din's outstretched hand and pondered it for a moment. "Your mind is occupied with a momentous matter in which there is much danger to you, your family, and your people."

Mu'ayyid al-Din nodded apprehensively at these words. The dervish examined the Minister's palm as though he there read a finely scribed letter, then he raised his eyes to Mu'ayyid al-Din once more. "The dilemma in which you find yourself is easily solved, if only you wish it."

"Explain yourself!" Mu'ayyid al-Din demanded.

"You must first consider your own interests and those of your people. Above all, you must free yourself of the feeble illusions of the weak-hearted and the irresolute. Are you capable of this, Mu'ayyid al-Din?"

Mu'ayyid al-Din wondered at the stranger's uncanny powers of divination. He abruptly withdrew his hand from the Sufi's firm grasp. "Tell me first, what is your name?"

"I am a trusty messenger to a great minister."

Mu'ayyid al-Din now realized that his suspicions had been well-founded and that the man was no Sufi but a disguised envoy. "And who has sent you?" he frowned.

"A true friend who bears you and your people nothing but good will has sent me. But it seems you know not how to profit from the many advantageous opportunities offered you," he added severely.

"Do you dare to threaten me? Explain yourself, man! Who has sent you, I say?"

"I am the messenger of a great Khan who shall soon invade your country. Against his mighty hordes you shall be utterly defenseless."

His words struck Mu'ayyid al-Din like a thunderbolt. This was an envoy of Hulagu the Tatar, then, come all the way to Baghdad! He nonetheless thought it wise to equivocate until the man should openly declare himself. "And who may this great Khan be?"

The envoy frowned in displeasure. "It is my Lord Hulagu! Do you not know him, then? He has repeatedly bidden you to divest yourself of the ties that bind you to your puny Caliph, confederate of slaves and singers, and yet you remain mute. He has now sent me to you as a most sincere counselor. It cannot be lost on you that the great Khan would never have sent his royal envoy on such a mean and perilous mission unless he were convinced of the legitimacy and the success of his cause. I now call upon you in the name of my Lord, the greatest of Sultans, to rally to his side against this tyrant of the House of 'Abbas. You shall have delivered yourself and your Shi'ite brothers from the yoke of injustice and oppression, and you shall sit at the right hand of the future lord of this land.

"Be not faint of heart!" he continued in a thunderous voice. "Why do you bow your head, as though your conscience crushes you, as though you tremble to disappoint your Caliph's trust? These are nothing but exaggerated and futile considerations. Has he not failed your own hopes? I have been here in Baghdad for days now. I know of all that transpired between you and the Caliph and his ignoble son. I have watched you grumble and complain. Why lack you the resolve to save yourself, man? If you continue to resist the Khakan, you and your kin are lost and shall surely perish along with your feeble master." His eyes took on the cast of flinty steel as he delivered this final prediction.

Mu'ayyid al-Din trembled under the sheer force and audacity of this threat. This man was a foreigner who dared to penetrate alone and unaided into the land of his most bitter enemies. He discerned in the man's face a courage and dignity not to be found in the common run of men. But Mu'ayyid al-Din's pride would not allow him to give way so easily. "Pray convey my gratitude to your master for his generous offer, and tell him that I am unable to comply with his request," he haughtily replied. "It seems he believes that the Empire is inferior to the task of repulsing him. He is mightily mistaken in this. Our army is neither small nor weak, and we are confident of victory, should war be declared."

The envoy laughed out loud at Mu'ayyid al-Din's earnest speech. "I have presented myself to you in the guise of a soothsayer and a mind-reader, and verily, I divine the thinking that lies behind your proud words. You yourself remain unconvinced of what you have just said. Your attempt to conceal the corruption and turmoil that plagues your armies is futile. Listen now to my advice and know that we do not wish to imperil your person in any way, nor do we ask you to perform any prodigious undertaking. Doubt not that we shall conquer this country, come what may. If you act for us, you shall prevent much bloodshed and destruction. We shall inflict punishment only on those who deserve it for having brought about the iniquities that afflict these lands. The people are not to blame, especially the Shi'a, who have suffered for generations at the hands of your Caliphs—most particularly the present laughingstock. As it may be difficult for you to retract your last words in defense of your master Al-Musta'sim, I shall not require an immediate answer from you. I only hope to offer sound counsel, and I shall give you sufficient opportunity to reconsider. My Lord the Khakan does as he wills. Not long ago you received his official letter of warning. If you hearken not to his demands, he shall descend upon your lands like an unchained storm. Know that he is all-powerful and ever-triumphant; he is the Victorious One. If you love your country and kin, send word of your allegiance to the Great Khan. You shall thereby be saved and your influence shall be paramount in his government. And now, forgive me if I have overtaxed your patience." As he rose to go, he reached into his pocket and produced a fine reed cylinder which he presented to Mu'ayyid al-Din. "This is a letter to you from my Lord. Open it only after my departure."

The emissary left Mu'ayyid al-Din in a state of wonder and great turmoil. He hurried to the terrace, and after having watched him disappear through the outer doors, he returned to his chambers and unrolled the scroll. This is what it said:

*Know, oh Mu'ayyid al-Din, that the messenger with whom you have just spoken
is Hulagu himself. He has offered you sound counsel; be counseled therefore! Do*

not attempt to pursue him, for you will certainly fail. While it was in our power to leave you to your ignorance, we have chosen to enlighten you and advise you. Consider your situation well and beware of spies. Send your reply in the manner previously agreed upon.

Mu'ayyid al-Din re-read the paper in astonishment. He could barely believe the evidence of his own eyes and ears, so strange was the interview in which he had just participated. He bowed his head in deep thought as he considered the implications. "Hulagu himself, the Great Khan of the Tatars, served by hundreds of thousands of men! So little does he trust any one of them to do his work that he comes in person, disguised, and at great personal risk, to speak with me. He could have easily sent a real messenger, but such is his vigilance and kingly zeal that he came himself. Surely he must know all our secrets better than we ourselves. He knows the size of our army and the state of relations between its generals and the Caliph. He knows all! How unlike he is to our sovereign, who cares more for a missing slave-girl than for the defense of Baghdad. These are certain signs of our coming extinction, while the Khan's actions bespeak assured victory. So it was with the Arab conquest of Byzantium," he mused. "Our great caliphs and generals, the Companions of the Prophet amongst them, were wont to take matters into their own hands. They depended on none but themselves, and holy war was their only occupation; they were few, and yet they defeated the vast armies of the Caesars and the Khosraus. Those days are legend, but alas, every empire must come to an end."

This gloomy prediction caused Mu'ayyid al-Din to hang his head in shame. "It shall not be so!" he declared out loud. "The Abbasid Empire shall endure only if its government can be reformed. We must have a new Caliph."

Night had now let down its veils. He placed the letter under his pillow and called for his evening meal. After he had eaten, he retired to bed earlier than was his habit in order to take some much-needed rest from the day's exertions, but his mind continued to rage. His stubborn loyalty to the Caliph would not leave him in peace. He dreamed much that night, and only woke the following morning to the voice of the muezzin and the hubbub of the Mustansiriyya students as they went off to make their forenoon prayers.

He was greatly tempted to keep to his bed and give free rein to the thoughts that devoured him. It is easier to think in the morning when the mind is clear and truth closer at hand. Mu'ayyid al-Din finally resolved to ignore Hulagu's threats and to pursue the path of reform on which he had set his heart. The decision comforted him, and he quickly rose and began to dress, while his harried thoughts wandered to the slave-girl Shwaykar. He wondered whether he had acted wisely in this matter. He would have preferred to hand the girl over immediately to the Caliph, but Sahban had stood in his way, and truth be told, the man's reasons were sound. It occurred to him to send for Sahban in order to make sure that he had carefully concealed the girl's hiding place, but on second thought, he decided to wait for him to come of his own accord.

Wishing to rest and to attend to some private business, Mu'ayyid al-Din remained at home all of that day. The sun set and his evening meal was served, but still there was no sign of Sahban. As he prepared to retire for the night, he suddenly remembered the letter that the Dervish had delivered to him the day before, and he resolved to destroy it so that it should on no account fall into the wrong hands. He searched the place where he had hastily thrust it under the pillows of his bed. The letter was not there! He searched in his pockets, and in every possible nook and cranny, but could still find no trace of the missing letter. His heart beat violently with cold dread. Had spies overheard his conversation with the mysterious messenger? Had the letter been stolen and delivered to the Caliph?

A New Guest

WHILE HE WAS THUS ENGAGED, Mu'ayyid al-Din suddenly heard a violent knock at the outer door. The Chamberlain arrived to inform him that Sahban and a companion wished to pay him a visit. Mu'ayyid al-Din breathed a sigh of relief. At last, Sahban! He wondered who his companion might be this time. A few moments later, a smiling Sahban entered and greeted the Minister effusively. Then he slowly moved aside and solemnly presented his guest, a tall man of noble bearing whose head and face were tightly wrapped in a veil. Only his eyes and the bridge of his nose remained uncovered and Mu'ayyid al-Din could see that his skin was dark like that of an Abyssinian slave. The majestic visitor crossed the room slowly as Sahban stood by in respectful silence. Mu'ayyid al-Din wondered at this ceremony. "Who is this guest, Sahban?" he whispered.

"You shall know presently, my Lord," Sahban replied carefully under his breath. He then rushed forward to seat the visitor on a large chair in the center of the chamber and begged him to remove his veil, to which the man graciously consented. Mu'ayyid al-Din watched him closely as he unwrapped the silken cloth and his heart jumped in his chest the moment he saw the naked face glowing in the lamplight. "My Lord Imam!" he cried, "Imam Ahmad! How have you accomplished this feat, Sahban?" and he fell upon the thin brown hand to kiss it.

Sahban laughed and said, "It was your own wish that brought him here."

"Woe unto you!" Mu'ayyid al-Din cried. "Did I ask you to abduct his Excellency and bring him here? How did you accomplish it? He is a prisoner, his palace surrounded by guards and spies. Indeed, Sahban, you are an extraordinary fellow!"

"You did not ask me to bring him to you simply because you did not think me capable of it! After our conversation of yesterday, I supposed that you would like to see him and to personally assure yourself of his good will."

"Of course, of course," Mu'ayyid al-Din murmured in bewilderment. "And yet I would not, in fact, have believed it to be within your power. By God, you are a brave and intrepid fellow—though you lack patience and foresight," he added wryly.

"What I lack, my Lord, your own deep wisdom and craft completes."

Mu'ayyid al-Din ignored this pointed compliment and gave his undivided attention to his royal guest, for the Imam Ahmad was uncle of the Caliph and son of his grandfather, Al-Zahir, by an Abyssinian slave. He had by this time reached middle-age and his demeanor was serene and stately, as becomes a great prince in his later years. Mu'ayyid al-Din solemnly and respectfully seated himself on a pillow at the Imam's feet and proceeded to welcome him. Sahban, too, drew close and began to speak. "My Lord, I am a hasty man who loves neither prolixity nor procrastination, and indecision is abhorrent to me. Yesterday, your confidence in his Excellency Imam Ahmad pleased me greatly. Our opinions of him are in perfect accord; proof, in itself, of excellent judgment. Here, then, is the concerned party—I have not yet spoken to him of our project, but I have extracted him from his prison."

"How did you accomplish this?" Mu'ayyid al-Din demanded. "How did you dare?"

"I managed it with God's help, and I must confess that I yet hope to succeed in an undertaking that is infinitely more difficult. It is my opinion that this wise and righteous Imam must become Caliph instead of that—"

The Imam quickly but firmly interrupted Sahban's speech. "Say no more, my son. Our Caliph Al-Musta'sim Billah would be inoffensive were it not for his dissipation and his son's outrageous domination over him. It is possible to correct these faults. Do not close your hearts to him."

"You are indeed the best of men, my Lord," Sahban replied. "As for our Caliph, I am convinced that his case is hopeless and he must be removed. You are more deserving of the Caliphate than he, for you are the brother of Al-Mustansir—may God have mercy on his soul—, an upright, pious, and assiduous man, as his acts did attest, quite unlike that—"

Once again Imam Ahmad interrupted, this time with a gentle rebuke. "If I had known that you brought me here only to hear you speak thus, Sahban, I would have preferred to remain in my prison. We are all my nephew's loyal subjects, and if he has erred, it is our duty to counsel him. I have spoken my mind."

The Imam's careful rejection of Sahban's impetuous proposal did not in the least surprise Mu'ayyid al-Din, though he guessed him to be even more desirous of the Caliphate than Sahban was of transferring it to him. His rebuke was merely the habitual practice of astute politics on his part; a mixture of caution, cunning, and foresight—all qualities of the utmost importance in the present circumstances. "My friend Sahban is merely expressing the feeling of all Muslims, your Excellency," Mu'ayyid al-Din politely explained, "especially those of our Shi'a brothers, for they have suffered bitterly under your nephew, as everyone knows. I do not, however, see the wisdom in rushing so precipitously down the path our friend proposes. We have yet to take a single step in the direction of our hopes." He then turned to Sahban and continued. "You have escorted his Excellency here from his palace, but where shall he now be lodged? If his absence from the Firdaws Palace is discovered tomorrow, we shall be the first to fall under suspicion, and you well know that the Caliph's men wreak havoc as they please."

"Fear not," Sahban quickly replied. "I shall return him to his palace tonight. I have arranged it so that no one will even notice his absence. I brought him to you so that you might personally inform him of our design to remove the Caliph. Did we not agree that his Excellency Imam Ahmad would be the most worthy Abbasid to replace Al-Musta'sim? Well, here he is, and there you are." And he turned once again to the Imam. "Your Excellency, I beg you to lift the veil between us. Pray spare us the encumbrance of guarded pleasantries and speak clearly. If we succeed in toppling the government and installing a new Caliph—his son, of course, being out of the question—would Imam Ahmad deign to accept the Caliphate? And would he swear to uphold justice for the persecuted Shi'a?"

In spite of the abruptness of this bold question, Mu'ayyid al-Din was beginning to see the wisdom in openly sounding out the Imam. He was now inclined to accept the fact that great projects require audacity and resolve as much as forethought and deliberation. He bowed his head and waited for the Imam's response. It was not long in coming. "My sons, if the Caliphate is offered to me, it is in the interests of all Muslims that I not refuse it. Such a refusal would be sinful and would moreover result in sedition and great turmoil at the very heart of the Empire." He stopped and carefully considered his words. "Know that if I were to become Caliph, my first duty would be to dispense justice and to serve all those of the Prophet's House, peace and blessings upon him, who have been oppressed by the present government."

"May God bless his Excellency," Mu'ayyid al-Din replied. "If God favors our aspirations, the entire Muslim community shall profit. We thank his Excellency for speaking his mind, and let me add that I sorely regret his having been burdened with the dangers of coming to us this night."

"There is no danger," Sahban rejoined. "The Imam may stay away from his palace for days if he so chooses. No one shall notice his absence, for I have left in his place a man who resembles him greatly. None but his closest attendants shall know the difference, they are so like. I was able to accomplish this thanks to my friendship with the Palace Steward, a man who desires to be rid of this Caliph even more than we do. No one has been left untouched by the crimes of Al-Musta'sim and his son. Rest assured, my Lord. And if you fear spies, we shall leave you this very minute." Sahban rose and invited the Imam to do the same.

Mu'ayyid al-Din saluted them with words of deepest respect. "His Excellency the Imam has honored the house of his servant. I beg him to act as he sees fit, and to aid us in the endeavor of serving him faithfully."

The Message

MU'AYYID AL-DIN accompanied his guests to the outer door. Upon returning to his rooms he immediately resumed the search for Hulagu's missing letter. He finally gave up, exhausted, and cold dread crept through his veins, for he knew full well that he was surrounded by enemies who awaited the slightest excuse to denounce him. He retired for the night but was unable to sleep a wink, for darkness magnifies fancy and inflates the specters of anxiety. He rose the next morning, greatly fatigued.

Nothing is so oppressive to a man as the indecision caused by a conflict between feeling and reason. One of these must triumph for the crisis to pass and the mind to be set at rest. So it was with Mu'ayyid al-Din, who was torn between two perspectives. His reason warned him that the corruption of the government would lead the Empire to ruin. Only the overthrow of the Caliph could prevent this fate, and only a mighty and conquering hand like that of Hulagu could in turn achieve this goal. This rational judgment was not unmixed with a stifled desire for revenge against the Caliph's son and the Sunni faction he represented. On the other hand, his heart and his conscience reproved him for contemplating treachery against the master to whom he had sworn an oath of fealty.

Hulagu's missing letter added yet another consideration to Mu'ayyid al-Din's uneasy reflections. If it had been deliberately stolen, as he suspected, then it would not be long before it fell into the hands of his enemies and he would almost certainly be accused of conspiracy. While the actual contents of the letter were perhaps not enough to sustain such a grave charge, they at least proved the existence of an ongoing correspondence between the Empire's deadliest foe and its First Minister.

The Caliph may well decree his imprisonment or execution—especially if Abu Bakr had his way—and it would then be impossible to save himself. In circumstances such as these, Mu'ayyid al-Din reflected, it would be wise to pre-pare for the evil before it came to pass. He considered writing to Hulagu at once, but his whole being rebelled at the thought. The great danger that awaited him should he do nothing was ever-present in his mind, however, and his torment threatened to overwhelm him. The instinct of self-preservation finally won the day, and he resolved to at least prepare the messenger that would take word of his capitulation to Hulagu, should the need for this arise. He summoned his Steward and a certain one of the slave-boys that lived in the palace. The Steward pres-ently arrived, accompanied by the slave in question, a dim-witted mute who had recently been bought from Turcoman traders.

Mu'ayyid al-Din examined the boy from head to toe, then instructed the Steward to shave his head. This Steward had long been attached to Mu'ayyid al-Din's household and he was privy to his master's secrets, great and small. More-over, he was genuinely fond of the Minister and exceedingly protective of his interests. He immediately understood the purpose of his master's command.

Once the task of shaving the boy's head had been completed, Mu'ayyid al-Din turned his attention to his faithful servant. "You have understood my pur-pose?" he demanded.

"I have, my Lord, and I am ever at your service."

"Then bring the needles and the kohl and shut the door securely."

The Steward did as he was ordered, and returning, seated himself on a chair and instructed the boy to kneel before him. Mu'ayyid al-Din now came forward with a bit of paper in his outstretched hand. He nodded to the Steward, who took it and silently read the brief sentence that it contained: Advance with your armies and your stores. The Steward understood that this was a message to Hulagu, and he was secretly glad of it, for he hated the Caliph and his court with the passion of a true Shi'a. He bent over the boy and began the operation of tattooing the words onto the smooth scalp with the needles and the kohl. When he had finished, he raised his expressionless eyes to Mu'ayyid al-Din and smiled.

The Minister now instructed his Steward to keep the boy in a safe place until the hair should have grown back to cover the tattooed message. If and when he should finally decide to send for Hulagu, he had only to dispatch the boy on his deadly journey. The Khan, knowing that the messenger had been sent by Mu'ayyid al-Din, would duly shave his head and read the words thereon inscribed, after which the boy would be put to the sword. In those days, this was the safest way for politicians to correspond in secret. Mu'ayyid al-Din had prepared his letter. If he should decide not to send it, he would simply keep the boy in his household with his hair fully grown. He hesitated still, and his conscience held sway over his will, for he yet dared to hope that the present state of affairs might be peacefully resolved.

A measure of tranquility descended upon Mu'ayyid al-Din once he had taken this precaution, and he returned to his duties and to the daily business of the Empire with a lighter heart. He mounted his mule and rode to the Palace of the Crown to examine his correspondence and to sit in council, but the missing letter continued to haunt him throughout the day. He closely watched the faces that surrounded him at court, but saw nothing there to excite his alarm. He returned home at the end of that very long day encouraged and in fairly good cheer.

Arrogance

DAYS WENT BY and Mu'ayyid al-Din almost forgot Hulagu and the missing letter; nor did any inauspicious news of Abu Bakr reach his ears. From this he inferred that all was well. He hoped that the young Prince had repented of his ways, having finally understood the fratricidal dangers that beset the Empire. One morning, however, well before the call to prayers, Al-Musta'sim's messenger came to summon the minister to the imperial palace. He dressed in haste and mounted his mule, all the while wondering what could be the reason for a summons so early in the day. Recalling Hulagu's letter, his fears returned and he struggled to preserve his composure until he should reach the Palace of the Crown and discover what lay in store for him. When he arrived, he was directed to meet with the Caliph in the Special Assembly Chamber. Seeing that Abu Bakr and the Dawadar were also present, his heart trembled, but he took refuge in God and resolutely greeted the company.

Al-Musta'sim returned his greeting and bade him be seated. Then he abruptly handed him a letter that had been lying beside him on the royal couch. Mu'ayyid al-Din took it. As he read its contents, he quietly breathed a sigh of relief.

From the Great Khakan Hulagu, Sultan of sultans, to Al-Musta'sim Billah the Abbasid. We grow weary of your procrastination, though verily we have been patient. Is it not time for you to see the light and to acknowledge our worth? We sent you emissaries to request aid against the Isma'ili murderers. Though we fought them in your name, you declined our alliance. Your refusal has proven the weakness of your judgment. We then wrote to reproach you for this failure and you sent an indifferent reply that did nothing to assuage our wrath; and you attached to this miserable reply an even more miserable gift that is only fitting for one such as yourself. Do you suppose, then, that we are in need of money? You would have been well advised to send us an Imperial envoy, to whom we would have graciously listened. And now, nothing will satisfy us but an official apology delivered in person by yourself, your Minister, or your Dawadar. Woe unto you if you fail to submit.

Now that his personal safety was assured for the time being, relief was quickly followed by dismay. Mu'ayyid al-Din glanced at the Caliph and saw that he was lost in thought. He wondered whether his master would now finally be guided by him and agree to conciliate the Tatar invader. The Caliph emerged from his reverie. "What is your opinion, Minister?" he demanded.

"It is for my Lord, Commander of the Faithful, to judge these matters," Mu'ayyid al-Din deferentially replied.

"Does the insolence of this Tatar please you? What shall be his punishment?"

These unexpected words threw Mu'ayyid al-Din into great confusion. The Caliph was even now miscalculating his true position. "I beg my Lord's permission to speak frankly," he began. "This man now wields great power. We know from our spies that he has crushed the Persians and many other peoples in fierce warfare. His armies are vast and his arms and stores, abundant. If we do not reply favorably to his letter, he will most certainly attack Baghdad."

Abu Bakr now spoke up. "Attack Baghdad?" he scornfully demanded. "And what if he does? Can his recompense be anything but failure and disgrace?"

Mu'ayyid al-Din flexed his jaw and ignored this silly retort. "My Lord, I am of the opinion that we must conciliate Hulagu until we can adequately prepare for war."

"How can we conciliate him?" the Caliph asked. "The scoundrel demands that I myself appear before him, or my Minister or Dawadar in my stead. Would it not have been better to engage with him before matters came to such a pass?"

The Minister was pleased by this tacit admission on the Caliph's part. "It would indeed have been wise, my Lord," he replied. "And may I remind you that the humble servant who stands before you suggested that very course of action when last we received a letter from the Tatar. I expressed my fears to the Commander of the Faithful and I begged him to send rich gifts of slaves and jewels—such baubles are enough to satisfy these barbarians. But the Dawadar protested and accused me of faintheartedness and cowardice. He accused me of stooping to appease the enemy. His Highness chose to ignore my counsel, and sent a trivial sum of gold that only angered Hulagu. This letter is the result."

Hearing himself accused, the Dawadar rose to his own defense. "I have not changed my mind, your Highness," he haughtily declared. "I still believe our Minister would have us submit in shame to this tyrant and conciliate him at any cost, thereby rendering him yet more greedy and proud."

The Caliph turned to him. "And what is our Dawadar's opinion, then? Shall you go to this savage, as he demands?"

"Yes, I shall go to him, but at the head of an army, if his Highness permits!"

Mu'ayyid al-Din was stunned by the man's sheer arrogance. The Dawadar knew full well that the treasury was almost empty and that the Caliph had been obliged to cut the soldiers' pay. Mu'ayyid al-Din had counseled him to do just this in order to collect the necessary tribute for Hulagu and avoid the threat of war. Baghdad's army had formerly boasted a hundred thousand soldiers. Mu'ayyid al-Din had caused eighty thousand to be dismissed, leaving only twenty thousand to defend the city, and the Dawadar was aware of this, as was the Caliph. Would they fight the Tatars with this miniscule army, then?

"How do you propose to take the war to him when you only have twenty thousand men?" the Caliph demanded.

"Of course these numbers are insufficient. We shall conscript more," the Dawadar dismissively replied. "The monies that our Minister has amassed from the pay of the dismissed recruits will be sufficient to re-staff the army." He glanced sharply at Mu'ayyid al-Din. "May God forgive the Minister for having made such a grave mistake in the first place. The troops are deeply aggrieved by it."

The Caliph was about to interject a word in his Minister's defense when Abu Bakr quickly intervened. "Why should the Minister care whether the troops be displeased or content? The only thing that interests him is Hulagu's satisfaction."

The Accusation

THIS INNUENDO shook Mu'ayyid al-Din profoundly, and the missing letter once again came to his mind. He studiously ignored the youth's impudent remark, however, and turned once more to the Caliph. "Sire, I am still convinced of the wisdom of my earlier opinion. The money we have conserved will suffice to satisfy Hulagu and avert war. You are the General of our armies," he added, turning to the Dawadar. "If you disagree with me and continue to insist that the troops may yet be made ready for war, then the matter shall be decided by the Commander of the Faithful."

The Caliph stared at Mu'ayyid al-Din. "I would know the opinion of our Minister."

"I maintain that we must conciliate Hulagu with the means at our disposal in order to avert war," he firmly declared.

"And yet he demands that I go to him, or that I send one of you in my place!"

"His Highness shall send whichever one of us he sees fit," Mu'ayyid al-Din replied.

Abu Bakr let out a contemptuous laugh. "I do believe that our Minister dearly hopes to be sent on this mission to his friend the Khakan," he sneered.

Al-Musta'sim wondered at this untoward speech and he glared disapprovingly at his son. Abu Bakr now rose and his face took on a serious expression. "I speak the truth, father. Ask your Minister. Is there not between Hulagu and himself old friendship and established correspondence?"

Mu'ayyid al-Din blinked in surprise and directed a reproachful glance at the Caliph.

"You have no right to speak such words, Ahmad," the fond father chided.

Abu Bakr silently extracted a letter from his pocket and handed it to his father. "This letter is my witness."

Al-Musta'sim took the letter and read it slowly, once, twice. Then he looked up in stunned silence at his Minister. "Do you recognize this letter?" he demanded.

Mu'ayyid al-Din made a monumental effort to remain calm and collected. He looked at the letter. "I know it, my Lord. It was stolen from me."

Al-Musta'sim threw the letter at him. "It proves our son's accusation. You have corresponded with Hulagu."

Mu'ayyid al-Din bent down to pick up the letter while he considered his words carefully. "Yes my Lord. But does it prove that I have conspired with him? Does he not complain of my refusal to serve his ends?"

Abu Bakr now spoke. "It is clear from this letter that the exchange between you is long-standing. Was it not your duty to inform the Commander of the Faithful of it? How should we know what has passed between you? Most likely you have already agreed to deliver the city into his hands and some trifling differences have arisen over the manner in which the treachery shall be accomplished. This is not the conduct of a loyal minister devoted to his master, as you hypocritically claim to be."

Mu'ayyid al-Din was at a loss how to respond. He began to speak, but the Caliph silenced him with a wave of his hand. Anger was now visible on his face. "Abu Bakr speaks truly. I did not expect this of you, Mu'ayyid al-Din. You should have informed me of any communication between yourself and our enemy when first it arose."

Mu'ayyid al-Din again attempted to defend himself, but Al-Musta'sim again commanded his silence. "I have long supported you against the rumors that surround you, but now it seems that your detractors did not lie. I can see no reason for your silence regarding this correspondence with Hulagu, other than that you thereby expect some great benefit to yourself."

Mu'ayyid al-Din could no longer hold his tongue. "I saw no purpose in speaking to his Highness of matters that would only vex him. It is my duty to serve him faithfully and to defend the sacred institution of the Caliphate. Is there then anything in this letter that indicates treachery? If so, then this slave is the hostage of his master's will."

Al-Musta'sim shifted uneasily in his seat. "So it shall be," he mumbled. "And now answer me this. Would it also have vexed me if you had revealed the whereabouts of the slave-girl?"

Mu'ayyid al-Din was taken aback by this sudden question. "Which slave-girl, your Highness?"

"Ahmad's slave-girl. The one who caused all that trouble at Karkh."

"Forgive me, your Highness, but I perceive not the relevance to our present discussion."

"Your ingenuousness surprises me," the Caliph replied. "Were you not aware that the massacre of Karkh took place because of her? Because Ahmad discovered that she was hidden there, and the people of Karkh refused to give her up?"

"Yes, my Lord."

"And on that day you told us that you knew nothing of her whereabouts?"

"It was so, my Lord."

"How dare you persist in this lie when she is concealed in your own house?"

Mu'ayyid al-Din started at this fresh and unexpected accusation. "In my house?" he repeated incredulously.

"Indeed. Or at least in the house of your kin in Qadhimiyya. Ahmad recovered her from there yesterday with the aid of our Dawadar—without resorting to violence this time," he added ruefully.

Mu'ayyid al-Din suddenly felt a ray of hope descend upon him. He would use his knowledge of the girl's true identity as a weapon against Abu Bakr!

"Is the Commander of the Faithful certain that his information in this case is accurate?" he sardonically inquired.

"Here is Ahmad, and the Dawadar stands there. They are the ones who recovered her yesterday," the Caliph replied.

"Has the Commander of the Faithful seen the girl?" Mu'ayyid al-Din continued.

"No, I have not seen her, but I trust in their testimony."

Abu Bakr now rose and feigned great anger. "Do you accuse me of being a liar, sir?" he demanded.

"I cannot answer to that," replied Mu'ayyid al-Din. "But I do know that I am no liar. As you have charged me with treason and insubordination, you are obliged to show evidence sufficient to prove your accusations. If you do so, I am prepared to submit to the executioner at once."

"There is no need to prove them," Abu Bakr said, "for we all know them to be true." He reseated himself and, playing nervously with his mustache, assumed a detached and contemptuous look. The last thing he wanted was to be obliged to produce the girl before his father, and he now regretted ever having mentioned the affair. He could not have known, however, that Mu'ayyid al-Din was aware of her true identity.

"Would it do any harm to have the girl brought here so that we may see her and hear her testimony?" Mu'ayyid al-Din pursued.

"It would not," the Caliph replied. "Where is she?" he asked, turning to Abu Bakr.

"It would be unseemly to bring a slave-girl into the Assembly Room of the Commander of the Faithful," Abu Bakr persisted. "Does his Excellency truly deem her presence amongst us to be of any importance?"

"It is exceedingly important," the Caliph said. "Our Minister stands charged with treason and falsehood, in part due to this woman. We must therefore have her testimony."

Abu Bakr rose impatiently from his seat. "I do not agree," he emphatically repeated. "Hulagu's threats against us are our present concern. Our father has seen both letters, and that is enough." Having summarily dismissed the subject of Shwaykar in this fashion, he turned on his heel and strode towards the doors of the Chamber without having first requested and received the permission of his sovereign to withdraw. His father merely looked on in mournful silence. Though this precipitate departure was not disagreeable to Mu'ayyid al-Din—for he still greatly feared the harm the boy was capable of inflicting upon him—he clearly felt the present necessity of exposing the outrageous theft that he had committed before the Caliph. He therefore marshaled his resolve and called out after the youth. "Ahmad!" The boy turned and raised his brows sardonically. "Yes?"

"I insist that we conclude this matter of the slave-girl."

"Let us forget her. I willingly forgive our Minister for this minor dereliction of duty."

"And yet I do not forgive myself," Mu'ayyid al-Din wryly declared. "I would that the girl be brought before us and prove this charge of treason that has been leveled against me. This is my right."

Abu Bakr's only response was to laugh breezily and stalk out of the room with a flourish.

Mu'ayyid al-Din turned to the Caliph. "Will his Highness command the girl's attendance? The Dawadar has seen her, for he was with Prince Ahmad at the time of her recovery from the house of my kin in Qadhimiyya, as he claims."

The Caliph turned to the Dawadar as though giving him leave to speak. "Do you doubt the words of his Excellency Abu Bakr?" the latter demanded of Mu'ayyid al-Din.

"I doubt neither his words nor yours. But I nevertheless beg his Highness the Caliph to summon the girl immediately."

"I see no harm in this request," the Caliph said to the Dawadar. "Bring her to me."

Now, the Dawadar saw no reason to resist this direct order, for he knew nothing of the real connection between the girl and the Caliph. He had wondered at Abu Bakr's refusal to comply with such a simple request and had put it down to the folly and pride of youth. He rose accordingly and spoke. "I shall bring the girl by direct order of my Sovereign, his Highness the Commander of the Faithful."

The Caliph nodded and the Dawadar bowed and immediately withdrew. He was not long gone, for the house in which they had lodged Shwaykar was close to the Palace of the Crown.

"The slave is at the door, my Lord."

"Let her enter," the Caliph said.

Mu'ayyid al-Din watched the door attentively, for fear that another girl had been brought in place of her whom he sought. He recognized her at once, as soon as she set foot in the Audience Hall, and he fell back, assured. Shwaykar advanced tremblingly into the Caliph's presence and stood perfectly still before him with bowed head. The Caliph now spoke to her. "Were you not concealed in Qadhimi-yya and recovered only yesterday by our General?"

"Yes, Your Highness," she meekly replied.

"Who was it that hid you there? Speak the truth!"

"Who dares to lie in the presence of the Commander of the Faithful?" she murmured. "A man named Sahban hid me there, my Lord."

"Was it not the Minister Mu'ayyid al-Din that hid you?"

"No, Your Highness. Neither did he know that I was concealed there."

"Have you had prior interactions with our Minister?"

"Yes, Your Highness."

"How did you meet him? Who took you to him?"

Shwaykar trembled and hesitated, for she divined in these questions a trap set for the man who now stood watching her closely and who had shown her nothing but kindness. In truth, she was reluctant to tell any part of her story to the Caliph.

Mu'ayyid al-Din finally broke his silence. "I beg his Highness to ask the girl her name and from whence she comes to Baghdad. I also beg his Highness to inquire as to the reason for her concealment."

"And what is the relevance of these questions to the matter at hand?"

"His Highness shall see presently that they are of the utmost relevance."

"Very well," the Caliph sighed as he turned to Shwaykar once more. "What is your name and your city of origin?"

Shwaykar understood from Mu'ayyid al-Din's intrusion that he wished her to speak the truth. "My name is Shwaykar and I was sent from Egypt to serve as a singer at the court of the Commander of the Faithful."

The Caliph was struck dumb by this revelation. Was this then the singer that had been lately stolen from him? His astonished eyes flew first from Mu'ayyid al-Din to the Dawadar; then he resumed his questioning. "Shwaykar, the slave of Tree of Pearls?"

"Yes, your Highness. I am she."

"And you were coming to join my household?"

"Yes."

"By whom were you captured? Where were you hidden all this time?"

"It was your Highness's son, Prince Abu Bakr, who seized me, and I am presently housed under his roof."

The Caliph stared fixedly at the girl. "Are you not the slave who caused the incident at Karkh?"

"I am that slave, my Lord. I had escaped in order to save myself."

"But how did my son manage to take possession of you?"

"At the outskirts of Baghdad a band of soldiers descended upon the caravan that brought me from Egypt and claimed that they were come from the palace of the Commander of the Faithful to take me to him. I was given up to them, and they took me to a palace which I later discovered to be that of Prince Abu Bakr."

The Caliph now flew into a great rage and the Dawadar stared at the girl in amazement. He sorely regretted having brought her into the presence of his master, for he feared that Abu Bakr would suffer the wrath of his father. Mu'ayyid al-Din kept his silence, but his heart jumped for joy at this victory. Shwaykar, meanwhile, was somewhat heartened at the prospect of leaving Abu Bakr's house and entering that of the Caliph, though she still cherished her dearest hope of being finally returned to Egypt and Rukn al-Din.

A Father's Love

HAVING FINALLY ASCERTAINED THE TRUTH, the Caliph clapped for a page and ordered him to take Shwaykar to the Custodian of the Imperial Harem, and he charged the page to make sure that she be honored and given every possible comfort. He then turned to the Dawadar. "You have just heard that Ahmad was aided in this criminal exploit by men from amongst our own troops. Is this proper? Is it fitting that our men conduct themselves thus? Is this not treason?" he spluttered angrily.

The Dawadar understood this outburst as a personal reproof, and he was now obliged to lay blame on the Caliph's son in order to defend himself. "I assure you, Your Highness, our troops were not acting on my orders but on those of Prince Abu Bakr. They could not have refused a direct command from his Excellency."

"And why not?" the Caliph hotly retorted. "Do you defy me in order to obey my son while I yet live?"

The Caliph was exceedingly agitated. He huffed and gasped for air and gritted his teeth in fury. Mu'ayyid al-Din was almost inclined to believe that he would have ordered Prince Ahmad's execution, had he been present in person. How he wished that the Prince would come! As though reading his thoughts, the Caliph resumed his speech. "Where is Ahmad now?"

"I know not, my Lord," the Dawadar uneasily replied.

"Find him and bring him to me this instant!"

The Dawadar bowed and turned to withdraw. The Caliph glanced at Mu'ayyid al-Din with a contrite expression on his face. "We have doubted our Minister unfairly—may he be rewarded. Why did you not immediately inform me of the girl's true identity?"

"Because I did not know it myself until a few days ago, my Lord. I bade the man who brought her to me to hide her in a safe place until the opportunity arose to consult the Commander of the Faithful without the knowledge of Prince Abu Bakr. I thereby hoped to avoid any harm he might do. He is the son of the Commander of the Faithful and the army answers directly to him."

The Caliph shook his head sorrowfully. "To God we belong and to Him we shall return. Indeed, I committed a grave fault in giving this boy of mine his freedom. If he had been cloistered in the manner of his predecessors, he would not have acquired this evil nature, nor brought these calamities upon us. He shall be detained and placed under guardianship once again. I will teach him obedience—may God shame the wayward rogue!"

While they were thus engaged, there came at the door a great din in which they discerned the voice of Abu Bakr shouting angrily. "Are the hordes of women in his own house not enough for him? Must he lust after my own poor slaves? Let me enter!" The Chamberlain hurried in and awkwardly sought permission to admit the Prince.

"Has he come alone?" demanded the Caliph.

"Yes, Your Highness."

"How so? Is not the Dawadar with him?"

"No, Your Highness."

Abu Bakr stormed unannounced into the room, his whole body shaking with anger. At the sight of him, his father was constrained to invoke God's mercy, for the coming interview promised to be a stormy one. "What is this, Ahmad? Is this how one enters the presence of the Commander of the Faithful? Where are your manners? Know you nothing of the dignity of the Caliphate?"

Abu Bakr sat down uninvited. "You ask me about manners when I am the son of the Commander of the Faithful and have been raised in his lap? Perhaps this is the very cause of my wretchedness. People envy me because the Caliph is my father, but if they knew how he treats me, they would have nothing but pity." His voice grew thick as though he would burst into tears.

Now as soon as Al-Musta'sim heard his son's strangled sob and remarked the tear that sparkled in the corner of his eye, his anger subsided and his paternal affection began to get the better of him. A father's love does not submit to justice, nor does it acknowledge the principles of logic, nor require evidence and proofs. It is a tyrannical ruler whose actions most often fall outside the realm of law, and many of which contradict all common sense and reason. The father loves his son, is jealous of his wellbeing, and sees in him virtues undiscernible by others. He loves him not for reasons of utility or because the son objectively deserves such love, but rather he loves spontaneously, unconditionally, simply because the child is his own son. The heavy trials and tribulations involved in raising a child only increase this strange love. The father's compassion grows stronger in proportion to the son's unhappiness. No matter how angry a parent is, his sympathy will always be moved by the sight of his offspring in tears, as though those tears but fall on the fire of parental anger to put it out once and for all. The smoke that rises in its wake casts a lingering veil over the cause of the original resentment, leaving nothing but pity and tenderness behind.

Al-Musta'sim was the weakest of tender fathers. He was now tempted to forget the reasons for his anger, but he still held fast to his injured pride. "Is this how you speak to your father? Do you have the right to complain against him, when he has given you the one thing that the sons of Caliphs have ever desired, the freedom to command and forbid at will? Where is the Dawadar?" he added.

"I have not seen him," Abu Bakr petulantly replied. "But they told me that he came to my Palace and confiscated my slave. I cannot bear this insult, and so I have come here to you to lodge my complaint. You speak of freedom? What freedom is it that allows you to begrudge me a paltry slave-girl while your Palace abounds with them?"

"I have not begrudged you a slave-girl," Al-Musta'sim broke in. "I charge you with stealing a slave-girl sent expressly to me from Egypt."

"Sent expressly to you from Egypt?" Abu Bakr repeated mockingly. "You seek and acquire hundreds of slave-girls from all parts of the Empire, but if your young son lays a hand on one of them, you upbraid and repudiate him. Had I been the son of a commoner, my father would have treated me with more kindness than does the Commander of the Faithful." He swallowed hard and made a show of controlling his sobs. "Nevertheless," he continued, "you are our sovereign and you have rights where others have none. We are your slaves and all that we possess is at your command. A handful of other slave-girls yet remain to me—why don't you order the Dawadar to take them as well? Would that you had kept me imprisoned and never shown me the light of freedom! The babe lives in darkness, knowing nothing of the joys of light, and therefore never missing them. If you regret having freed my hand, here I stand before you—confine me or kill me! Death would be preferable, since I would thereby relieve you of a great burden." It now appeared that his struggle with the tears that threatened had failed, and he burst out sobbing while his father looked like he might at any moment join him.

Mu'ayyid al-Din watched this little scene in amazement. His joy at having got the better of Abu Bakr's scheming quickly evaporated, and he contented himself with the thought that he had at least escaped the Caliph's anger. He now urgently wished to quit the place, but was at a loss as to how to execute this purpose. He could not request leave to withdraw before the Caliph had exhibited an inclination to dismiss him: such is the prerogative of caliphs and kings. He began to fidget in his seat in order to draw the Caliph's attention to the superfluity of his presence. Al-Musta'sim had perhaps even more reason than himself to wish him gone.

The unfortunate Minister only succeeded in attracting the attention of Abu Bakr, who, having wiped his tears and blown his nose, now turned toward Mu'ayyid al-Din and resumed his speech. "I doubt not my father's affection for me," he craftily began. "I blame none but this Minister, who has imbibed a deep hatred of us with his mother's milk, for he is an 'Alawi and in his heart of hearts he rejects our right to the Caliphate!" And turning to address his father directly, he continued, "I wonder at my father's patience towards an individual who hates us and who seeks to overthrow our state by secretly consorting with our worst enemy. How is it possible that you believe the lies with which he attempts to excuse himself?" He snatched Hulagu's letter from Mu'ayyid al-Din's hand and cast his eyes over it. "You believe his defense and suppose him innocent of conspiring with our enemy. And yet in this letter, Hulagu calls him a friend and advises him to send his correspondence 'in the agreed upon manner.' Does this not prove a prior communication on the subject of treason? In spite of all this, Mu'ayyid al-Din the 'Alawi's words are taken for truth and those of my unhappy self are dismissed as lies." And he burst into tears once more.

Mu'ayyid al-Din could see that the spineless Caliph was deeply moved by his son's outburst and that he was quickly succumbing to the boy's clever ruse. He now realized that all his efforts had been in vain, and he wished for nothing more than to vanish from the conference, for he dreaded to hear the Caliph's inevitable rebuke. But it was too late. "I shall look into the matter of Ahmad and the slave-girl at another opportunity," Al-Musta'sim began. "As for your correspondence with Hulagu, Mu'ayyid al-Din, Ahmad speaks truly. How comes it that you consorted with our enemy for so long without telling us? I am confident of your loyalty, but trust has its limits . . . Yes, I trust you still, though Ahmad disagrees with me. He has spoken thus out of anger."

Abu Bakr brusquely interrupted his father. "I do not speak out of anger! You have always been aware of my suspicions regarding this Minister. Today, these suspicions have been proven!"

The Caliph was caught in a delicate position. He believed in the aptitude and loyalty of his First Minister and knew that he needed his services more than ever at this juncture in the Empire's affairs. On the other hand, he was unable to master his fatherly feelings and to quarrel with his son. He decided to put an end to his quandary by bringing the audience to a close, and he gave Mu'ayyid al-Din leave to withdraw with a heavy gesture of his hand. Mu'ayyid al-Din rose and, bowing deeply, took his leave in brooding silence.

Mu'ayyid al-Din was so incensed by this interview that he walked through the Palace's winding corridors in a blind haze and lost his way from the Diwan to the stables where his page awaited him. On the road home, the intensity of the emotions that besieged him—sorrow, despair, and fear—made him insensible to his surroundings. His Steward awaited him at the gate of his palace, as was his habit. When Mu'ayyid al-Din's absent gaze fell upon him, he recalled the slave on whose head the deadly message had been inscribed. Mu'ayyid al-Din inquired about the boy. "He is safely ensconced in my quarters," the Steward replied.

"And his hair?"

"It has covered his head. I shall bring him to you this instant if you desire it, my Lord."

"Good," Mu'ayyid al-Din curtly replied, and he mounted to his chambers, his body shaking and his thoughts full of the contemptible Abu Bakr.

No sooner had he thrown himself onto his bed than the Steward entered with the dim-witted lad in tow. Mu'ayyid al-Din gazed at the boy. He seemed barely human to the great Minister. He examined the boy's head and noted with satisfaction that the hair had indeed grown back and covered all traces of the secret message. "The words beneath this head of hair have the power to turn the world upside down," he mused. "Hulagu shall wreak my revenge on Abu Bakr. And am I to blame if I send this message? The Khan is unstoppable, and shall take Baghdad one way or the other. I am certain of his imminent victory. If I send the message etched on the head of this Turcoman, I shall be sure of my own life and those of the friends and family that I choose to save. If only I believed that we stood a chance of repelling Hulagu and his men, I should pay no heed to Ahmad's insolence. I should defend my country and my people with the last drop of my blood. I should indulge the Caliph's weakness and his son's recklessness. But it is impossible for us to resist the Tatars when our armies are only twenty thousand strong; twenty thousand, moreover, whose hearts are divided and whose objectives are at odds." He raised his eyes slowly to his trusty old servant. "Send the boy on his mission."

The Steward said nothing, but his heart leapt with joy as he led the boy out of the room. His instructions to the youth were simple: that he must go to Hulagu the Khan of the Tatars and present his insignia. The Khan would then give him further instructions. The Custodian added that a great reward awaited him upon his safe return, whereupon the boy rejoiced and prepared to embark on his journey like a sheep on its way to the slaughter.

Shwaykar in the Women's Quarters

SHWAYKAR RELUCTANTLY ACCOMPANIED the Caliph's page to the Imperial Harem. As she silently followed him from hall to hall, she struggled to summon forth her gratitude for this sudden change of residence, for Prince Abu Bakr had clearly signaled his intention of using her for a purpose other than singing. She had stubbornly refused to bow to his will, and Rukn al-Din's tender letter had only served to strengthen her resolve. Her beloved had sworn to rescue her! The faithful 'Abid had gone to great lengths to deliver the precious letter into her hands whilst she was kept under lock and key at the Prince's palace. 'Abid had, moreover, succeeded in helping her escape to Karkh, with the deadly consequences we have already recounted. He subsequently accompanied her to Qadhimiyya, and remained there after her hiding place had been discovered by Abu Bakr whereupon she had been forcibly returned to the Prince's palace.

The inhabitants of the Imperial Harem had all heard the news that the singing-girl destined for the Caliph and seized by thieves had been found and brought to the Palace of the Crown. A great horde of men and women had consequently gathered to gape at her as she made her way to her new quarters (the women outnumbering the men, it should be noted, as the female sex is more inclined to engage in this type of activity). The Imperial Harem contained thousands of slaves and concubines of different classes and functions. In the days and weeks after her initial disappearance, many of them had repeatedly begged the Custodian of the Imperial Harem to describe the famous singer to them, for a number of wildly divergent accounts of her person, her height, and the timbre of her voice were in circulation, and imaginations had run rife.

The Caliph's singing-girls were especially interested in this potential rival. They had spent long hours discussing every detail, both real and rumored, that they had heard concerning her—an all-too-human tendency, alas, particularly in the day and age of which we speak, when this kind of gossip was the sole occupation of cloistered womenfolk. The women of that epoch had neither books nor newspapers and magazines in which to interest themselves; neither did they have access to schooling or to the literary and scientific salons common today. Their only concern was to adorn themselves and to compete with each other for the affections of men.

The first person Shwaykar met upon arriving in the Harem was the Majordomo, the Chief of Eunuchs. She was taken to him in his chambers, where he sat proudly enthroned on a raised dais in the very center of the room. She kissed his hand and stood waiting silently for his commands, for he was, as she well knew, the undisputed master of the women's quarters and exercised an important political influence at the Caliph's court (rather like the Aghas of Yalzar in the time of the Ottoman Sultan Abdulhamid). The Majordomo demanded her name, her age, and the date of her arrival in Baghdad, as well as an account of her primary physical characteristics, and commanded that all this information be recorded in the Harem register in order to avoid any possible confusion, for the women under his charge were many and their names often quite similar.

Shwaykar was next taken to the apartments of the *Qahramana,* Custodian of the Imperial Harem. As she proceeded on her way to wait upon this august personage, she bowed her head bashfully to avoid the bold stares of the many eunuchs and slaves who stood by, gawking and whispering. A company of eunuchs stood at attention at the Qahramana's door, much like a company of royal guards. Shwaykar entered and cast a quick glance about her. She identified the Qahramana by the manner in which she occupied her couch and by the magnificent robes she wore. She was a middle-aged woman upon whose flaccid body the flesh was piled in heavy layers, much like the rouge that caked her face and the splendid jewels that hung on her neck and wrists. This woman was the undisputed Queen of the Harem. Each and every concubine and slave fawned upon her and curried her favor with flattery and gifts. Shwaykar approached her and bent to kiss her hand. The Qahramana placed a kiss on the girl's forehead and invited her to sit at her side. She then began to shower upon her the customary phrases of welcome which, if addressed to an untutored ear, would appear to be the most sincere expressions of affection and regard. Overuse and shrewd social custom had even by then conspired to render them meaningless, or worse yet, entirely false.

Shwaykar was greatly comforted by this gracious reception, however. She surveyed the room's elegant and rich furnishings, and taking note of the opulence and luxury in which the inhabitants of the harem seemed to live, she almost began to wonder whether she would not prefer to stay here in this marvelous place rather than return to Cairo. But her heart immediately rebelled at this ignoble thought, and she instantly paid heed to its call. "Fie upon you, woman!" she silently reproached herself. "Furniture and jewels were never wont to bring happiness to their owner! Only true love can secure life's joys." The Qahramana called for one of the eunuchs and ordered him to prepare a luxurious chamber for the Caliph's newest singing-girl. Then she turned to address Shwaykar. "You shall remain here with me until your rooms are ready to receive you, my dear. I have been awaiting your arrival for so very long and we were all frightfully concerned for your safety."

"Indeed, I am undeserving of this warm solicitude on your part, my Lady, for I am nothing but a lowly slave," Shwaykar gratefully replied.

The Qahramana chuckled good-naturedly. "You suppose I am not aware of your value, child? I have known everything about you for quite a while now. My dear friend the Custodian of the Righteous King of Egypt—may God have mercy on him—has told me much about you. Do you know her?"

Shwaykar recalled Sallafa and the bitter rivalry between her and her mistress, Tree of Pearls. She was surprised to hear of her friendship with the Qahramana of the Caliph's Palaces. "I believe you mean Sallafa, my Lady? I am indeed acquainted with her but would never have presumed to solicit her attention."

"On the contrary, my dear, she knows you very well. She it was who spoke to me of your magnificent voice, and she who suggested you as a suitable acquisition for his Highness the Commander of the Faithful. This is how I came to propose you to his Highness, and he duly requested you from the Sultan of Egypt, as you well know."

This revelation disturbed and confused Shwaykar. She was troubled by this heartless meddling on the part of her mistress's rival. And yet she could not help but feel flattered by the high opinion of her worth that Sallafa had shown in recommending her to the Custodian of the Imperial Harem. She could not have divined Sallafa's true intentions. "In truth, my Lady, Sallafa's recommendation is a great kindness for which I am greatly obliged. Had I known of it earlier, I would have thanked her most sincerely in Egypt."

"You may thank her now if you so desire," the Chamberlain complacently replied.

"Is she here then?" Shwaykar inquired.

"She is here. She arrived in Baghdad but a few days ago."

Shwaykar wondered at this coincidence and her face lit up with pleasure. She thought that this accident augured well and imagined that Sallafa's presence at Baghdad would be a great consolation to her until her dearly anticipated return to Egypt. She even dared to hope that Sallafa would aid her in this suit. "How fortunate I am!" she declared. "Where is my Lady Sallafa? I would kiss her hand and thank her for her beneficence."

"You shall see her shortly," the Qahramana replied, "for she inquired after you the moment she arrived from Egypt. Your late mishap grieved her sorely. As soon as we received news of your fortunate recovery, I immediately sent word of it to her. She rejoices, and she is coming to us presently. Here is her slave now. Where is your mistress, Aqhwana?"

"She is in her chambers, my Lady, and she has sent me to request the pleasure of the young lady's company. She longs to greet her in person."

The Qahramana laughed heartily and revealed a row of stained and broken teeth. "Will she see her, then, before she sees the Commander of the Faithful himself?"

"That is her request, my Lady. The decision is yours."

"Very well," she replied. "Our guest Shwaykar shall go with you to our friend Sallafa, for she is equally anxious to see her and to thank her. Tell Sallafa not to prolong the interview, however, for the girl must be properly prepared for the Caliph by the ladies' maids. She must be fit to be presented to the Commander of the Faithful this evening, when he shall hear her sing for the first time. I believe he shall wax exceedingly impatient if we detain her further. Go to Sallafa, Shwaykar. You are amongst friends here and you must put your trust in me, for you are like my own daughter."

Shwaykar rose and followed the slave Aqhwana down endless corridors dotted with the doors to seemingly innumerable apartments. She shivered slightly, for she sensed rather than perceived the many invisible figures they hid, faceless people who yearned to catch a glimpse of her as she passed by. Some doors were flung wide open, while others opened just a crack, and heads suddenly poked out and then withdrew as quickly as they had appeared. Shwaykar stared straight ahead of her until she finally reached Sallafa's apartment. Aqhwana entered first to announce her arrival.

Sallafa rose to greet Shwaykar with a warm smile that only increased the young girl's shyness. She bent to kiss her hand but Sallafa prevented her from taking it. "Welcome to my dear Shwaykar," she smiled. "I thank God that He has gratified me with the sight of you in the Caliph's palace: a blessing that has ever been my fondest wish. Tell me, are you happy here, Shwaykar?" and she motioned for her to be seated on a cushion next to her own in the magnificently appointed room.

Shwaykar did as she was told and timidly raised her voice in reply to the great lady. "I thank you for your consideration and your kindness, my Lady. I am well taken care of, praise God."

"It greatly pained me to hear that you had been kidnapped on the road to Baghdad. I have only today discovered the cause of this outrage, and I thank God for your safety. How delighted I am to see you! Though you are indeed fortunate to have been called to Baghdad to reside in the house of the Caliph, I count him even more fortunate to have won a singer the likes of whom is not to be found in all of Egypt and Iraq."

Shwaykar was obliged to acknowledge her gratitude once again, but her heart remained mute with quiet despair. She would have preferred to remain close to Rukn al-Din, though in the barest of prisons, than to be separated from him by a Caliph's treasure.

Sallafa knew this, of course, but she feigned ignorance. Shwaykar was entirely unaware of all that had passed between Sallafa and her beloved Rukn al-Din. If she had divined the true cause of Sallafa's arrival in Baghdad, Shwaykar would have trembled and hated the sight of her. The Reader will recall that we last saw Sallafa in Egypt, furious at Rukn al-Din's refusal to bow to her will. She had resolved to be patient, however, for she hoped that Rukn al-Din might yet regain his senses and abandon Shwaykar, rather than court her certain revenge. Her spies had been busy at work discovering his intentions, and she had learned of his plans to travel to Baghdad. So it came to pass that she had hastened there herself in order to follow his movements from close quarters. She had heard of Shwaykar's abduction whilst in Cairo. This unexpected circumstance had suited her plans to perfection, and in truth, she had been much put out to learn that the girl had been recovered. She now set about devising another strategy to rid herself of Shwaykar once and for all, for she was convinced that the girl would be a nuisance to her as long as she remained alive.

Shwaykar's artless thanks confirmed her suspicion that the girl knew nothing of her own relations with Rukn al-Din. She could not help but silently gloat at the ease with which she would execute her nefarious plans. It suddenly occurred to her that Shwaykar might even prefer to remain in the Caliph's household rather than marry Rukn al-Din. She therefore desired to know her thoughts on the matter, and watched her face closely as she spoke. "It seems that you have forgotten Egypt and its people, my dear," she lightly sighed. "That it should be so is only natural, after all. She who lives in these palaces in closest proximity to the Commander of the Faithful would have no reason on earth to think twice about Egypt!" Poor Shwaykar was at a loss to reply. The lover is jealous of his secret, and keeps it from all but those whose sincere affection and devotion he may be sure to trust. Shwaykar dared to hope that Sallafa was such a person, for had she not striven to procure this high honor for her? Perhaps if she were to confide in her, Sallafa would help her to quit Baghdad and return to Egypt. Shrewd Sallafa noticed the indecision in Shwaykar's lovely eyes. "Why do you not speak, my dear? It seems that you are over bashful in my presence. Do you not trust my confidence?"

"I beg your pardon, my Lady. I only fear that you may laugh at my thoughts."

"Laugh? Nay, my dear, Sallafa would never stoop to abuse fair Shwaykar's confidence in a manner so unbecoming to the high esteem and affection in which she holds her. Speak, I pray you."

Shwaykar blushed and hung her head as she nervously twisted a plait of her hair around her finger. "Many are those who long for the chance to live in these magnificent palaces, and many are those who must envy me for the great honor with which I have been blessed. But . . . my Lady, I wish with all my heart to return to Egypt." The words came tumbling out before the poor girl could stop them.

Sallafa feigned astonishment. "Return to Egypt? Does some tie of affection yet bind you to that country? You are betrothed to a young man there, perchance? Even if it were so, you shall surely find a better suitor in Baghdad. Once the Caliph hears your singing and your accomplished playing on the oud, he may well favor you with rewards the like of which you could only dream in your former life."

"My happiness lies not in proximity to caliphs," Shwaykar replied with winning simplicity, "nor in marriage to a prince or nobleman, but in love equally exchanged." She blushed shyly and turned to rest her confused gaze on a splendid tapestry that hung on the opposite wall and displayed a complex and cunning design of brilliantly colored birds of all shapes and sizes.

"If your heart is taken by a youth in Egypt, beware, and do not be deceived," Sallafa continued. "It might be that the young man in question took another to wife as soon as he received news of your departure. And even if he has remained true to his troth, merely think on the future, Shwaykar. Nothing is easier for a man than to divorce a wife he once held most dear, in the blink of an eye. Trust no man born of woman, my child. Sallafa speaks to you from long experience."

The radiant smile that instantly sprang to Shwaykar's lips upon hearing these words bespoke a crushing victory over such trifling arguments. She had boundless faith in her beloved Rukn al-Din. "The young man that I love is unlike those of whom you speak, my Lady. I am confident of his constancy. He shall soon come to this city to seek me."

Sallafa laughed lightly while her heart raged at the joyful innocence of these heartfelt words. "And what is the name of this singular young man, pray tell?" she archly inquired.

"His name is Prince Rukn al-Din Baybars al-Bunduqari. Surely you know him, my Lady? Not a soul there is in all of Cairo that does not know his worth. Am I then wrong to love him as I do?" Her eyes shone as she said this, and she fell upon Sallafa's hand to kiss it. "By God, my Lady, you and you alone can save me. You caused me to be brought to this city, and you surely have the power to send me back to Egypt." Sallafa struggled to control herself. Shwaykar's plea had aroused her own thwarted passion, as well as her spite. "I know Prince Rukn al-Din," she murmured, "and verily, he is a most excellent prince. If you are sure of his love I shall do my best to aid you, for I have grown very fond of you, my child, and wish for nothing but your happiness."

Shwaykar believed her. "Truly, my Lady? You shall return me to Egypt? Thank you, oh thank you! Deliver me as soon as possible, I entreat you!" and she fell upon her hand, but Sallafa pulled the weeping girl to her bosom in a viper's embrace.

"You must be patient, Shwaykar. This is only your first day in the Commander of the Faithful's palace and he expects to hear you perform this very evening. Rest assured, however, I shall leave no stone unturned until I have devised a way to send you back."

Shwaykar's mind was now at ease. She put all her hopes in Sallafa and thanked God for having brought them together in this place.

The Subterfuge

SALLAFA PACED THE ROOM, frowning deeply as though pondering a momentous problem. "Listen closely," she suddenly said. "If you insist on returning to Egypt, then we must not waste a single moment. Once the Commander of the Faithful has heard you sing it will be exceedingly difficult to remove you from Baghdad."

Shwaykar was now more than ever convinced of Sallafa's solicitude and the sincerity of her offers of assistance. "And what course of action does my Lady advise? I am the hostage of her will, and shall do anything to which she commands me."

"We must commence this very instant. You shall complain of a headache and a sore throat. I will inform the Qahramana that you are severely indisposed. Then I shall contrive to have you removed to a nearby palace that the Commander of the Faithful has placed at my disposal. Once you are safely there it will be much easier to smuggle you out of the city."

Shwaykar was unable to prevent herself from falling at Sallafa's feet to kiss them. "Thank you, my Lady, thank you! I am sure I already feel the onset of a terrible headache!" Sallafa produced a scarf that she proceeded to wrap tightly around the girl's head. That very instant, the slave Aqhwana entered the apartment. "The Qahramana has sent me to inform my Lady that she grows impatient for Shwaykar. She would have her returned at once, for the Commander of the Faithful is expected shortly."

"Look at the poor child," Sallafa said, pointing at the prostrate Shwaykar. "She has taken gravely ill of a sudden. Look how she shakes and shivers. I have given her a physic but it has had no effect. The Qahramana shall be obliged to make her excuses to the Commander of the Faithful until the girl recovers." Aqhwana left to take the dire news to the Qahramana, who promptly came in person to see the stricken Shwaykar. "How can this be?" she demanded of the maid in a

160

loud, rasping voice as she waddled heavily into the room. "His Highness is due to arrive at any moment. He has long awaited the arrival of this particular singing-girl. How can she take ill, now that she has finally been delivered to us?"

Her restless eyes fell upon Shwaykar lying prone on a couch. Sallafa hovered anxiously over her. Her color had changed dramatically and she moaned softly from time to time while Sallafa bestowed tender caresses on her shivering body. The Qahramana took note of all this and felt pity for the girl. "Very well then," she sighed. "The child shall be moved to the infirmary and placed under the care of our chief physician."

"Do not trouble yourself, my friend," Sallafa quickly replied. "Let me take care of my wretched countrywoman," she said as she gently covered Shwaykar with a blanket and felt her cheek and forehead. "I shall nurse her back to health in my own palace, and with more solicitude and affection than any physician can show her."

The Qahramana sighed again in resignation. "Do as you see fit, Sallafa. Only be quick about it. His Highness is likely at the end of his patience." As she took her leave, she mentally prepared her excuses to the Caliph, who had no doubt promised himself an exceptional evening of entertainment after having so long waited to come into the possession of his prize. As fate would have it, the Caliph's own page accosted her as she made her way back to her apartments to inform her that his Highness wished to see her immediately. She hurriedly turned her steps to the Imperial Wardrobe and found the Commander of the Faithful dressing in preparation for his evening of revelry on the Terrace. "Where is the new singing-girl?" he demanded abruptly as soon as his eyes fell upon the Qahramana. "We have finally taken possession of her after long delay, thank God. Have you put her voice to the test? Have you heard it? They say that it is the most exquisite and artful of female voices in the Empire. It is high time that I take some rest from the tiresome business of governing. May God forgive that rascal Abu Bakr, for he is the sole source of my many cares." Al-Musta'sim chattered on in this manner while his attendant dressed him in a fine, diaphanous gown and wove a small turban around his head. The Qahramana stood respectfully silent and waited until he finished speaking. The moment finally came when she had no choice but to break the unhappy news. "His Highness's slave, Shwaykar, has fallen ill."

"Ill?" he roared. "I parted from her but a few hours ago and she was then the picture of health!"

"She has contracted a fever that she fears will kill her, my Lord. His Highness's servant, her countrywoman Sallafa, has taken charge of her."

Al-Musta'sim frowned. He tossed aside the silk sash that his servant had given him to wind round his waist and wearily threw himself into a chair. "Good God," he sighed. "One aggravation after another. This slave is indeed a wellspring of ill fortune. She has caused nothing but trouble from the moment she left Egypt! And now that we have finally found her, she has taken ill." He lowered his eyes in thought for a moment, then resumed. "Would that she had remained with Abu Bakr, and that we had not grown angry with him on her account. Do you suppose that her malady is fatal?"

"I know not, your Highness. She complains of a severe headache and pains in her throat. She is likely to recover in a few days. If she does not, another can easily take her place. His Highness possesses many singing-girls. Shall I prepare one of them now for his evening's pleasure?"

"Very well," the Caliph gloomily replied. "I am in need of rest after the day's trials. Have you been informed of our dispute with Abu Bakr?" he added sharply.

"Indeed, your Highness. If his Highness permits me to speak, his Excellency Prince Ahmad was wrong to have acted as he did in purloining his father's prized possession. And yet he is but a fond youth who only dares to make a natural claim on his beloved father's generosity." This last expression soothed Al-Musta'sim. Indeed, he had only questioned the woman in order to receive this very answer, for he regretted the rough manner in which he had used his son. He knew that his Qahramana adored Abu Bakr and that she was fully aware of his own partiality towards the youth. Al-Musta'sim was given to discussing many private and public matters with her, in spite of the fact that she was confined to the Harem. She knew of all that took place at court and did not hesitate to interfere quite frequently in the politics and intrigues that there reigned. Al-Musta'sim himself invited her meddling, and was given to all sorts of vain strutting and preening in her presence. The result of all this was that she held great influence over the Caliph. Such is the sad state of affairs in all declining states.

The Caliph's heart was pleased by her defense of Abu Bakr. "You speak truly," he nodded. "It is only his filial fondness that makes him act thus. The Dawadar has encouraged the boy's recklessness, rather than curbing and taming it as is his duty."

The Qahramana disliked the Dawadar, for he was at heart a rough soldier who treated her rudely and looked down upon her as a slavish female. She therefore immediately agreed with the Caliph's assessment. "Indeed, your High-ness, the Dawadar should have restrained my Lord Abu Bakr, out of loyalty and affection for the Commander of the Faithful. His loyalty is false, however. His Highness will no doubt agree that while it is possible to exchange his Dawadar for a better one, he has only one son." She laughed out loud at this little joke, which pleased her no end. The Caliph responded with a similar laugh. He had perfectly understood the meaning behind the pleasantry. "Send for Abu Bakr," he said in between chuckles. "I wish him to attend this night's entertainment so that we may recompense him for the sorrow we have caused him today."

The Qahramana bowed deeply in reply and took her leave.

A Newcomer

MEANWHILE, MU'AYYID AL-DIN, having sent his unwitting messenger to Hulagu, was once more plunged into mental turmoil. Remorse and relief competed for dominion over him, though relief was foremost. He remained cloistered at home all that day, and for many days after, as well, for the staggering nature of the deed he had committed and the anxiety that continued to haunt him left him ill-disposed to see or speak to another living soul. The Caliph's unusual silence doubled his apprehension. During Mu'ayyid al-Din's lengthy absence from court, the Commander of the Faithful had never once summoned him, nor even inquired after his health. Mu'ayyid al-Din inferred that the Caliph had changed towards him, and he clung to the solitude of his quarters like a condemned man who awaits news of his fate.

One day while he was thus occupied, he heard a familiar knock at the inner gates. It was Sahban, finally come in his turn, after a long and somewhat disquieting absence. Mu'ayyid al-Din was particularly glad to see his blustering young friend walk through the door on this occasion. He welcomed him warmly and bade him be seated at his side. "What news, Sahban?" he inquired uneasily, after a close examination of his guest's face. "I perceive dark clouds gathered above that fine brow of yours."

"You are not looking so well as the last time I saw you, either, my Lord," Sahban moodily remarked. "But why should this change of condition surprise you? Your own counsel shall lead us down the path to perdition soon enough." He bit his fleshy lower lip in frustration.

Mu'ayyid al-Din understood this remark as a criticism of his stubborn loyalty to Al-Musta'sim. He gave a bitter little laugh. "My dear friend, the next world may well be a better place than this one."

"Perhaps, but let us at least be avenged before proceeding there."

"It shall be as you wish," Mu'ayyid al-Din solemnly replied.

Sahban was taken aback by this unexpected answer. "When?" he eagerly demanded.

"Sooner than you think. Who knows? Tomorrow perhaps."

Sahban was now genuinely baffled. He rose and began frantically pacing the room. "What mean you, my Lord? Surely, you have mistaken my words."

"I have understood you perfectly. Do you not wish to be rid of this tyrant, though it be at the price of seeking outside aid?"

"I do!"

"It is done. We have only to await the result."

Sahban looked about him fearfully. "You have written to Hulagu?" he whispered.

"I have. You would have known it many a day since, had you come to me sooner. I would know your opinion, Sahban," he added thoughtfully.

"My opinion?" Sahban joyfully declared. "I have wished for nothing else! If my hopes are fulfilled, I would happily drop dead on the spot this very minute! But I come to you today with discouraging news, though it shall never be a real obstacle to us."

"Speak!" Mu'ayyid al-Din demanded.

"The Imam Ahmad has been moved to another prison. It may be that his absence of a fortnight ago was discovered. In any case, they have taken him to a palace near the Kalwadhi Gate in the southern part of the city, and they have doubled his guard. But let them do as they will," he shrugged dismissively. "He shall be our Caliph wherever they take him. We shall have no difficulty releasing him when the time comes. After the Tatars enter Baghdad and capture Al-Musta'sim, you shall guide them to Imam Ahmad's prison and he shall be invested with the Caliphate on the very spot. Oh, what a joyful day that shall be! And then we shall have our 'Alawi state! My heart's one true desire!"

Mu'ayyid al-Din stared at him in wonder. He almost envied Sahban his seemingly endless optimism and his unshakeable, though entirely unjustified, confidence in the certainty of success. A man of this character may well err and fail, but he is yet closer to true happiness than the cautious or suspicious man who grasps happiness in his hand while doubting its existence. For Sahban, the simple fact that Mu'ayyid al-Din had written to Hulagu meant the war was already won. The many great dangers and obstacles to come simply did not occur to him. "We pray God to favor us in the coming battle against the tyrants," was all Mu'ayyid al-Din could think of to say as he pondered his friend's strange disposition.

While they were thus occupied, another knock was heard at the gates. Though in the normal course of events, Mu'ayyid al-Din never paid much attention to the daily commerce between his household and the outside world, this past week his anxious ears were constantly strained for the slightest signs of movement. He now fixed his eyes on the door to the apartment in which they conversed, and sure enough, shortly thereafter Sahban's servant entered.

"Where do you come from, boy?" Sahban demanded of him.

"I have come from the house, master. A stranger asks for you. He insisted that I bring him to you immediately."

"Who is this stranger? And where is he now?"

"He refused to tell me his name, but he is here and awaits permission to enter."

Sahban turned inquiringly to the Minister. "Let him enter," Mu'ayyid al-Din said.

The boy promptly returned with a young man dressed in handsome traveling clothes. Sahban recognized him immediately. "Prince Rukn al-Din!" he cried, and hurriedly rose to welcome him.

Mu'ayyid al-Din had been expecting this visit since the day that Sahban had brought Shwaykar to him. He was glad to meet the excellent young man again after so many years, and he graciously rose to greet him in his turn. "Welcome to Prince Rukn al-Din," he exclaimed warmly. "I have been following your intrepid career in Egypt from a great distance and I am all the more pleased on the occasion of this happy meeting."

"You flatter me, sir, for I am but a humble servant of the Sultan and have done nothing to merit such generous recognition," Rukn al-Din replied. "If praise be due, it belongs to my Lord Minister Mu'ayyid al-Din al-Alqami, he who holds the reins of the Abbasid State in his capable hands and guides its affairs with his wisdom and sagacity."

"Prince Rukn al-Din's fame precedes him," Sahban politely declared. "He is a great hero whose valiant deeds in the wars against the Franks I have recounted time and again to my Lord Mu'ayyid al-Din. May he know equal success against the enemies that even now threaten the health and prosperity of the Imperial State," he added meaningfully.

Mu'ayyid al-Din was by now used to Sahban's rash speech. He ignored this last remark, as did Rukn al-Din, who was the Minister's equal in prudence and caution. Sahban was somewhat embarrassed by their studied silence and he immediately changed the subject. "When did you arrive at Baghdad, my Lord? And how did you find my place of residence?"

"I arrived this morning," Rukn al-Din replied. "You yourself told me in Egypt that you reside in Qadhimiyya. As I am not entirely unfamiliar with Baghdad, I dismissed my servant and entered the city disguised as a common traveler. At Qadhimiyya I inquired after you, and was told that you were to be found at the house of his Excellency the First Minister. I have come to see you on urgent business and to pay my respects to his Excellency, whose brilliant reputation travels far and wide throughout the Empire."

"You are most welcome, dear Prince," Mu'ayyid al-Din replied in response to this compliment.

Sahban now resolved to broach the subject of Shwaykar, for whose sake Rukn al-Din had come to Baghdad. "Permit me to speak of the mission with which you charged me in Egypt, my Lord. His Excellency the Minister is aware, in part, of its details. He holds you in particularly high esteem and is anxious to serve your interests."

"You speak of Shwaykar, no doubt," Rukn al-Din replied. "I had long expected a letter from you on this subject," he added reproachfully, "and having received none, I have come in person to hear the results of your research."

Sahban flushed at this gentle rebuke, and he hastened to apologize and to offer his excuses. "You speak truly, my Lord. But I have not tarried out of negligence. As soon as I arrived in Baghdad I managed to discover Shwaykar's whereabouts. I attempted to rescue her from her persecutors, but my attempts have so far failed. What use would it have been to write to you with no concrete results? The Minister is aware of the difficulties that have beset us in this matter."

"Where is she now, then?" Rukn al-Din demanded.

"She was in the Caliph's household only two days since. But she has disappeared again, my Lord!"

"How can this be? Explain yourself, man," Rukn al-Din replied. "By whom was she first abducted?"

"She was seized by Abu Bakr, son of Al-Musta'sim, without his father's knowledge. We managed to free her and take her to a hiding place in Qadhimiyya with the intention of bringing her to you in Egypt as soon as circumstances permitted, but Abu Bakr discovered her hiding place and seized her once again by force of arms. His father subsequently discovered the truth of her whereabouts and demanded her restitution. All this is a long story, but the most important thing that you will surely wish to know is that Shwaykar has not changed since leaving Egypt, my Lord. She remains entirely devoted to you. Her only concern is for your good opinion; her only wish, to return to your side. I am certain that she lives in the Caliph's own harem against her will. We must save her, but patience is necessary, for we are on the threshold of a momentous event which shall turn Baghdad upside down and whose echoes will reach as far as Egypt, Andalucía—the whole world! A great event," he added meaningfully, "from which the resolute and judicious man may well profit."

Mu'ayyid al-Din feared that Sahban intended to use this introduction as a prelude to divulging their plans. He broke in hastily before Sahban could continue. "Wonder not, young Prince, at the remarkable nature of the narrative you have just heard. Our Caliph prefers to spend his time scouring the Empire for new singing-girls, while the enemy approaches the gates of the city and our armies languish in disarray."

"I heard much talk of the Tatar Khan's advance at the outskirts of Baghdad. They say his mighty army is less than two days' march away from the capital. Have you made no preparations to meet him?" Rukn al-Din asked.

"Indeed, we have done the best that can be done, but I shudder at the coming battle, nonetheless. A fortnight ago news reached us that Hulagu's army under the leadership of his greatest general, Baiju, had reached Tikrit and crossed the Tigris to the western bank in the direction of Baghdad. Precious time was lost in debating the appropriate strategy for the defense of the city. By the time the Tatar army had arrived at Dujayl, no solution had yet been decided. Their army numbers approximately thirty thousand mounted men. The Dawadar, Mujahid al-Din Aybak, shall ride out to meet them at the Caliph's command, but our army is small by comparison and we are uncertain of success. Moreover, dissension at the Abbasid court is rife. Our Caliph is weak. He is led by his son and his Commander in Chief, both of whom are inexperienced and foolish men. Verily, we fear that God has decreed the end of this Empire."

"Fear not such an outcome!" Sahban passionately declared. "Rather pray that it should be so! This prince is aware of our true situation. I have already spoken with him in Egypt about the future restoration of a Fatimid Caliphate there."

Mu'ayyid al-Din was greatly wroth at Sahban's headlong recklessness in speaking so openly, but he clenched his jaw and maintained his outwardly calm demeanor. "I doubt that the Prince sees eye to eye with you on this fantastical subject, Sahban." He turned to Rukn al-Din and looked him steadily in the eye. "For the present, we must be content to replace a lackluster Caliph with one who will exert himself for the good of the Empire."

Rukn al-Din returned the Minister's unswerving gaze with cool composure. Ibn al-Alqami's prudence and resolve pleased him. "His Excellency the Minister's proposal must strike any intelligent man as a sensible one," he began, "particularly those who would gladly reach deep into their own purses in order to avoid great bloodshed. Once you have decided on a course of action, I undertake to guarantee its successful implementation in Egypt." He secretly resolved, however, to make this promise of aid conditional on his own elevation to the Sultanate.

Mu'ayyid al-Din divined, and approved, the deepest thoughts of this gifted and ambitious young man. He now regretted having acted so precipitously in summoning the Tatar hordes and thereby imperiling the mighty Abassid Caliphate. For what if Hulagu were not content to depose Al-Musta'sim and allow the Imam Ahmad to be invested in his place? He shuddered at the thought. "We shall gratefully consider your offer of aid, good Prince, and we pray that our efforts shall bear fruit," he said aloud.

Rukn al-Din now deemed it proper to return to the subject of Shwaykar. He turned to Sahban. "And what of Shwaykar? How shall I recover her? I have neglected country and duty and travelled to these distant lands for her sake. Shall I then return without her? Impossible!"

"My Lord, the eunuch who brought you Shwaykar's letter, 'Abid, is lodged under my roof at present. It was he who aided her flight from Prince Abu Bakr's palace and he is, moreover, attached to the harem of the Imperial Palace. Two days ago he came to inform me that Shwaykar was suddenly taken ill and removed from the Imperial Harem to an unknown location. If she had escaped, she would have no doubt immediately come to us. 'Abid is even now trying to discover news of her. He has most likely returned to our house in Qadhimiyya. Do you wish to go and speak to him in person?"

"Let us go at once," he replied. "I will not rest until I have found her. Only then will I be at liberty to turn my attention to the urgent political business that presently claims our attention. Away with us, Sahban." He rose and begged leave to withdraw, which was cordially granted by Mu'ayyid al-Din.

The Tatars

BAGHDAD WAS MUCH CHANGED since Rukn al-Din had last seen it in the days of his youth. The neighborhood of Qadhimiyya lay on the other side of the Tigris from the Minister's palace. With Sahban as his guide he crossed the bridge to the western portion of Baghdad, where the city that Al-Mansur had built five and a half centuries earlier had lain. Nothing now remained of those magnificent structures but a few ruins. A noisy market and rows of dilapidated buildings had sprung up in place of the glorious Imperial complex of old. Rukn al-Din was suddenly distracted from these observations by the sight of a group of terrified people running towards the bridge that he and his companion had just crossed. Recognizing one amongst them, Sahban called out to him. The man detached himself from the crowd and hurried towards them. His legs were covered in thick mud up to the knees, as though he had just been wading in the turbid river.

"Why all this hurry, man?" Sahban inquired.

"It's the Tatars, master Sahban—the Tatars are upon us!"

Sahban caught his breath at this revelation. "Have they even now arrived?" he demanded. "Where are they camped?"

"Here," the man replied, his voice shaking. "Here, at the very gates of Baghdad!"

"And the Imperial Army?" Sahban demanded. "They went forth to do battle at Dujayl with the Dawadar at their head . . ."

"These Tatars are of the evil race of *djinn*," the man babbled on. "None can stand in their way. I was near Dujayl the very day they descended upon it. No sooner had word of their coming spread than the people, terrified, took flight towards the city with their women and children, in a state to be much pitied. Grown men threw themselves into the river for fear of the invader. The boatmen will only take those who can pay them handsomely across the river to safety.

They are greedy for coin and gold. One woman even paid her fare with a richly embroidered robe. We were told that the Caliph's army had come to vanquish these devils, but alas, they were utterly routed by the Tatars, who gave chase to those who retreated and killed or captured thousands. During the night, the wily devils dug a canal in which those who fled were drowned in a sea of mud. Only those who threw themselves headlong into the river were saved, I amongst them." He paused to gain his breath and pointed to the thick mud that covered his legs.

Anger mounted steadily in Rukn al-Din's breast as he listened to this ignoble account of the Imperial Army's rout.

"And the Dawadar? What has become of him?" Sahban demanded.

"He has retreated to Baghdad with what's left of the army, defeated and broken, like our very own hearts, master. May God have mercy upon us!"

Sahban briefly pondered the narrative he had just heard. "What do they look like, these Tatars?" he continued.

"Devils, one and all! They gobble up our men like so many sheep. I have never seen such creatures in all my life. Hurry and quit this road, master, for they are surely close to Baghdad by now and perhaps they have already entered the city. I have heard that a company of them is camped at the Azudi Hospital and another has arrived at the *Mabqala* near al-Rusafa. Only the Tigris stands between them and the royal palaces now. Hurry, master, flee the Tatar arrows that fall like rain. Nay, never have I seen the like in all my life!" He said this and hurried off as though pursued by all the legions of hell.

Sahban turned to Rukn al-Din, whose eyes had by now grown red with rage. A dark and furious frown creased his brow. "What ails my Lord Prince?" he lightly inquired, barely able to suppress the victorious smile that hovered over his lips.

"What ails me, you ask? Woe to you, Sahban! Have you no love for your native city, man? Is this the comportment of the Imperial Armies? Do the troops flee the savage face of the Tatar and hide under their beds? Were I but mounted with my doughty men at my back I would show these cowards how a battle is joined!"

Sahban laughed and, taking Rukn al-Din by the shoulder, turned into a narrow alley. "Your valiant sentiments are useless, my Lord. This dynasty's days are numbered. Their empire is spent, their tyranny at last come to an end. If God had willed their victory, He would have long ago opened their eyes and led them down the straight path. But their conduct has been like that of a blind man who stumbles about and knows not what he does. Let us leave them to their fate. Only God can deliver them, if He pleases."

A peculiar-looking arrow of a kind that Sahban had never before seen suddenly fell to the ground before them. He picked it up and upon closer examination discovered it to be inscribed with writing in Arabic letters. This is what it said:

The 'Alawi Chiefs and all those who do not resist us shall rest secure in their lives, their women-folk, and their property.

Sahban handed the arrow to Rukn al-Din, who read it in his turn. "It seems that the Shi'a have allied themselves with the Tatar invaders," he muttered.

Sahban only shrugged in response to this complaint. "The Shi'a have been ill-used, my Lord. Is not the persecution they have already suffered for generations enough? If the Tatar are to be victorious and the 'Alawis serve them justly, neither they nor we should be blamed."

Rukn al-Din was forced to acknowledge the reason in Sahban's words and the futility of railing against the dictates of fate. He once again reminded himself that he would do better to concentrate his energy and wits on finding Shwaykar and returning her safely to Cairo. They wove their way through a spiderweb of narrow, abandoned alleys in order to avoid the crowds of fleeing refugees that were now everywhere to be seen. Finally they reached the Azudi Hospital and in the near distance spied the banks of the Tigris and its immediate hinterland spread out below them and covered, like a great carpet, with the Tatar encampment: horses, tents, banners, and prisoners. Sahban stopped to contemplate the impressive sight. "Do you see the Tatar, the strength of his body and the roughness of his hands? See how he rolls up the cuffs of his trousers and how his eyes seem about to pop out of his head? These men have spent days and nights marching, on their feet, sleeping only rarely and taking nothing but mare's milk for nourishment—just like the first Muslim Bedouins, who needed nothing in the world but their camels for transportation, food, shade, and company. So it is with the Tatar and his horse. They say that a Tatar soldier can even outrun his mount! As for the soldiers who defend Baghdad, they have grown used to vain comfort and emasculating luxury, like the Byzantines before them. Can we struggle against fate, my Lord? The end is decreed for one and all and God alone does as He wills. Let us continue on to Qadhimiyya to find the good 'Abid and seek news of Shwaykar."

Rukn al-Din returned no reply to this discourse, for the sight before him had rendered him speechless. Mighty indeed was the Tatar, he reflected. Only a miracle could now save the Mother of Cities from ruin.

They left the Azudi Hospital behind them and descended towards Qadhimiyya. Rukn al-Din could not help but remark the difference in mien between the people of this quarter and the residents of the other towns they had passed through. Here, in Qadhimiyya, a measure of tranquility reigned and the inhabitants went about their business calmly, nay, almost cheerfully, as though the coming Tatar victory were their own, or as though the Tatars were a Shi'ite dynasty that had come to liberate them. Men love anyone who gives them succor, no matter how distant the ties that bind them, and they hate those who strip them of their rights, though it be their own brothers. A few men approached Sahban to greet and congratulate him heartily on the imminent collapse of the House of 'Abbas. Sahban graciously returned their greetings, but he repressed all outward signs of joy in the fearsome presence of Rukn al-Din.

'Abid

FINALLY, THEY ARRIVED AT SAHBAN'S HOUSE. Sahban welcomed his guest and bade him be seated in the reception room while he went to inquire after 'Abid. A few moments later, he reappeared with the gentle eunuch. As soon as he saw Rukn al-Din, tears sprang to his eyes and he grasped the Prince's hand to kiss it. Rukn al-Din was astonished at this peculiar behavior. "What news, good 'Abid?" he inquired as he withdrew his hand and motioned to him to sit by his side. "Where is Shwaykar? What has become of her?"

"My Lord, as I promised you in Cairo, I have exerted the utmost effort on my mistress Shwaykar's behalf. Once I had found her, I did not part with her for a single second. This time, however, was different. The soldiers seized her and I could do nothing about it."

Rukn al-Din was somewhat baffled by this confused account. "But where is she now?" he continued.

"The last definite report that has reached me is that she is currently detained in the Palace of the Crown."

"Brother Sahban has informed me of this. He also told me that you went to seek more news of her but yesterday. What have you discovered?"

'Abid stared at his feet morosely for a moment before replying. "The accounts of the Harem eunuchs with whom I spoke differed. They all agreed that she had been taken gravely ill on the day of her arrival at the palace, that she was consequently unable to sing for the Caliph, and that she spent that night in the quarters of a royal concubine from Egypt by the name of Sallafa."

Rukn al-Din started violently. "Sallafa?" he cried. "Sallafa is here in Baghdad?"

"Yes my Lord, they say that she was until lately the Custodian of the Righteous King's Palaces in Egypt and that she has great influence at the Palace of the

Crown thanks to her friendship with the Palace Qahramana and the Majordomo. Even the Caliph himself is said to respect and esteem her."

Rukn al-Din now feared the worst. He well recalled the threats that the slave Sallafa had hurled at him on the occasion of their last meeting. This unexpected encounter with Shwaykar could only spell disaster. "And since then?" Rukn al-Din continued breathlessly.

"I have had different accounts of what happened after that night. Some say that Sallafa took my Lady to a palace at which she lodges near the Kalwadhi Gate. Others contradict this report and claim that she remains sequestered at the Palace of the Crown." 'Abid hesitated for a moment and his expression grew dark. "There are some who deny both claims."

Rukn al-Din urged him on. "What do they say? Speak!"

"They say that Shwaykar has simply disappeared, they know not where, nor how she was made to vanish."

"Sallafa has murdered her!" Rukn al-Din cried.

"God forbid, my Lord! They say that Sallafa is my Lady's dearest friend, that she showed her uncommon favor and that she spared no pains to secure her comfort and wellbeing when she was taken ill." Rukn al-Din shook his head impatiently and turned to consult Sahban on this dangerous turn of events.

Sahban was otherwise occupied, however. He had moved slightly apart during the first part of this conversation to discuss the Tatar advance with some of his men, and upon rejoining the company had remained plunged in deep thought. He was unaware of Sallafa's enmity towards Shwaykar, but he was well acquainted with the former's boldness and malice, as the Reader knows. "Sallafa is a wicked woman," he said to Rukn al-Din. "She cares not for the consequences of her evil actions. I know her well. If she has come to Baghdad, her presence at the Caliph's palaces is certainly an evil omen. If once she resolves on a course of action, she dashes into it with all her being. Be not fooled by her kindness to Shwaykar or by her pretense of friendship, for if she perceives a benefit to herself in doing the girl harm, she shall not hesitate."

Rukn al-Din agreed wholeheartedly with this assessment. Fear and fury made his chest rise and fall like that of an angry lion. He rose precipitately to take his leave, but Sahban held him back. "What do you intend to do, my Lord?"

"Intend?" he replied distractedly. "I intend to look for that cursed woman. By God, if she has laid a finger upon Shwaykar I shall sever her head from her body!"

"Calm yourself, my Lord," Sahban replied. "You shall not so easily find her now, for she is at the Caliph's palaces and under his protection. But these very palaces shall soon open their doors to one and all. Then we shall be free to deal with Sallafa as we wish, and with many others besides. By God's grace we shall find Shwaykar hale and hearty and all will be well," he chuckled. "Come with me now. I would show you something to lighten the mind and sustain the soul."

They quit the house and Sahban led his guest to a nearby mosque whose spiraling minaret commanded a breathtaking view of the entire city. He pointed to the eastern part of Baghdad, where the royal palaces stood. "Look at al-Rusafa, my Lord, from whence we have just come. There lies the Imperial complex with its palaces, schools and gardens. The great wall that surrounds them to the east boasts a number of gates and towers, among them an immense tower at the southeastern corner, the 'Ajami tower. If you look closely you will see a vast field of tents and banners spread behind it. These are the tents and banners of the great Khakan."

Rukn al-Din gasped in wonder. "Hulagu is even now in Baghdad?"

"He came from the east at dead of night and besieges Baghdad from the direction of the 'Ajami Tower. I have only just heard that his great General, Baiju, has entered Baghdad from the west. There are two other divisions besides this and the one we have already seen: one at the Azudi Hospital and the other at the *Mabqala,* quite close to the Palace of the Crown. Do you still hope for an Abbasid victory?" he added maliciously.

"The Imperial complex is well fortified," Rukn al-Din replied uncertainly. "The Tatars will not take it as easily as you think, my friend. The great wall of which you speak is stalwart, as are the soldiers that defend it."

Sahban merely shrugged. "We shall see. But now let us descend. I shall go to consult our wise Minister on the best course of action in these new circumstances. Pray wait my return, my Lord. I shall not tarry." Sahban left him in the care of 'Abid and the rest of his servants, and departed on his mission.

Rukn al-Din and Sahban

NOW FINDING HIMSELF ALONE, Rukn al-Din was plunged into gloomy reflections on Baghdad's imminent fate. He was inclined to believe that the Tatars would be victorious in the coming battle. If they did indeed manage to take the city, would they overthrow the government and bring down the Caliphate? Or would they retain the sacred institution and simply replace one Caliph with another? His own ambitions in Egypt would certainly be aided by the current weakness of the Sultanate. He was fully aware that he would need the support of the Caliph in Baghdad to secure the throne of Egypt, however. His thoughts turned to the glory and might of Baghdad, the very center of the entire Muslim world from its easternmost lands to the farthest west. No king could sit securely on his throne without the sanction of Baghdad, for the common folk revered the Caliphate as an article of their deepest faith.

The present perils that beset the Imperial city grieved him mightily, and he wondered at the illusions that dominate the minds of men. Power, as Rukn al-Din well understood, depends most keenly on illusion, through which it bends and shapes the populace to the will of the ruler. An extraordinary idea suddenly occurred to him, and his heart leapt with excitement. Why not move the Caliphate itself to Egypt? Cairo would then become the beating heart of the Islamic world that no prince or sultan, however independent, could do without. Had Rukn al-Din been a man like Sahban, he would have danced for joy and imagined himself already seated on his Egyptian throne and supported by an Egyptian Caliphate, while the princes and monarchs begged his favor. But our worthy prince was pessimistic about the future, and was inclined to dwell on any and all possible impediments to his plans and ambitions. He preferred to assume failure. The many obstacles to this farfetched plan now crowded in on his mind and he pushed them aside with a deep sigh, preferring for the moment to return to the immediate problem of finding Shwaykar.

'Abid had twice interrupted him during these solitary reflections: once to call him to table, and a second time to prayer. Shortly before sunset, the eunuch came to inform him that Sahban had returned from his visit to Mu'ayyid al-Din. Soon thereafter, Sahban himself appeared with furrowed brow and angry eyes. "What news, Sahban?" Rukn al-Din began. "Have you seen the Minister?"

"I have not," Sahban glumly replied.

"And why not?"

"He is not at home. He left shortly after we took our leave of him. I was told that Al-Musta'sim sent him to Hulagu's encampment. It seems that the Caliph has finally awoken to the dangers that beset him. His faith in our Minister's ability is apparently renewed, and he has secretly sent him to negotiate with the Tatar."

"It has come to this, then . . ." Rukn al-Din murmured as he considered the consequences of this new development.

"The Caliph's decision to send Mu'ayyid al-Din on this mission is the best decision he has taken in many a month, though I fear it comes too late. Our Minister—may God preserve him—has influence with Hulagu and can negotiate an outcome that shall suit both parties."

"I do not understand what you mean by the Minister's influence over the Tatar. Was there previous acquaintance between them?"

"I shall not hide from you that the Minister and Hulagu have secretly corresponded. Hulagu proffered alliance and promised him many benefits in consequence. For many a month Mu'ayyid al-Din hesitated, bent as he was on further attempts to reform Al-Musta'sim. When he had finally despaired of success, he wrote to Hulagu, for the sake and safety of his kinsfolk and of the Shi'a of Baghdad." Catching sight of the look of astonishment on Rukn al-Din's face at this revelation, he added, "Our Minister only pretended his surrender. It is no treachery, my Lord."

"Mu'ayyid al-Din has betrayed his Caliph!" Rukn al-Din thought to himself in bitter irony. "And so the mighty Empire doth fall." He held his tongue, however, and continued to question Sahban. "What course of action do you then suppose the Minister and Hulagu will decide?"

"I believe they will depose Al-Musta'sim and crown the Imam Ahmad, Al-Mustansir's brother, in his place. He is the scion of the Abbasid Dynasty most worthy of the Caliphate. For this reason, Al-Musta'sim fears him. He is a prisoner in his own palace, surrounded by guards and spies. We have nonetheless managed to see and parley with him. We have discussed the future of the Caliphate, and he has promised us nothing but good should it fall to his lot." Sahban paused and glanced slyly at Rukn al-Din. "I doubt not that he would help you to acquire the Sultanate of Egypt, should you choose to pursue it, worthy Prince, for amongst all your peers you are surely the most deserving of it."

Rukn al-Din realized that Sahban was covertly inviting him to join forces against Al-Musta'sim and assist in the installation of Prince Ahmad as Caliph. But were the truth to be told, the ambitious youth desired much more than this— he desired nothing less than the removal of the Caliphate itself to Cairo! He dissembled, however, and was content for the moment to give his tacit support to the planned succession. "Where is the Imam at present?" he inquired.

"He was confined in the Firdaws Palace, close by the Palace of the Crown. Since then he has been moved to a fortified palace near the Kalwadhi Gate. I know where it is, and can easily extract him from his prison when the time comes. We must first eliminate Al-Musta'sim. No one shall stand in our way, especially should Hulagu himself, Khakan of the Tatars, decree it. The people have grown weary of the weakness and indecision of our present rulers."

"An excellent plan," Rukn al-Din replied distractedly. "May God aid you in its execution." The mention of the Kalwadhi Gate had reminded him of Sallafa's mysterious presence in Baghdad. He recalled that 'Abid had told him that she had taken Shwaykar to a palace near this very Gate. His fears for Shwaykar's safety now returned in full force. Was she alive or dead? Did Sallafa still intend to harm her?

Rukn al-Din was more than ever determined to find Shwaykar and carry her back to Egypt as quickly as possible. If, however, she had fallen victim to Sallafa's wicked plots, then he intended to have his fullest revenge. In the meantime, his continued presence in Baghdad could only prove useful for his political ambitions.

That night when he finally betook himself to the quiet refuge of a warm bed, the lovely, tear-stained face of his betrothed haunted his dreams and gave him no peace.

An Important Message

THE NEXT MORNING 'Abid brought him a message. "My Lord, Sallafa's page is at the door and would speak with you on urgent business."

Rukn al-Din shivered imperceptibly, as though a sudden shadow had passed over the sun's warming rays. "Let him enter," he replied.

The boy entered and bowed deeply. "A note from my Lady to your Lordship," he said, and placed a slender scroll in Rukn al-Din's hand. *From Sallafa to Prince Rukn al-Din,* it began. *It has come to my knowledge that you are presently in Baghdad, as am I. There is a matter of great importance that I wish to discuss with you. Pray come to my palace at the Kalwadhi Gate. My messenger shall guide you. Peace.*

After he had read the note, Rukn al-Din handed it to Sahban, who strongly advised him to ignore it. "I cannot," he replied. "I have no choice but to accept an interview with that she-fox in order to ascertain Shwaykar's whereabouts. Besides, man, what can she possibly do to me? It is unbecoming of me to fear her whilst I carry my trusty dagger at my side. But tell me, in which direction does her palace lie?"

"It is far, my Lord," Sahban replied. "The longest part of the journey will be that portion that takes you to the Tigris Bridge that we crossed yesterday. Soon after the crossing you shall arrive at the Kalwadhi Gate. If you insist on going, my horse is at your service. 'Abid shall accompany you mounted, and this messenger on foot."

"I shall go immediately." Rukn al-Din rose with a look of stony determination. He disappeared into his chamber to change his clothes, and armed himself with two daggers. He then swiftly quit the house and mounted the horse that 'Abid brought to him. Rukn al-Din again observed the joyful expressions exhibited by the people of Qadhimiyya as he rode through its streets. Spite against their Sunni neighbors was evident in the passing snatches of conversation he heard around him.

The pride of Baghdad's Sunni population had derived from the Abbasid Caliph and his government, and the coming upheaval of the Sunni State had, in consequence, greatly diminished the Sunnis' collective confidence and sense of security. Outside Qadhimiyya, the mood changed drastically. Fear and dread ruled the streets, and Rukn al-Din saw many tight knots of men, seated or standing, avidly piecing together contradictory information from passers-by and anxiously discussing the latest rumors and reports.

He arrived at the aforementioned bridge and crossed over to al-Rusafa, where the streets were much calmer. In spite of the occasional crash of an enemy catapult, the inhabitants felt secure in their proximity to the Imperial Palace, for official propaganda did not cease to celebrate the might of the Imperial Army and the strength of the Imperial fortresses. The artillery fire from across the river was fairly negligible, and frequent cease-fires allowed people to circulate in the streets and markets. But the damage it caused was terrible to behold. If a projectile fell on a house, it clove the structure in two. If a man were its unlucky victim, it killed him instantly. These projectiles were round flint boulders whose diameter measured approximately half a meter. They were fired by the siege engines from the Tatar encampment, aiming at the Gate's towers or at the surrounding palaces. The soldiers stationed in the towers responded with catapults of their own. These antique machines were the cannon of those days.

Rukn al-Din's journey finally ended on the eastern bank of the Tigris. The messenger stopped and pointed to a palace on the riverbank surrounded by an enclosed garden. He entered through the gate on his mount, and the messenger preceded him to announce his arrival. Rukn al-Din descended and handed the reins of the horse to 'Abid, ordering him to wait and above all to be on his guard. He walked on into the garden, his heart pounding in anticipation of the coming interview, his mind's eye calling up the image of Sallafa on the day when they had last met.

The Meeting

A PAGE EMERGED FROM THE PALACE and beckoned to him to follow. There, at the doors of the sumptuous edifice, stood Sallafa, arrayed in her most magnificent robes and jewels and armed with her most effective arts of seduction. Rukn al-Din marshaled his prudence and his abiding love for Shwaykar. He greeted her, and she returned the greeting with effusive words of welcome. She invited him into a hall sumptuously furnished with *mokado* carpets, tapestries, and couches. "Who would have thought that we should meet again in this country?" she began as she beckoned him, with a beguiling smile, to be seated.

"Indeed, the coincidence is a marvel of marvels, my Lady," Rukn al-Din replied.

"Coincidence? Do you suppose that we meet now by chance?"

"Yes my Lady, for it did not occur to me that you had reason to travel to Baghdad."

"Perhaps so. For myself, however, wretched and desolate as I am, no course of action is too farfetched. I would give my comfort and my very life to encounter Rukn al-Din, wherever he may be." Sighing deeply, she continued, never once taking her opaque, restless eyes off his, "I have watched and considered your every step in Egypt, Rukn al-Din." Rukn al-Din began to grow uneasy at this inauspicious introduction, and he attempted to change the subject. "I thank you my Lady, for your good opinion of me," he began. "I have received your letter and have come at your request. I come to you, in turn, with a query, and I beg that you shall answer it honestly."

"Speak," Sallafa replied.

"I have heard that Shwaykar was lodged of late in this palace, and I call upon you to enlighten me as to where she may now be found." The many fears he entertained on Shwaykar's behalf danced before him, and he steeled himself for the reply. Sallafa dawdled over her answer. "Poor girl," she murmured.

"Why speak you so? Where is she, my Lady?" It was all he could do to keep from crying out in despair.

Sallafa sighed sadly. "She is not here, good Prince. You must recall that I once considered her a rival, and that I desired to be rid of her in order to enjoy sole possession of your affections. But when I became acquainted with her engaging person at the Caliph's palace, I regretted the torment that I may have caused her, for she is truly a sincere and kind-hearted girl."

Rukn al-Din grew exceedingly impatient with these evasions. "Sallafa, this is not the answer I require of you. What has happened to her? Where is she?"

"I have already told you that she is not here."

"I understand, but where is she, then? Speak!"

She glanced reproachfully at him. "By God, how hasty you are! Can a prince such as yourself, who seeks the throne and finds himself on the verge of acquiring it, be so impatient of receiving a short communication regarding a slave girl? Listen then—I shall tell you what has befallen the poor wretch. I saw her on the first day that she arrived at the Palace of the Crown, and I was greatly taken by her and regretted having been the author of her suffering. She, too, took comfort in my presence and she recounted her story to me from beginning to end. She spoke touchingly of her love for you, and how she could not bear to be separated from you, even if she were a favorite in the Caliph's palace. I advised her to feign illness and was able to convince the Caliph's Qahramana of the truth of her claim. I persuaded the woman that the girl was in dire need of a change of air. The following day, I came to this, my temporary abode, and I sent for her." She swallowed and fell silent.

"And then? Did she come?" Rukn al-Din prompted.

"Believe what you will. She is dead—that is all that matters," Sallafa suddenly blurted out.

Rukn al-Din rose furiously from his seat. "Nay, she is not dead," he declared. "You have hidden her somewhere."

"She is dead, Rukn al-Din, and you must believe me when I say that I do most sorely regret it. The sailors in whose charge she was sent informed me that she had fallen off the boat that carried her here and drowned, despite all their efforts to save her. Recover your reason, Rukn al-Din, and submit to God's will. Shall you indulge in womanish behavior and weep over the loss of a slave, while Sallafa stands here before you and offers you her person and a rank that no Sultan of Egypt has dared yet dream of?"

Shwaykar was truly dead then! Rukn al-Din's mind reeled from the blow. In spite of Sallafa's pretense of innocence and her claims of friendship for the wretched girl, he yet suspected her role in the tragedy. His heart clamored for revenge, but he could not be sure that she was, in fact, the author of so heinous a crime. He resolved to exercise his cunning and discretion in hopes of discovering the truth, and he therefore made a monumental effort to hide his anguish beneath a mask of stony self-possession. "Poor Shwaykar," he murmured. "Her death is a great loss to me."

Sallafa, who had been watching Rukn al-Din closely, was heartened by this measured response. "Poor child, indeed," she echoed, "it has weighed sorely upon me, as well. But what is to be done? We must submit to the decrees of fate. And now, great Prince, do you wish me to inform you of the glory to which, with my aid, you shall soon be raised?"

Rukn al-Din said nothing, but once again took his seat at Sallafa's side.

She was delighted that he had yielded to her so easily, and her face glowed with triumph as she spoke. "You have surely heard of the tumult that has befallen the government due to the Tatar siege. Hulagu's forces are camped at the 'Ajami Tower. The Dawadar, Commander of the Imperial Army, was unable to prevent their advance. His Highness, Commander of the Faithful, is sorely wroth with his General and intends to replace him. The Caliph's Majordomo has consulted me on the matter of a suitable candidate for the post; a champion who will restore the honor of the Abbasid Army and drive back the enemy from the gates of Baghdad. I have thought of none other than you—for you are always in my thoughts," she added, smiling. "None but you can rescue the Empire. If you become the Commander in Chief of Baghdad's army, your ambition shall thereafter know no bounds. I shall personally guarantee you Egypt's throne, or another, should you so wish. My only condition is that you acknowledge my love and my right to seek your own. Say then that you love me, or at least that you love no other!"

Rukn al-Din bowed his head in silence for a moment while he gathered his thoughts and struggled to master his conflicting emotions. We know him to be one of those supremely ambitious men who seek their own interests above all. We know that his love for Shwaykar was not unmixed with pity for the trials and travails she had been obliged to endure through no fault of her own. He had truly wished to make her happy. But now that she was dead, it would be unmanly to die in her wake. Though her death afflicted him greatly, and though his heart forbade him to love her mortal enemy, he felt it would be folly to ignore the dizzying prospects now offered him. He was convinced of Sallafa's great influence at Baghdad—he had already seen the proofs of it—and he knew that she was supremely well equipped to aid him in the realization of his greatest aspirations. But the dangers of the alliance she proposed were many, and mortal. He needed time in which to think in peace and solitude. "I am not fit to accept such a position, my Lady. Let us not speak of it now. We shall defer this discussion to a future occasion."

"This is a matter that cannot be postponed, Rukn al-Din, for the state is at war. Do you not hear the missiles that fall upon our palaces day and night? As for your suitability, I do not hesitate for an instant to put my full confidence in you. The only excuse that remains to you, cruel man, is that of my love. I have only asked that you accept it. How would you act if I were to demand that you return it, cold-hearted one!" She broke off peevishly and hearkened to the sound of voices in the outer vestibule. "Listen . . . the Majordomo has arrived. He comes for your answer. Do not confound me before him, I beseech you! We will postpone these matters of love till after you have seized your prize—and many others that I shall lay at your feet!"

At the Palace of the Crown

A SERVANT ENTERED to announce the Caliph's Majordomo, and Sallafa rose to meet him at the door. She welcomed him effusively and escorted him into the hall. Pointing to Rukn al-Din, she said, "This is the Prince Rukn al-Din al-Bunduqari, who vanquished the Franks and repelled them from Egypt. I have spoken to you of him at great length, and we are indeed fortunate to have him here with us in Baghdad. We were only now engaged in discussing the grave matter that you confided to me but yesterday."

The Majordomo glanced briefly at Rukn al-Din and inclined his head in greeting. The young man's intelligent mien and noble bearing pleased him well. "We shall be grateful to discover in Prince Rukn al-Din the superior martial qualities sought by the Commander of the Faithful. We hope that he may recompense us for the shame heaped upon us by the previous Dawadar. Let us go to the Palace of the Crown this very hour."

Rukn al-Din attempted, with many delicate and well-turned expressions of gratitude, to decline this great if precipitate honor, but the Majordomo dismissed his excuses as issuing from over-excessive modesty. He continued to press the Prince, who, finding that his protests were useless, was obliged to submit to the mighty Imperial officer in good grace. As they took their leave of their hostess, Sallafa threw Rukn al-Din a look full of passionate languor and pressed his hand in a parting salute. "I confess that I am delighted to have succeeded in fulfilling the charge laid upon me by our most excellent Majordomo. Brave Prince, you shall, with God's aid, deliver the state from the grave dangers that threaten it." She drew closer and whispered in his ear. "As for myself, should I now die, I shall depart this world knowing that you submitted to me in this, though the knowledge of it only increases the fires of longing that burn in my heart. If we are fated to meet again, you shall have a token of their ardor."

Sallafa's impassioned farewell struck a reluctant spark in Rukn al-Din's heart, but he let no sign of this escape. He returned her salute and silently followed the Majordomo into the courtyard. Once outside the palace gates, they mounted their beasts and proceeded to the Palace of the Crown, with 'Abid trailing behind on his mule.

Rukn al-Din passed the short distance to their destination wrapped in deep thought, for his interview with Sallafa had once again confounded him. Shwaykar was dead, Sallafa claimed innocence, and he now found himself on the point of taking an important step in the direction of his dearest ambitions. Had he acted rightly? He had stayed his hand and refrained from seeking the blood of Shwaykar's mortal enemy. He was a sensible and realistic young man, however, and he decided that revenge would yet be his, should he ascertain beyond the shadow of a doubt Sallafa's complicity in his betrothed's death.

The three men rode on in silence. Rukn al-Din was oblivious to his surroundings, and he paid no attention to the frenetic comings and goings of passers-by nor yet to the distant explosions made by falling canon. Upon arriving at the Palace of the Crown, however, he found its residents in a state of utter chaos and great terror, for much of this incessant bombardment was directed at the Imperial compound itself. Being unsure of Palace protocol, he watched the Majordomo in order to be guided by his movements. When he dismounted, so too did Rukn al-Din, and he proceeded to follow the Majordomo on foot until they reached the Commons Gate. The Chamberlain met them there, and the Majordomo requested permission for an audience with the Caliph. As soon as this had been granted, they entered the Reception Hall.

The Majordomo gave the customary greeting and then addressed the Caliph. "I beg the Commander of the Faithful to permit me to introduce Prince Rukn al-Din Baybars al-Bunduqari. His Highness will recall that I have already spoken to him of this Prince and of the excellent qualities that would make of him a most suitable Commander of the Armies of Baghdad in these perilous times. Sallafa, the Royal Chamberlain of Al-Salih of Egypt's Palaces, has testified to his renown as a warrior and a leader of men."

Rukn al-Din noted that the Caliph was withdrawn and pensive. His head was bent as though the cares of the world lay upon it, and a deep frown creased his brow. He was entirely alone in the reception hall, as though wishing to avoid any and all company and diversion. The words of his Majordomo raised him from his lethargy. He gestured for his guest to be seated. "Welcome to Prince Rukn al-Din. Does the Majordomo speak truly, then?"

"His good opinion, if nothing else, equals truth, your Majesty. I, however, hesitate to endorse his claims, for I am nothing but the lowest of officers."

The Caliph was pleased by these modest words. "Nay, you are a valiant warrior whose fame is justly celebrated throughout our Empire. Moreover, I have the highest confidence in the testimony of Sallafa, the Royal Custodian. Young Prince, we are at war with a foreign invader, the enemy of all Muslims, for if he should prevail here—God forbid—Egypt, too, shall surely suffer. You are charged with annihilating him in defense of the Abbasid Caliphate and the Sultanate of Egypt, and you shall triumph, God willing. If we had but known of your merit heretofore, we should never have confided the leadership of our armies to this Dawadar. He has brought nothing but shame upon us. May God grant that you shall be the means by which we shall erase this blot on the name of the Imperial forces." He shifted nervously in his seat as he said this. Rukn al-Din remained silent and respectfully waited for him to finish his speech.

"We erred in ignoring the counsel of our Minister Mu'ayyid al-Din. Had we given him our ear, we would not now be obliged to seek parley with the enemy and to sue for peace: a suit of which the outcome is far from certain. May God forgive Abu Bakr," he murmured sorrowfully, almost to himself. "He abused the natural right of a son and muddied our heart against our Minister. And now, listen closely, Prince. I hereby raise you to the rank of Dawadar of the Imperial Army," he solemnly declared. "If you succeed in repelling the enemy, your reward shall be equal to your success."

Rukn al-Din bowed deeply. "The defense of the Abode of Peace and the Commander of the Faithful is the duty of every Muslim," he replied. "I shall exert the last drop of my blood to this worthiest of ends, and may God be my support."

The Chamberlain now entered and announced the presence of the Minister Mu'ayyid al-Din. Upon hearing this news, the Caliph's face lit up and his eyes glinted with curiosity. As soon as Mu'ayyid al-Din entered, Al-Musta'sim, unable to restrain himself and too eager to give the customary greeting, cried, "Tell us, Minister, what news do you bring?"

"Good news, God permitting, your Highness," Mu'ayyid al-Din replied.

"Be seated and speak," the Caliph commanded.

The Minister did as the Caliph bade him. He was out of breath and his face was drenched in perspiration from the haste he had made in returning to the Imperial Palace. "Your Highness, I met with the Khakan of the Tatars, Hulagu, as you commanded me, and exposed to him the injustice of this aggression against us at great length, in addition to which I made clear to him that we do not fear him in the least, but only wish to prevent further bloodshed. He replied coldly, and after much discussion he refused to end the siege unless his Highness, the Commander of the Faithful, comes in person to sue for peace. He promised that his honor and dignity would be preserved and respected, and that the Caliphate would be upheld and honored. This, he said, is the Khakan's custom in dealing with the great kings he meets in battle. He informed me, moreover, that he cares not a fiddle for the game of king-making, but only for the honor of his troops; and furthermore, that he considers the Commander of the Faithful's refusal of aid in the war against the Isma'ilis, and his subsequent silence in response to the Khan's letter of reproach, to have been the gravest of insults. The Commander of the Faithful's continued silence in the face of the Khan's most recent demand for the capitulation of myself or the Imperial Dawadar is considered by the Khan to be yet another insult added onto the first two, an insult that can only be righted by the submission of the Commander of the Faithful himself. The Khan repeated that the Commander of the Faithful, along with the princes and officers of his entourage, shall be given every honor, as befits their rank most high. Finally, the Khan notified me that if we comply with these conditions, he shall willingly grant his eldest daughter to Prince Abu Bakr in marriage."

Mu'ayyid al-Din was severely discomfited by the news he brought the Caliph, and his face glistened with beads of heavy perspiration as he spoke. The Caliph, however, received the news in immobile silence, his head bowed and his brow furrowed, as did Rukn al-Din. Once Mu'ayyid al-Din had finished, the Caliph raised his head and sighed deeply. "If only I had listened to your counsel from the beginning, we would never have reached this pass. I dare to hope that we may yet be victorious over the Tatar and repel him from our lands, now that we have given the command of our armies to Prince Rukn al-Din."

Mu'ayyid al-Din, who had up until this moment not perceived Rukn al-Din's presence in the Imperial audience chamber, and who was unaware of the Dawadar's disgrace, turned to look at him in surprise. "Rukn al-Din is indeed worthy of your confidence, your Highness, and we may yet have victory at his hands. But

I fear that our troops are weaker than we suppose, and that if we refuse Hulagu's terms, we may miss a final opportunity to sue for peace. We have been offered a treaty that will stanch the blood-letting. The decision belongs to his Highness." He bowed deeply and fell silent.

"Does the tyrant truly insist that I go alone to his camp?" the Caliph repeated incredulously.

"By no means, Your Highness. He has agreed to allow the Commander of the Faithful's favorites and counselors to accompany him to the pavilion that shall be raised for them at the Kalwadhi Gate on the riverbank. Hulagu shall meet Your Highness there, and the matter will come to a close."

The Caliph was inclined to accept the Tatar's terms, but first he turned to consult the Majordomo. This personage quickly gave his approval of the scheme, for he shrewdly saw that this was the Caliph's own inclination.

The Caliph now made his will known, after which he turned to Rukn al-Din once again. "You have heard our Minister's counsel. We have failed to accept it in the past, and this failure has brought us nothing but grief. We now intend to rectify our past mistakes, but we nonetheless consider Prince Rukn al-Din to be one of our leading commanders and we shall recompense him well for his service to us." Rukn al-Din bowed deeply and the Caliph turned to the Minister. "Once the pavilion is raised, we shall go forth. You are charged with this matter, Mu'ayyid al-Din."

The Minister bowed deeply and requested permission to withdraw, and with this the council came to an end. Mu'ayyid al-Din signaled to Rukn al-Din to follow him home.

The Caliph's grave capitulation had shocked Rukn al-Din, and he could not help but suspect Hulagu's true intentions. He feared the Caliph was walking into a trap. He kept his misgivings to himself, however, and rode to the Minister's palace with 'Abid by his side to act as guide. He counseled himself to be patient, for he knew that he would no doubt get to the bottom of the matter soon enough.

The Truth

RUKN AL-DIN was escorted into Mu'ayyid al-Din's private chambers and found the Minister, who had arrived, himself, but a few moments earlier, restlessly pacing the room with furrowed brow and an expression of the greatest distress on his face. Sahban sat silently by, waiting for the Minister to acknowledge his presence with a word. Mu'ayyid al-Din nodded at Rukn al-Din to be seated and, coming to an abrupt halt before him, finally spoke. "Oh Prince, fate shall now take its course!"

Sahban leaned forward eagerly. "What mean you by this, my Lord?"

Mu'ayyid al-Din turned upon him. "It shall take the course that you have long desired, and not the one for which I had hoped, nor Prince Rukn al-Din," he cried bitterly.

"My Lord, I beg you to explain these grave words," Rukn al-Din said.

"I was unable to persuade Hulagu to preserve the Abbasid Caliphate. He is intent upon its destruction."

"Its destruction?" Rukn al-Din cried, aghast. "Does he intend to kill every last Abbasid?"

"This is indeed what his tone and manner implied, though his words affirmed the opposite." The revelation was like music to Sahban's ears, and he chuckled softly to himself, as does one who cannot believe his sudden good fortune. "You laugh because you consider not the consequences," Mu'ayyid al-Din sternly upbraided him. "If the Abbasid Caliphate ceases to be, Islam itself shall vanish from these lands."

"Nonsense!" Sahban declared. "We shall reconstitute the Caliphate."

"You are a fool and a knave!" Mu'ayyid al-Din cried impatiently. "If you hope to restore the Fatimid state, you hope for the impossible and would resurrect the dead." Sahban fell into a sullen silence at this stinging rebuke, but he continued to gloat in his heart over what he perceived to be a great Shi'ite victory. Meanwhile, Mu'ayyid al-Din turned his attention back to Rukn al-Din. "You have kept your silence, Rukn al-Din," he remarked. "I would have your opinion."

"If this tyrant truly intends to destroy the Abbasid line, he shall cause a breach in the Empire of Islam that shall be most difficult to repair. But why, then, did you tell the Caliph that Hulagu intends to spare him?" he added.

"This was Hulagu's pledge to me," Mu'ayyid al-Din moodily replied. "I do not trust him, however, for his eyes spoke otherwise. He has given me his ensigns and has urged me to hang them from the doors of homes that I would protect, and particularly those of the Shi'ite quarters of the city. His men will respect them as tokens of amnesty. Does this not prove his true intentions?" he demanded, as if to himself. "In any case, we must prepare for the worst." He walked to the far end of the room and returned with a number of yellow banners on each of which a red dagger had been painted. He gave one to Rukn al-Din. "Take this. You may have need of it." He then gave the rest to Sahban. "Hang these at the entrance of our people's quarters in Karkh and Qadhimiyya. Be discreet, so that none shall notice what you do."

Rukn al-Din folded the banner that Mu'ayyid al-Din had given him and reluctantly tucked it underneath his cloak. The thought of using it was repugnant to him, for he was a valiant and battle-hardened warrior whose doughty sword spoke for him and his men. But he was also a pragmatist and knew the importance of giving every situation its due. He took his leave soon thereafter, lost in a welter of turbulent thoughts. 'Abid brought him his horse, and he mounted with no particular destination in mind. Then it occurred to him that he would do well to seek out Sallafa for one last and decisive interview. On the way to her residence, he carefully reconsidered his own ambitions in light of Mu'ayyid al-Din's awful revelation of Hulagu's true intentions. Such is the nature of all men and women in all times and places. Those fine words that describe the virtues and that flow so easily from the pens of poets—generosity, kindness, unity, courage, charity, and so forth—are most often nothing but so many different terms that revolve around a single sense: that of self-interest. Collective action, though it be ever so virtuous, can never succeed unless its ends benefit the individual members of the enterprising group.

Rukn al-Din pondered the deepest ambitions of his heart, all of which revolved around the Egyptian Sultanate, and he saw a clear connection between this and the passing away of the 'Abbasid state. He consequently turned his thoughts to the advantage he might draw from the present circumstances, and the unlikely idea that had dawned upon him the day before returned to haunt him. Why should he not aspire to make Egypt the capital of the Abbasid Caliphate? A feeling of tranquil confidence descended upon him as the idea grew and took root in his mind. His thoughts quickly turned to the Imam Ahmad, and he resolved to seek him out and rescue him, if possible, from the coming slaughter. If Hulagu truly intended to murder every last member of the House of 'Abbas, he, Rukn al-Din, would shelter and maintain the last remaining scion. Once Sultan of Egypt, he would declare the Imam the new Caliph of the Abbasid Empire at Cairo. His heart leapt with joy as he contemplated this happy conclusion to his plans.

He proceeded on the road to the Kalwadhi Gate lost in thought. Only the great bustle and commotion that reigned at the Gate succeeded in awaking him to his surroundings, for it was here that the pavilion in which the Caliph was to meet Hulagu was being erected. Rukn al-Din recalled that the Imam Ahmad's place of imprisonment was nearby. He called 'Abid to his side. "They say that the Imam Ahmad, the Caliph's uncle, is imprisoned in a palace near here. Do you know where it is?"

"I believe it to be this one, my Lord," and he pointed to a palace behind the one that Sallafa occupied.

"Do you have any acquaintance amongst his servants or guards?"

"No, my Lord, for he was brought here not long ago. But if you wish it, I can easily infiltrate the household. Do you wish to pay him a visit now?"

"First I would see Sallafa once more. I shall not tarry long in this country, and I must do my utmost to discover Shwaykar's true fate. Do you wish to return with me to Egypt, faithful 'Abid?"

"To accompany you thence would be the greatest honor, my Lord," 'Abid gratefully hastened to reply. "But what of Shwaykar? Can she be truly dead? And if she be yet alive, you shall surely not leave without her?"

Rukn al-Din slowed the pace of his horse and smiled wanly. "You are indeed a true and loyal fellow, 'Abid," he replied. "Fear not. We shall get to the bottom of this matter, and then my hand shall be guided by the dictates of courage and constancy."

Rukn al-Din's horse sauntered slowly on the riverbank while 'Abid kept abreast of him. The horse reached a fragrant clump of bushes and stopped to nibble at the tender shoots. Rukn al-Din had fallen silent and 'Abid now spoke. "My Lord, my counsel must surely be beneath your notice, but I beg leave to speak freely, nonetheless. I have heard of this Sallafa that she is the most evil of women, and the most cunning, for even the Caliph cannot deny her any favor. You shall be alone in her palace, and she might easily betray you, or summon a band of villains to overpower you."

Rukn al-Din was touched by this solicitous consideration, yet another proof of the eunuch's devotion. "Do not be afraid, good 'Abid. You shall wait and watch in the palace gardens. If you notice the least unusual circumstance, sound the alarm by calling out to one of the passing boatmen who ply their trade on this river. As soon as I hear this call, I shall be forewarned. Above all, do not leave our mounts unattended, and make sure that they are saddled and ready for instant flight."

'Abid bowed in obedience, and they entered the garden. The guard hastened to inform Sallafa of Rukn al-Din's arrival, and after having changed into her most sumptuous gown, she descended to meet him and led him into the reception hall, with many smiles and words of welcome. "I hope that you have succeeded in your suit, my Lord," she said as she motioned for him to be seated.

"And what suit may that be, my Lady?" Rukn al-Din replied.

"Why, did you not go this very morning to the Commander of the Faithful in the company of the Majordomo to receive the command of the Imperial Army? Has the compact been sealed?"

"Nothing of the sort transpired. It seems that you have not heard of the treaty between Hulagu and the Caliph."

"Indeed?" Sallafa replied uneasily. "And what are its terms?"

"The Caliph sent his Minister Mu'ayyid al-Din to Hulagu to negotiate a truce. He returned from that mission during my audience with the Caliph and informed him that nothing less would pacify Hulagu than that the Caliph himself go out to meet him at Kalwadhi Gate. If you look from this window, you will see the carpenters erecting the pavilion in which the appointed meeting shall take place. The war is now over and the Caliph has no further need of a Dawadar—at least for the present."

Sallafa rushed to the window and looking out, saw that all was as he had said. She wrung her hands and slapped her cheeks in despair. "Woe unto him! Has he fallen so low? The Commander of the Faithful goes forth from his Imperial

Palace to pacify the wrath of his most bitter enemy? Farewell then to the Caliphate and its subjects!"

Her eyes shone as her mind worked quickly to calculate the consequences of this unprecedented development, while Rukn al-Din waited for her to continue. Finally she spoke. "There is no longer any reason for us to remain in this country. We must depart instantly. All my jewels and personal possessions are yours to dispose of. Let us not waste a single moment!"

"Where would you go, my Lady?" Rukn al-Din replied.

"To Egypt."

"Alone?"

"We shall take whom you will of servants and retainers."

He stared at her intently for a moment. "And what of Shwaykar?" he demanded.

"Have I not told you, Rukn al-Din, of Shwaykar's misfortune?" she impatiently replied.

"My heart refuses to believe you in this, Sallafa. I came from Egypt to Baghdad to seek Shwaykar and I shall not return without her!"

She tossed her head in irritation, but forced a smile to her lips. "What would you have me do, my Lord? I cannot bring her back from the riverbed where she has surely by now become food for the fish!"

"Nay," he answered coldly. "She is not dead. I am certain that she is alive and hidden in some place. Look for her, perhaps you shall find her. I shall not go to Egypt without her," he repeated.

Sallafa's exasperation grew at these strange words. "What mean you by this?" she demanded. "Surely you jest, sir. Shwaykar drowned in the Tigris, I tell you. If you do not believe me, come, and I shall show you the proof of what I say." She took his hand and led him through a corridor and to a chamber that gave out onto the river. She proceeded to a cabinet, unlocked it and withdrew a purse from which she took out a clump of long hair. She presented this to him and he immediately recognized it as belonging to Shwaykar.

"Is this not the hair of Shwaykar, the poor wretch who died in the flower of youth?" Sallafa demanded.

"Indeed, it is! But how did it come into your possession?"

"The boatmen whom I charged with carrying Shwaykar hither from the Palace of the Crown brought it to me. They informed me that the boat in which they were traveling overturned in this place," and she pointed to a spot on the river just below the window by which they stood. "The men tried to save her by plucking at her clothing and her hair, but she drowned and naught but these locks were left in their grasping hands."

Rukn a-Din's breast rose and fell as he struggled to contain the anger that boiled within him. He lowered his eyes as he considered his next step, for he was sure that Sallafa had actively sought Shwaykar's death. She placed her hand on his shoulder and smiled coquettishly. "You believe me now, I suppose. Oh, Rukn al-Din! If you only knew of the great love I bear you. It is high time that you take note of it and that you return to your senses. You must understand that I will stop at nothing to please you. You are already aware of the lengths to which I went to make you the Caliph's Dawadar and the greatest commander in all the lands of Islam. Do not be angry that this has not come to pass, for I have prepared Egypt's throne for you and have cleared the path to it. Nothing remains for you to do but to return to Cairo and seize the scepter."

Tree of Pearls and ʻIzz al-Din

THE WORDS "EGYPT'S THRONE" set his heart pounding anew and cooled his wrath. He wished her with all his soul to prove the truth of her words. He therefore remained silent as she gazed curiously at him and finally, taking his hand, she led him to a small terrace overlooking the Tigris. She nodded for him to be seated and seated herself beside him. The river's clear waters rippled delightfully before them but Rukn al-Din saw nothing of this natural beauty, for he was greatly wrought up. Every muscle in his body was tensed to spring instantly and at the slightest provocation.

"I suppose you would like to know the details of my claim, and of all that I have accomplished to ready Egypt's throne for the reception of Rukn al-Din," she began. "Oh, if you but felt the raging force of my love, cruel man! But you shall, once you hear of the great deeds I have effected for love of you."

She shifted in her seat and toyed with one of the long braids that lay on her shoulder as she gazed out at the river. "When you left Cairo, Al-Ashraf sat upon the throne with ʻIzz al-Din Aybak as his Regent."

"So it was," Rukn al-Din solemnly confirmed.

Sallafa laughed lightly. "They are both departed, and Tree of Pearls with them."

"Departed? Whence?" he demanded, greatly puzzled by this enigmatic statement.

"To the underworld!" she cried.

Rukn al-Din started. "Surely you lie! How can such a thing have come to pass?"

"God forgive you for accusing me thus, Prince. Sallafa does not lie—unless it be to serve her one and only master. Verily, in this cause I have committed acts much worse than falsehood. I have betrayed and I have murdered for Rukn al-Din, and yet he still begrudges me a warm word or look." Her eyes brimmed with real tears and a sob escaped her lips as she spoke these words. Rukn al-Din resolutely ignored the small pang of sympathy that her tears evoked and steeled himself to hear the rest.

"You left 'Izz al-Din content in his role of Regent to the child-king and Tree of Pearls resigned to her lot. If matters had remained so, it would have been impossible for Rukn al-Din to seize power. And even should he have made such a move, the most he could have hoped for would have been the Regency, for the House of Ayyub monopolizes the throne. I intend to raise Rukn al-Din to the Sultanate, just as I promised him. Shall I tell you what I have done?"

He leaned forward eagerly to hear the rest of her speech, and she continued. "I believe you are aware of the place I held in 'Izz al-Din's heart and my influence over his mind, for I was the cause of his gaining the Regency after Tree of Pearls was deposed. I caused her to be deposed and I caused 'Izz al-Din to be invested. I caused the Princes to choose an Ayyubid Sultan. I did all this to prepare your own way to the throne, cruel one. I recounted all this to you when we spoke in Cairo, but you paid me no heed. I came close to despairing of you, to hating you even, and I resolved to avenge myself on your cold obstinacy, but my heart would not obey. I remained true to my love and continued to seek your interests by any means. First, I induced 'Izz al-Din to destroy the boy-king, al-Ashraf. He threw the child into the deepest and darkest of dungeons where he shall soon expire, if he be not already dead. 'Izz al-Din then seized the throne and none dared to challenge him. Egypt is now free of the Ayyubid yoke, Rukn al-Din!

"Once this had been accomplished," she continued, "I proceeded to plot 'Izz al-Din's removal to make way for my own beloved. This was no easy task, thanks to the number and strength of his men. I made Tree of Pearls herself, his former paramour, my instrument in this. I caused her to be informed by a few of her slave-girls that 'Izz al-Din was to be married to the daughter of the Ruler of Mosul, Badr al-Din Lu'lu'. I prevented 'Izz al-Din from seeing Tree of Pearls for some months, and this led her to believe in the truth of the rumor. You are well acquainted with that woman's crude and ruthless heart. As she brooded over this second betrayal, her fury grew and multiplied till she prevailed upon some attendants to strangle the usurper in his bath. It was later put about that he had fainted in the bath and died of an epileptic fit."

"'Izz al-Din is dead?" cried Rukn al-Din.

"Dead, never to return," she replied. "As is Tree of Pearls."

"How can this be?" Rukn al-Din was now thoroughly astonished.

"When 'Izz al-Din died, his son Nur al-Din Ali was elected to the throne. I had a hand in the upbringing of this youth, and he hearkens to my counsel. Once he was crowned Sultan, I revealed to him that Tree of Pearls had plotted against his father, and I encouraged him to seek revenge. He charged the women of his house with this mission, and they beat her to death with their clogs and threw her corpse into the Citadel's moat. The dogs ate half of her lifeless body and the remains were buried in the Cemetery of our Lady Nafisa."

Rukn al-Din stared, aghast, at the woman before him. "You were the cause of all this?"

"I was," Sallafa proudly replied, "and I executed each link in the chain of my design for your own sake. Now, if you go to Egypt, you shall find none to oppose you. I hold Nur al-Din in the palm of my hand. If you command it, I shall have him murdered as well, and make you Sultan of all Egypt."

This abominable conduct in a woman horrified Rukn al-Din, and yet the thought of so easily possessing the throne was near to tearing his heart from his breast. He hung his head and reflected for a moment, and his eyes fell upon the dear locks of hair that Sallafa had carelessly cast aside. The image of Shwaykar now returned to his mind, and he recalled that it was Tree of Pearls who had first received their vows. The wretched woman before him had confessed to having caused the death of many, and his heart told him that she had also engineered the murder of Shwaykar. Indeed, what should prevent her from murdering him if once she doubted his friendship or despaired of his love? He was at a loss as to how to proceed. Sallafa grew impatient with his silence, and spoke again. "See you not what crimes I have committed for your love, cruel Prince? And you still call me to account over a slave-girl whom you might easily replace for a hundred dinars? Put this coldness aside. Let us forget the past and quit this place for Egypt. Your final happiness is my only desire. Take all I possess."

Rukn al-Din reflected that if he submitted to her he would become Sultan and his most cherished ambitions would thereby be fulfilled, but no sooner had the thought crossed his mind than he pushed it away in horror. Shwaykar's image and all that she had suffered through his own fault lingered before him. He suddenly rose, and Sallafa rose too, believing that she had finally convinced him to surrender to her love. Rukn al-Din reached out to take the clump of hair in his hand and he stared at it intently. "I suppose your pity for the owner of these locks still troubles your conscience," she rallied him. "But what good can it now do you? Here is the hair of a woman who lives and speaks and wants nothing but your good will," and she teasingly held out one of the luxurious black braids that fell over her shoulders.

"Is she really dead then?" Rukn al-Din repeated morosely.

"Good God, man!" she cried in frustration. "Have I not told you so time and again?"

"You only repeated the account of the boatmen. Perhaps they lie."

"Nay, they lie not! And why on earth should they?"

"They have some motive . . ."

She gazed at him furiously with a mixture of violent longing and keen exasperation that gave her eyes a fiery cast. "You have constrained me to prove the slave's demise beyond the shadow of a doubt," she finally declared. "She is dead. I am the one who planned her execution! This too I did for your sake, and for mine, for I will brook no rival for your affections. Like the others, the girl was sacrificed to your own interests."

Upon hearing this awful confession, Rukn al-Din could no longer control himself. With a quick glance he ascertained that the hall beyond the chamber that they occupied was empty of attendants, and looking out the window next to which he stood, he saw 'Abid motioning for him with a rapid gesture of the hand to mount the attack. He swiftly withdrew his dagger and plunged it twice into her heart. Sallafa fell to the floor and expired instantly. He sheathed his weapon, and grasping the locks of Shwaykar's hair in his hand, he hurried from the room.

The Imam Ahmad's Palace

'ABID HURRIEDLY MET HIM at the gates with their saddled mounts. "May your right hand ever be firm!" he exclaimed. "You have avenged my Lady! Mount, my Lord, and let us leave this place." Rukn al-Din instantly did as he was bidden, and they made haste to quit the empty palace gardens.

"Why did you signal to me to hasten Sallafa's execution?" Rukn al-Din asked 'Abid as soon as they had left the palace well behind them and slowed to a brisk trot.

"My Lord, I discovered beyond the shadow of a doubt that she was the agent of my lady Shwaykar's death. I then contrived to empty the palace of its servants and retainers so that you were free to act. But I feared that the wily woman would yet convince you of her innocence, and that you would continue to postpone her chastisement."

"God bless you, 'Abid. Sallafa did murder Shwaykar. She confessed it to me with her own cursed lips. But tell me, how did you manage to make this discovery?"

"I insinuated myself into a company of her servants and we conversed on sundry subjects. I boasted to them of the many wicked deeds that I had committed in the service of my master—murder, theft, and the like—and this, as I had hoped, excited the tedious vanity of one present, who proceeded to boast in turn of how Sallafa had charged him and another lackey with conveying Shwaykar hither from the Palace of the Crown, and how she secretly ordered him to make the journey at night and to seize the first opportunity to throw her into the Tigris. The opportunity did not present itself, however, until they had almost arrived at their destination, for an unknown vessel trailed behind them for most of the way and observed their movements. At last the scoundrel resolved to take his chances: he cut off a few locks of my lady's hair, threw her overboard and took the trophy to his mistress as proof of having executed his commission. I then asked him if he had seen the lady drown with his own eyes and he replied that as it was so dark, he had seen nothing, but that he doubted not that the lady had met a watery death."

Rukn al-Din's conscience was greatly soothed by this vivid account of Sallafa's perfidy, and he told himself that she had indeed merited the sudden death that he had dealt her. A new hope had also now taken hold of him: that Shwaykar might yet have been saved by the grace of God. But he said not a word of this to 'Abid, and only urged him to quicken his pace in the direction of the Imam Ahmad's dwelling.

The sun was beginning to set as they continued on their way, when suddenly they spied a great company of Hulagu's troops galloping from the direction of the Ivory Tower to the Kalwadhi Gate and sending the terrified populace scrambling for cover. 'Abid led Rukn al-Din's horse away from the commotion and towards the Imam Ahmad's place of confinement. Rukn al-Din's thoughts were divided between Shwaykar on the one hand, and the terrible fate awaiting the Caliph and his family on the other. He wished to cast his eyes one last time over Baghdad in the soft light of dusk, and so he and 'Abid climbed a hill overlooking the Kalwadhi Gate and its environs all the way to the Ivory Tower. There he saw the Tatar hordes advancing towards the city, and a small company of them moving in the direction of Sallafa's palace and scaling its walls. 'Abid turned to Rukn al-Din. "Do you see, my Lord?" and he pointed to the palace.

"It seems they are intent on pillage, and I fear they will find none to oppose them. Only Sallafa, lying drenched in her own blood. Her servants shall surely share in the plunder and the killing. Thus is the end of all tyrants," he mused. "Would that it were given to me to witness the events that shall befall Baghdad on the morrow. But enough of this. We have no time to lose. Let us go at once to Prince Ahmad," and he turned the reins of his mount in that direction once more.

The gates of the palace were heavily guarded. 'Abid advanced and inquired whether the Imam was within. "He is," replied one of the guards, "but he is currently occupied."

"In what business?"

"He entertains a guest."

"Pray enter and seek permission for us to meet with him." 'Abid replied.

"He will see no one at present. The Commander of the Faithful has greatly restricted his company."

"We are strangers," 'Abid replied. "Night overtook us before we entered the city, and we now beg a place to lay our heads till the morrow."

"I must first request permission."

"Pray thee do so then," 'Abid replied.

"And what shall I say?"

"Tell his Lordship that we are travelers from Egypt and that we would pass the night under his roof."

The guard withdrew into the palace while Rukn al-Din remained mounted and 'Abid stood waiting at his side. After a long interval, he returned with another man who stared intently at Rukn al-Din as he approached. "Prince Rukn al-Din!" he cried. "Enter, my Lord, and welcome."

Rukn al-Din was somewhat surprised to discover that the person who now stood before him was none other than Sahban. He dismounted and passed with him into an empty and dimly lit hall in which not a living soul stirred. Rukn al-Din felt foreboding from this deathly silence, and he waited for Sahban to address him. Sahban remained silent, however, and so Rukn al-Din began. "Have you been long in conference with his Excellency the Imam, Sahban?"

"I arrived but an hour ago."

"Prince Ahmad is within?"

"He is, my Lord Rukn al-Din. He is dressing, and will go out shortly with the Caliph and his family to meet Hulagu at the Imperial pavilion."

"And who has counseled him to do so?"

"He goes, as do all the Abbasid Princes, at the Caliph's command."

"Shall you then allow him to depart with them?"

"And why should I prevent him? Let him go with the rest," he shrugged.

Rukn al-Din now perceived that Sahban truly welcomed the extinction of the House of 'Abbas. He was opposed to the fellow's fanatical dreams of a Fatimid restoration, as has been previously explained to the Reader, and he resolved to prevent Prince Ahmad from quitting his palace on this night of all nights. He stopped Sahban and said, "We must not allow the prince to be led to his death."

"He is not called to his death. The decree in which the invitation is inscribed merely states that he shall go out to Hulagu along with all the sons of his house."

Rukn al-Din grasped Sahban by the shoulder. "You know full well the truth that lies behind this treaty. We heard it together from Mu'ayyid al-Din's own lips but yesterday. Let the prince live."

"Is his preservation of such import to you then, my Lord?"

"Its importance to me is of no matter. Neither should his death be to you. Take me to him."

"Perchance he has already betaken himself to his appointment . . ." he stammered evasively.

"You lie, Sahban." He bristled with anger as he said this. "I charge you to produce him instantly!"

Sahban grew uneasy at Rukn al-Din's change of manner, and he hastened to appease his sudden wrath. "I perceive that I have angered you unnecessarily, my Lord," he mumbled. "If Prince Ahmad is yet to be found in the palace he shall certainly be happy to receive you." They had by now arrived at the doors of the Prince's private chambers. Sahban knocked, while Rukn al-Din stood waiting. He heard the prince say, "I have almost finished dressing."

"There is no need for ceremony, your Excellency," Sahban called, "for here is a guest who merely wishes to speak with you.

The doors opened to reveal Prince Ahmad sitting within. He had finished dressing in his robes of state, excepting the black turban, emblem of the Abbasids, which he still held in his hand. "Prince Rukn al-Din Baybars al-Bunduqari, whom I have only just mentioned to you this hour, has come from Egypt to meet with your Excellency," Sahban began.

Prince Ahmad smiled graciously. "Welcome to the valiant Prince. You shall be an honored guest of our house," and he motioned for him to advance into the chamber where he sat. "My attendants shall do their best to make you comfortable here until I return shortly from the audience with Hulagu."

"His Lordship must under no condition quit the palace this night," Rukn al-Din hastened to reply.

"The Commander of the Faithful himself requires it," Prince Ahmad replied in some perplexity at this outburst. "It is a condition of the peace that he has signed with Hulagu. I fear that my absence would cause some unforeseen mischief. I have consulted with Sahban, and he agrees."

"I believe he has now changed his mind," said Rukn al-Din as he glanced meaningfully at Sahban. "Ask him, my Lord."

Prince Ahmad turned to look curiously at Sahban, who swallowed and prepared to forswear his earlier counsel. "I have indeed changed my mind, your Excellency, for Prince Rukn al-Din has convinced me of the imprudence of your quitting the palace. It is best that his Lordship remain here this evening, and we shall wait and see what the morrow brings."

"And how shall I explain this to the messenger?" the Imam replied.

"Tell him that you are ill-disposed, your Excellency," Rukn al-Din suggested.

Sahban was greatly put out by Rukn al-Din's sudden arrival and the consequent faltering of his plans. He dissembled, however, and soon begged leave to withdraw, claiming that pressing business obliged him to return at once to Qadhimiyya.

This precipitate departure aroused Rukn al-Din's suspicions and he deliberated as to its possible consequences. He resolved to exercise the utmost prudence and cunning to protect the Imam from any plots that Sahban might devise against him. As soon as Sahban had withdrawn, Rukn al-Din turned to Prince Ahmad. "Has his Excellency long been acquainted with this Shi'ite?" he asked.

"It is so, my good Prince," he replied.

"And are you convinced of the sincerity of his affection?"

"He has never given me cause to doubt it."

"Do you then believe that the Shi'a are devoted to the interests of the Abbasid Caliphs?"

Prince Ahmad only bowed his head in silence.

"My Lord Imam, we are this very moment at the threshold of a great revolution in the affairs of the Caliphate. Does my Lord permit me to speak openly and boldly to him?"

Prince Ahmad was somewhat taken aback by the somberness of his guest's words. "Of which revolution do you speak, my friend? It is true that we feared revolt and sedition before this treaty between the Caliph and Hulagu, but we may surely now expect that our affairs will return to their proper course."

Rukn al-Din smiled sardonically at this speech. "My Lord's informants have been cruelly deceived, and if the primary source of his information be Sahban, then he has deliberately engaged in falsehood, for he is fully acquainted with the true state of affairs of the Caliphate, a condition that must inspire terror and disgust in all righteous souls—may God be our refuge and may He save the Imam Ahmad from its consequences."

The Imam was greatly affected by these words. The terrible apprehension they provoked increased in proportion to his admiration and awe of their speaker. He was now anxious to hear more. "I perceive the utmost gravity in every word that I have heard and every gesture that I have observed. Speak, Prince, explain yourself. I place my full confidence in you."

"If his Excellency had been guided by Sahban and gone out from his palace this night, not a single scion of the House of 'Abbas would be left in Baghdad!" His eyes shone feverishly in the flickering lamplight as he said this and produced a strange effect on the Imam. Rukn al-Din appeared to him almost to be a prophet who had only just descended from the heavens. "What mean you by this?" he anxiously demanded.

"Once they are conveniently assembled in the Imperial pavilion, Hulagu intends to put to death every living member of the House of 'Abbas under guise of this so-called peace treaty!"

A violent fit of trembling seized Prince Ahmad upon hearing this terrible declaration. "Did Sahban know of this?" he murmured.

"He did," Rukn al-Din replied solemnly.

"God's curse upon the villain!" he cried, "and may God bless you, my son. I shall never forget this favor as long as I live. And yet how my heart bleeds over the destiny of my kin and my people! Are you absolutely certain of what you have told me?"

"I am, my Lord. Tomorrow all shall be clear as the light of day. Would that the first light of dawn prove me wrong, that the peace be a real and enduring one, and that no mischief befall his Lordship the Imam. Should he by any chance fall into harm's way, my constant sword shall attend him, and my very life is his ransom."

The Imam's estimation of Rukn al-Din rose all the more at these valiant words and he resolved to submit to him in all matters, for had he not saved him from certain death? He proceeded to praise and thank him most warmly, though he was truly at a loss as to how to discharge the deep debt that he now owed the mysterious prince. Rukn al-Din interrupted him respectfully. "I have not finished, my Lord," he quietly interposed.

"Speak, friend," the Imam replied.

"If the House of 'Abbas disappears from Baghdad tomorrow, you shall be the last living Imam. You must not appear before the populace, but remain in hiding until God should decree that the Abbasid standard be raised once more in a free Muslim land. Cairo, once the capital of the 'Alawi Fatimids, shall be the new capital of the House of 'Abbas!"

The Prince's astonishment increased at these consecutive tokens of favor, and he saw that it was time to reward Rukn al-Din with a pledge of his own. "If God most high wills in His wisdom that the Caliphate should pass to me, then none other than Prince Rukn al-Din Baybars shall have the Sultanate of Egypt," he solemnly declared.

His words were music to Rukn al-Din's ears. His face betrayed not the slightest mark of his inner agitation, however, and he only replied, "The Sultanate must go to the worthiest prince amongst us, my Lord. As for the Caliphate, it is a hereditary right that can neither be bestowed nor transferred."

"Can there be anyone in Egypt more deserving of the throne than yourself, brave Prince?" the Imam cordially replied. He then fell into a gloomy silence as he pondered the astounding news he had just heard recounted. The murder of Al-Musta'sim and of all his kin at one fell swoop was almost more than his heart could bear, and his eyes filled with tears. "I beg your indulgence, Prince Rukn al-Din," he murmured sorrowfully. "I grieve for my beloved Baghdad."

"I share his Excellency's grief," Rukn al-Din replied. "But he is surely not ignorant of the causes of this great catastrophe, namely, the corruption that has overtaken the state, the weakness and licentiousness of the Caliph, and his unfortunate overdependence on hypocrites and flatterers. It seems clear that God has deprived him of His divine favor in order to bestow it on one more deserving."

Prince Ahmad only sighed and dried his tears. "Evening has overtaken us, my friend. Let us perform the evening prayer together while our meal is being prepared. We shall dine in each other's company, then retire to our beds for the night."

"I am at my Lordship's command in every matter but that of sleep. His Excellency shall go to his bed when he pleases. I shall remain awake through the night to keep watch. Sahban's hasty departure has aroused my suspicions, and we are in troubled times, as my Lord well knows."

His vigilance and zeal greatly pleased the Imam. "Here is a born leader of men," he thought to himself. "God bless you, Prince," he said aloud. "But why do you fear Sahban?"

"He has failed in his plot to send you to your death, and the overly easy manner with which he took his leave of us disturbs me," Rukn al-Din replied. "If he had quarreled with me or bitterly opposed my intervention, I should have been more tranquil. His silence can only augur ill, for it means that his rancor shall seek another outlet."

"But surely he is incapable of such treachery?" the gentle Imam wondered.

"It may be that I have judged him too hastily," Rukn al-Din mused, "but I nonetheless intend to remain alert. And now if my Lord desires it, I shall gladly accompany him to prayers." Prince Ahmad rose and the pair went to the private oratory of the palace, after which they returned to dine, while Rukn al-Din admiringly took note of the Imam's evident piety and sincere devotion.

Discovery

THEY SAT DOWN to take their supper, and Prince Ahmad showed his guest the utmost consideration and hospitality, all the while warmly endeavoring to express his gratitude at having been saved from certain death. "Thank me not, your Excellency," Rukn al-Din said to him. "It is surely only God's reward for one of your own many acts of goodness."

The Imam Ahmad smiled and bowed his head in contemplation. "Indeed, it may be so," he began. "Perhaps God did send you to me this night in reward for a kindness that I did but of late perform by His own command."

The Imam's modesty pleased Rukn al-Din, and he waited to hear the rest of his speech. "I thank Him for this good fortune, for it is one of His blessings, and it has been bestowed upon me in the midst of an existence awash with hardship and distress. My only crime was to have been a scion of the House of 'Abbas and a potential successor to the greatest of thrones. How I have complained to God of this, and wished that He had made me a man among common men! The Caliph, however, was not content to confine me to my home, but ordered that I be brought to this palace and placed under lock and key. God doth work in mysterious ways, for it was by this act of cruelty that I was permitted to save the life of a fellow human being. I was brought here in a small vessel at dead of night. My stout guards showed me nothing but the greatest kindness and respect, but sorrow and despair strangled my heart, and my soul silently raged at the tyranny to which I was obliged to submit. I sat apart in the bow of the vessel and watched the dark waters rippling past. From time to time my gaze would turn to the passing boats coming and going around us, and the sound of the sailors' calls or snatches of their song brought a small measure of comfort to my dark thoughts. A silent vessel glided near to us on the waters. The only sign of life it emitted was the weak light given off by a lamp that hung in its prow. A few minutes before we were to dock on the other side of the river, I heard a piercing scream and saw a dark shape plunge into the waters. Suspecting some crime to be afoot I called the captain of our boat and requested him to follow the mysterious vessel. He was under orders to deliver me forthwith to my prison and so was unable to comply with my petition, but after a thorough search of the waters around us, he discovered a half-drowned person, struggling to stay afloat and calling weakly for help. By God's will we were able to save the unlucky soul as it struggled to take its very last breath."

Rukn al-Din listened to this narrative with growing wonder and impatience, for he began to hope that the drowning person in question was none other than his beloved Shwaykar. Finally, he could control himself no longer. "Is she alive?" he cried out. The Imam was taken aback at this eager interruption, and even more so that Rukn al-Din had somehow divined the sex of the person of whom he spoke. He begged his guest to explain this strange insight.

"I know her, my Lord—I know her!" he cried, and he eagerly urged the Imam to continue his narrative.

"The sailors applied themselves to the task of reviving her until she recovered. We saw that her hair had been shorn and we questioned her on the train of events that had brought her to this sorry pass, but she was unable to speak and so we refrained from all further attempts at disclosure."

"It is Shwaykar, my Lord! Shwaykar! Allow me to see her, I entreat you. Is she not here?"

"No, my son, she is not. Had I known that she be of such importance to you, I would surely have detained her."

"Your Excellency, I entreat you to tell me where I may now find her."

"No sooner had we arrived at our destination than I gave instructions that her wet clothing be replaced and that she be permitted to rest. Once she had recovered, I begged her to explain her situation and to allow me to offer her any assistance that she might require, but thanking me profusely, she declined to reveal her history. The sailors guessed from the vessel that carried her that the girl was an Imperial slave who had fallen from favor and been sentenced to death by drowning. None of us dared to reveal the circumstances of her rescue to a soul, however. I asked her again if she knew anyone in Baghdad with whom she desired to take refuge. She replied that she wished to be taken to our friend, Sahban the merchant. We disguised her in the costume of a male servant, her shorn head making this undertaking easier to accomplish, and we sent her in the company of one of our men to Qadhimiyya and Sahban's house this very morning. When Sahban came to me today he had not yet received intelligence of her arrival."

Rukn al-Din was overcome by this unexpected news and his heart beat with joy that Shwaykar had escaped death's clutches. Her presence in Sahban's house disturbed him not a little, however. Imam Ahmad was now desirous of discovering the nature of the connection that bound Shwaykar to Rukn al-Din, and he urged his friend to tell his story. Rukn al-Din then narrated the history of the liaison from its beginnings in Egypt; of Sallafa's perfidy; and of his fruitless inquiries in Baghdad. Imam Ahmad now greatly regretted having sent Shwaykar to Sahban's house, though in truth he had nothing with which to reproach himself, having been entirely unaware of her true identity.

Pandemonium

AS THEY WERE THUS ENGAGED, they heard a great uproar in the palace gardens. The Imam Ahmad was greatly alarmed by the sudden din, but Rukn al-Din had been expecting it and was only surprised that it had taken this long to transpire. He signaled to the Imam to remain calm, and swiftly made his way to the palace doors like a lion bracing for an enemy attack. One of the guards had rushed inside and barricaded the doors. Rukn al-Din saw that the man was terrified.

"The Tatar, my Lord!" the guard shouted when he saw Rukn al-Din. "They have entered the gardens and demand that we deliver his Excellency the Imam into their hands."

"Go out to them and inform them that I shall meet them personally," Rukn al-Din resolutely commanded.

"But they want none but the Imam, and they threaten to attack the palace and to kill every last one of its inhabitants if we do not deliver him."

The Imam, who had hurried to join his protector, overheard this conversation, and he now implored Rukn al-Din to submit, for he preferred to go with the Tatar in peace rather than bear the burden of the general massacre that must ensue.

"Take comfort, my Lord," Rukn al-Din calmly replied. "Not one of these men shall touch a single hair of your head as long as the blood continues to run through my veins."

"And why imperil your life thus, my son, if these Tatar are to triumph come what may? They outnumber us and are much better armed."

"They shall never triumph, God willing," was Rukn al-Din's only reply. He climbed up to a small aperture above the door and looked out at the gardens. They were bristling with men, some carrying flaming torches that lit up the dark, others wielding swords and quarterstaffs. The noise and tumult were great. At the head of the crowd stood a man that looked, from his attire, to be their leader, and

Sahban stood next to him. The sight of Sahban confirmed Rukn al-Din's earlier fears, and his blood boiled with fury at this craven treachery. "Sahban!" he called out to him.

Sahban looked up and saw Rukn al-Din. The armed men that surrounded him had made him bold. "You must give up the Imam," he shouted in reply. "The Khakan himself now demands it. You cannot hide him away any longer, Rukn al-Din."

"I shall not surrender him."

"The Khakan has ordered his immediate arrest. If you refuse to deliver him, these soldiers will attack the palace and take him by force."

"It is you and none else who has instigated this laughable little scene, Sahban. I advise you to withdraw with your men, my friend."

"I do not understand your defiance, Prince. This affair concerns you not."

"Neither does this treachery become or serve you in any way."

Sahban hesitated and bit his lip. Rukn al-Din was a formidable foe, and with the men of the palace could well mount a successful resistance to a siege. Sahban was pressed for time, moreover, and hoped to conclude the affair as quickly as possible. He consequently decided to try another avenue of attack. "I would inform you, Prince Rukn al-Din, that Shwaykar, for whose sole sake you came to this distant country, has once again come under my protection. I shall deliver her to you safely when you leave this palace."

This veiled threat cast an icy chill over Rukn al-Din's heart.

"Now, open these doors," Sahban resumed, "or we shall force them, and you know full well what the consequences shall be for the Imam—and for yourself," he added darkly.

Upon hearing this exchange, the Imam Ahmad resumed his attempts to induce Rukn al-Din to submit, but the young prince would not listen and, calling for his weapons, prepared, with the handful of guards that remained indoors, to defend the palace and its precious tenant.

Not receiving a response to his last ultimatum, Sahban resumed. "I have warned you repeatedly, Prince, and again I say, surrender! You and all those within this palace are at the mercy of these soldiers, and unless you take heed you shall never again see Shwaykar."

If this threat had been calculated to weaken Rukn al-Din's resolve, it had the exact opposite effect, for the fury and contempt it inspired only strengthened his heart and steadied his determination. Suddenly a familiar voice rang out loud and clear in the midst of the din. "Do not believe him, my Lord! Shwaykar is safe with us!" Rukn al-Din recognized his trusty servant 'Abid's speech. 'Abid now turned to Sahban and pointed an accusing finger at him. "It is you who have incited the Tatar against us!"

Sahban drew himself up in outraged dignity. "Away with you, knave! I only execute the command of the Khakan himself."

"Lies!" 'Abid's voice rang out again for all to hear. "The Khakan has given me and every one of the inhabitants of this palace his personal amnesty—and here is the proof. Look!" As he said this he withdrew the yellow banner of amnesty that Mu'ayyid al-Din had given Rukn al-Din, and unfurled it where he stood. As soon as the Tatar soldiers caught sight of the fluttering standard they fell respectfully silent and began preparing to withdraw from the garden. Sahban watched in dismay as they slowly quit the scene of the stillborn battle, and having no other choice, he scurried after them, shamed and defeated. Rukn al-Din watched this ignominious retreat while his heart danced for joy at his triumph, and the Imam Ahmad embraced him and kissed his cheeks in thanks.

Rukn al-Din and the Imam Ahmad returned to the chamber they had so precipitously quit and impatiently waited for 'Abid to attend upon them. As soon as he breathlessly entered the room, Rukn al-Din fell upon him eagerly for news of Shwaykar. "She is here, my Lord. Upon hearing from the servant who accompanied her to Sahban's house in Qadhimiyya that she was yet alive, I immediately set out to retrieve her and return her here, for Sahban's conduct this morning did not augur well."

"May God bless you for being the true and devoted friend that you are," Rukn al-Din warmly declared. 'Abid was delighted by this generous acknowledgment on the part of his master. He bowed deeply and continued. "If you wish to see Shwaykar, pray come this way to the apartment where she is lodged." Rukn al-Din followed him eagerly and entered through the doors that 'Abid indicated. There she sat, still dressed in the robes of a young eunuch. As soon as she saw him she burst into tears of happiness and threw herself upon his knees, showering them with kisses. He gently raised her from the ground and kissed her forehead. "I thank God for your safety, my darling, and praise Him for his bounty," he whispered tenderly in her ear. "Our greatest thanks are also due to the Imam Ahmad, may God preserve him."

The Imam, who had followed in Rukn al-Din and 'Abid's footsteps to witness this sweet reunion, replied, "On the contrary, it is I who must thank you, my Prince. And I heartily congratulate Mistress Shwaykar on this happy outcome."

Rukn al-Din now turned to 'Abid. "How did you come to hear Shwaykar's story, 'Abid?"

"I was sitting in the garden and gazing sadly upon the locks of my mistress's hair when one of the servants asked me to tell the story of those locks. I unfolded the contours of the tragic story, and he sat staring at the color and texture of the hair. Suddenly, he jumped up and said, 'How similar are these particulars to those of the girl we found in the river!' I begged him to explain himself, and finally understood that Shwaykar was the girl who had been taken to Sahban's house. As fast as the speed of light, I flew to Qadhimiyya and brought her back, disguised as you now see."

Rukn al-Din thanked him again profusely, but 'Abid merely replied, "The Imam Ahmad must on no account stay here a moment longer. Though the Tatar have temporarily left us in peace, Sahban shall surely go to the Khakan or one of his ministers and inform them of the Imam's escape. On the way back from Qadhimiyya, I witnessed atrocities that would strike terror in the staunchest hearts."

"What have you seen, good 'Abid?" Rukn al-Din demanded. "Have the Tatar occupied the entire city?"

"My Lord, they have descended upon the Imperial Palaces with Hulagu in person at their head. The palaces have been ransacked and the women taken prisoner and bestowed as slaves upon the Khan's officers."

A shocked hush fell upon the company at this devastating news.

"And the Caliph?" the Imam Ahmad was finally roused to ask. "What have they done with him?"

"I have heard that the Minister Mu'ayyid al-Din convinced the Abbasid princes and the entire Imperial administration to go out to the Tatar pavilion and that they were all cruelly slaughtered. Then, at sunset, the Tatar attacked the palaces and murdered the remaining princes of the blood. The youngest ones they took as prisoners. Sword and fire rage through Baghdad as we speak, and the streets run red with blood. Baiju has crossed the bridge to Karkh, and his men are engaged in pillage, rape, and murder throughout the city. I have also heard that the Imperial Libraries have been emptied and their innumerable treasures thrown into the Tigris. His Excellency the Imam's name is on every tongue, for his absence from the Imperial pavilion was noted. His former residence, the Firdaws Palace, has already been searched, and soon he shall be sought throughout the city. This is why I urgently recommend that his Excellency quit this place immediately."

Terror struck the Imam Ahmad's heart at these words. Rukn al-Din turned to 'Abid. "You are a native of this country," he said. "Guide us therefore to a place where we may hide his Excellency until calm returns to these lands."

'Abid bowed in obedience and replied, "Gladly, my Lord. Leave this matter to me. Pray you order the servants to pack his Excellency's most essential possessions on the instant."

The Imam Ahmad gladly submitted to 'Abid's urgent counsel, and after his few possessions had been packed, the small company mounted just before dawn and were led out of the city by the faithful eunuch. The following day, when news reached them that the Tatar had discovered their flight and were following in hot pursuit, the Imam Ahmad, with 'Abid in attendance, took refuge with one of the hardy Arab tribes that roamed the adjacent Iraqi countryside, while Rukn al-Din, having assured himself of the Imam's safety, continued on his journey to Egypt with Shwaykar.

Epilogue

THE HAPPY COUPLE were married as soon as they reached Cairo. Nur al-Din, son of 'Izz al-Din, was now Sultan of Egypt, just as Sallafa had claimed. Rukn al-Din easily incited the princes against the boy-sultan and they invested Sayf al-Din Qutuz, a noble scion of the Kings of Khurasan, in his stead in 1259. Rukn al-Din, meanwhile, bade his time, and patiently set about laying his ambitious plans to seize the throne and transfer the Caliphate to Egypt.

In the following year, Hulagu marched upon Syria and sent his messengers to threaten Qutuz, Sultan of Egypt, whereupon the Sultan consulted his commanders and, Rukn al-Din foremost among them, they advised him to declare war. Hulagu was forced to withdraw from Syria with the greatest part of his army, thanks to the sudden death of his sire, Genghis Khan. The forces that remained met Qutuz's army in battle in Palestine, and the Egyptians were victorious. Before the Egyptian army had returned to Cairo in triumph, Rukn al-Din seized the opportunity that thereby presented itself and assassinated Qutuz, having previously conspired with a faction of the princes to this end. The princes agreed to elevate Rukn al-Din to the Sultanate, and he was crowned in Cairo in 1260 as Al-Zahir, the Manifest King. As soon as Rukn al-Din had firmly secured his throne, he sent for the Imam Ahmad from the deserts of Iraq. The Imam arrived at Cairo in the following year. He was invested as Commander of the Faithful under the title of Al-Mustansir Billah, and this is how it came to pass that the Abbasid Caliphate was reborn in Egypt.

Tree of Pearls

AN AFTERWORD

Roger Allen

WHAT'S IN A NAME? My own acquaintance with the woman known as "Tree of Pearls"—Shagret ad-Durr, to cite the Egyptian pronunciation of her name—goes all the way back to my graduate student days in Cairo in 1966. At that time I was Director of Music at the city's Anglican Cathedral and had diplomats as members of the choir, and was thus fortunate enough to be invited to live in a British embassy house. The house stood on Shagret ad-Durr Street in Zamalek, the tree-lined island community close to the center of the city that was then devoid of the multiple high-rise buildings that have now completely transformed its appearance. Needless to say, I was curious to find out about the person, and a female person at that, after whom the Cairene street in which I was living was named. Thus did I discover the history of this illustrious woman.

Tree of Pearls belongs on a relatively short list of Muslim women who played significant roles in the public life of their region and culture during the pre-modern era of Islamic history. Among those women we would also include two elegiac poets from the earliest period of poetic creativity: Al-Khansa' (d. after 644) and Layla al-Akhyaliyya (d. 704); two princesses of caliphal families: the Umayyad Wallada bint Mustakfi in Spain (d. ca. 1091), and 'Abbasa (9th cent.), the sister of the Abbasid caliph, Harun al-Rashid, in Baghdad; and the renowned Sufi, Rabi'a al-'Adawiyya (d. 801). If we were to expand the purview to include Middle Eastern women from various time frames and regions, we would also need to cite from pre-Islamic times Cleopatra of Egypt (d. 30 BCE) and Zenobia (d. ca. 274) of Palmyra in Syria; and, from the contemporary era, Benazir Bhutto of Pakistan

(d. 2007), Shaykh Hasina (b. 1947) of Bangladesh, and Megawati Sukarnoputri of Indonesia (b. 1947).

In the case of Tree of Pearls, Shajar al-Durr (the Library of Congress's preferred transliteration of her name), we are dealing with Egypt in the thirteenth century. In fact, she herself already had a female predecessor as de facto ruler of that particular country, namely Sitt al-Mulk (d. 1023), the sister of the Fatimid Caliph Al-Hakim bi-Amr Allah (d. 1021). However, the circumstances in which Sitt al-Mulk assumed power were somewhat different. Her Fatimid caliph brother was widely believed to have severe mental problems (perhaps diagnosable now as schizophrenia). He certainly issued some peculiar decrees in his lifetime: banning the pilgrimage to Mecca; requiring that Egyptians work at night and sleep by day; and ordering the destruction of the Church of the Holy Sepulchre in Jerusalem because he did not like the sound of bells. However, his ecstatic utterances proved to be inspirational for a community of his followers who, after his mysterious death, moved to the mountains of Syro-Lebanon, where they became the Druze community, regarding Al-Hakim as having gone into occultation. The actual circumstances of the caliph's death are obscure, in that he "disappeared" while indulging in his favorite pastime of star-gazing. Certain historians are of the opinion that his sister, Sitt al-Mulk, was involved in what was actually a case of murder. But whatever the truth of the matter, for the two years until her own death she became the de facto ruler of Egypt as regent on behalf of her young nephew, Abu al-Hasan 'Ali (known as Al-Zahir li-I'zaz Din Allah).

By way of contrast, when we consider the life of the later female ruler of Egypt, the woman renowned as "Tree of Pearls," we find ourselves dealing with the almost fabulous career of someone born a slave of Turkic origins who becomes the concubine and wife of a Sultan and accompanies him to Egypt. Her husband's death coincides with the arrival in Egypt of the European forces of the Seventh Crusade (led by King Louis IX) in 1249. Thus, in full collusion with Egypt's governing authorities, she conceals her husband's death and rules in his place before being declared "Sultana" in 1250. Her brief reign witnesses enormous amounts of political intrigue, as the defenders of Egypt, primarily the Mamluks (themselves manumitted slaves), fight against the Crusader armies and amongst themselves. In fact, her reign can be seen as marking the end of the Ayyubid dynasty that had ruled Egypt ever since the demise of the Fatimids in 1171 and the transfer of authority to a prolonged period of Mamluk rule.

War, political intrigue, murder, and a Muslim female ruler who is born a slave: these are clearly the elements of a potentially exciting historical novel, and Jurji Zaydan clearly relishes the opportunity. He has also borne in mind, no doubt, that the same events are also recounted in one of Arabic's most famous popular sagas, *Sirat al-Zahir Baybars,* Rukn al-din Baybars being the name of the Mamluk commander who not only crushes the forces of the Seventh Crusade (and captures King Louis) but also goes on to defeat the invading Mongol armies at the famous battle of 'Ayn Jalut (Goliath's Spring) in 1260. While aspects of the "story" in this popular account may be somewhat altered, the basic facts of Tree of Pearls's life remain the same.

Zaydan begins his novel, *Tree of Pearls,* in full educational mode, placing us in the historical moment and context and reminding us thereby of his overall pedagogical intentions as a combination of journal editor, historian, and novelist. As we read his novels, it is as well to recall that they originally appeared, like many of their European analogues, in serialized form: in his case, in the journal that he founded, *Al-Hilal* (still published in Cairo), and subsequently at his own publishing house, Dar al-Hilal. The introductory section of this novel also illustrates another interesting aspect of his compositional method as a student of history and historical novelist: he tends to study a wide variety of historical sources devoted to a particular period (always cited at the beginning of each novel) and then composes more than one novel based in the period in question. Thus, *Tree of Pearls,* originally published in 1914, comes directly after a novel about Saladin and the Assassins (1913)—a work to which he makes direct reference on the very first page of this novel (almost as though the "serial" started in one novel is being continued in the next). Similar earlier novelistic clusters include one devoted to Andalusian history and another concerning the early Abbasid caliphate.

The historical context of this novel is established from the outset: Al-Salih, Tree of Pearls's "husband," has died; the Crusaders have been defeated; and Baybars brings her the news of the assassination of Al-Salih's presumed successor, Turan Shah. In other words, the Ayyubid line is at an end; the date is May 1250. The beautiful Tree of Pearls sits with her songstress handmaid, Shwaykar, in her palace on the banks of the Nile, receiving this news. At this early stage in the narrative, the reader is also made aware of another essential element in a Zaydan historical novel: the existence of a love affair, in this case between Tree of Pearls and one of the Mamluk commanders, 'Izz al-din Aybak. Juxtaposed against this, her handmaid has been offered in gratitude to the Mamluk Baybars (who is to become the hero of the popular saga mentioned above). With the announcement that the Mamluks have decided to acknowledge Tree of Pearls as Queen of Egypt, the stage and the central elements of the story are set.

Fully the first third of the novel is concerned with a vividly characterized description of the multiple strands of intrigue connected with the power-struggles in Cairo that follow Tree of Pearls's coronation as queen: the cunning manipulations brought about by Sallafa, a rival concubine of Tree of Pearls, and the increasing rivalry between the Mamluk commanders 'Izz al-din Aybak and Rukn al-din Baybars. Then, in a typical Zaydanian narrative move—"and now let us take leave of these Egyptian intrigues for the time being and move our story to Baghdad, Capital of the Abbasid Caliphs"—the scene is transferred to another theater within the overall historical framework. Once again, Zaydan the educator introduces his readers to the history of the Abbasid caliphate and the topography of Baghdad, the purpose-built Abbasid city. The linkage to the earlier part of the novel is provided by reference to the Shi'i community in Baghdad, then suffering under the intolerant Sunni rule of the Abbasids. Sahban, a Baghdad-born Shi'ite now residing in Egypt, has traveled all the way back to his homeland from Egypt to discuss with his colleagues in Baghdad the possibility of restoring the (Shi'ite) Fatimid dynasty in Egypt, only to witness for himself the violence being wrought against his friends in the Baghdad Shi'ite community by the henchmen of the Sunni Abbasid Caliph al-Musta'sim—the last of the Abbasid Caliphs in Baghdad. Sahban immediately goes to see Mu'ayyid al-din, a Shi'ite minister of the Caliph, and the reader is thus introduced to another major element in the plot, one that will have an enormous impact on the city of Baghdad and the Abbasid caliphate—the Mongol assault on the city in 1258. Mu'ayyid al-din has received a mysterious dervish visitor who has assured him that the great Mongol Khan, Hulagu, has no desire to do harm to the Shi'i community but is instead intent on getting rid of the Abbasid rulers. Only when the dervish has departed, leaving behind a letter, does Mu'ayyid al-din discover that his nocturnal visitor was in fact Hulagu Khan in person. A Mongol assault thus seems to be imminent, and Mu'ayyid al-din sends a hidden message to the Khan to initiate it. Within the novel's narrative framework the very seriousness of the situation is cleverly emphasized by the insouciance and frivolity encountered at the caliphal court, where Mu'ayyid al-din's loyalty is tested by a dispute over ownership of the Egyptian songstress,

Shwaykar—Tree of Pearls's erstwhile companion—, who has been stolen on her way to the Caliph's palace by the Caliph's own reprobate son.

Now, again, the scene shifts. We remain in Baghdad, but move from the public domain to the interior of the caliphal harem. After Zaydan has provided the reader with a description of that institution's traditional hierarchy, we discover that Shwaykar's sworn enemy, Sallafa, is in Baghdad and indeed inside the harem quarters, still determined to thwart the interests and love of Baybars, he being someone for whom she herself nurses a strong passion. As the Mongol armies infest the city, the intricate web of interests and relationships is rendered that much more complicated by the arrival in the city of Baybars, himself. He is able to witness the size and efficiency of the Mongol army and is also aware of the tensions surrounding the Caliph and the contrasting interests of the Sunni and Shiʿi communities. In a climactic scene, Sallafa tries to win Baybars's heart by informing him of the details of her nefarious schemes in Cairo, whereby she claims to have orchestrated the deaths of ʿIzz al-din Aybak and Tree of Pearls, all in order that Baybars could become Sultan himself—and, of course, marry her. When Sallafa finally informs Baybars that she has also ordered the murder of his beloved Shwaykar, he stabs her to death. Little has she realized how closely her plans in Egypt have managed to mirror those that have been forming in Baybars's own mind. The novel draws to a rapid conclusion as the Mongols sack the city of Baghdad and obliterate the Abbasid family, and Baybars is at last reunited with his beloved—who has been rescued from drowning in the River Tigris—and returns to Egypt, taking with him the sole surviving Abbasid, whose function will be to legitimize his own rise to power.

The historical accounts of this particular period in Islamic history are themselves replete with incident: battles, murders, court intrigues, and contested successions—as we have already suggested, all of them offering fine material for an event-packed historical novel. The above précis shows how Zaydan, the historical novelist, frames the events in a serialized narrative, one in which the title character, Tree of Pearls, fulfills her role in the narrative sequence but then essentially disappears after the first third of the narrative. ("The Fall of Baghdad" might have been an equally appropriate title for this novel, albeit without the admitted attraction of using such an exotic name and character.) As is the case with his other historical novels—and, as I have suggested above, with the chronology of their composition—, individual chapters are provided with inviting titles (a reflection, no doubt, of their original positioning on the pages of the journal, *Al-Hilal*, where they first appeared). Then a scenario, a relationship, an intrigue is followed through in several successive chapters until a certain point, after which the scene and the characters change in an almost theatrical fashion. As is often the case with historical novels of the more "swashbuckling" kind, the character traits tend to be portrayed in bold colors: Sallafa, for example, and Sahban are shown to be truly evil and duplicitous; Shwaykar, the slave-girl songstress, is beautiful, sweet, and vulnerable; and Baybars is handsome and steadfast. In this and other novels, Zaydan relates history in an attractive fashion and occasionally indulges in some reflection on human nature and foibles, but not for him the extensive musings on history itself and the methods of historians, which are such a prominent feature of, for example, Tolstoy's historical novel, *War and Peace.*

Samah Selim, the translator of this novel, and I have been among those scholars who have spent some considerable time in recent years pointing out the need to re-examine and re-evaluate the cultural trends during the nineteenth century that are clustered under the general heading in Arabic of "*al-nahda,*" most often translated as "revival" or even "renaissance." Following his emigration from his native Lebanon to Egypt in 1883, Jurji Zaydan played a very prominent role in that process, although, like many indigenous trends in the cultural sphere, his role is one that has tended to be underappreciated within the broader context of the importation of Western ideas and literary genres. This has been particularly the case with regard to the earliest stages in the development of a novel tradition in Arabic, examples of which can be traced back to at least the middle of the nineteenth century in Syro-Lebanon—where Zaydan's remarkable series of twenty-one novels should occupy a prominent position, but mostly have not, at least thus far.

In such a context, a recent initiative started by the author's grandson, George Zaydan, is a most welcome development. The Zaidan Foundation, established in Washington, DC, has published translations of some of his novels and studies of his work.[1] Coupled with this excellent translation of *Tree of Pearls*, these translations and studies should help to reinstate Jurji Zaydan into his rightful position

1. The full series of Zaydan's work in translation has now been completed. Included are: *The Conquest of Andalusia, The Battle of Poitiers, The Caliph's Sister, The Caliph's Heirs,* and *Saladin and the Assassins.* All are available through the Zaidan Foundation on its website, at http://zaidan foundation.org/ZF_Website_HistoricalNovels.html.

as a major figure in the development of modern Arabic fiction and thereby offer a further contribution to the several studies that are now reassessing the relative roles of the imported and indigenous in cultural trends in the Arabic-speaking world during the nineteenth century.

Other titles from Middle East Literature in Translation